CW00872067

# Twisted FATE

FORTITUDE MEMORIES
BOOK ONE

TRACEY JUKES

**Cover design by** Sly Fox Cover Designs
**Formatting by** LJDesigns
**Editing by** Nikki Groom - The Indie Hub.
Karen Sanders - Karen Sanders Editing

# Twisted FATE

FORTITUDE MEMORIES
BOOK ONE

TRACEY JUKES

**Twisted Fate** is a work of fiction. Names, characters, businesses, places, events and incidents are either the products of the author's imagination or used in a fictitious manner. Any resemblance to actual persons, living or dead, or actual events is purely coincidental.



| | |
|---|---|
| **Cover design by** | Sly Fox Cover Designs |
| **Formatting by** | LJDesigns |
| **Editing by** | Nikki Groom - The Indie Hub. |
| | Karen Sanders - Karen Sanders Editing |

Lisa

♡

Tracey

# Dedication

*To my husband Rob and daughters Megan and Phillipa. It's thanks to you three that I managed to finish this novel, and for that I am truly grateful. I love you all more than you know x*

# Prologue

Screams, then what sounds like a car backfiring, but it's the sound of gunshots. Jumping from my bed, my feet get tangled in the sheets and I fall to the floor, winding myself. My heart's racing so fast, I panic at the thought of having a heart attack. Was it a dream? Then the same noise penetrates through my head. I don't like this. Dread swells within me. I can't breathe, and my palms feel clammy. More piercing screams echo through the walls, and realization hits me as I learn they belong to my family. This is reality.

Hearing my dad pleading with whoever is out there crushes me.

"Please don't hurt my family." Daddy's voice is tight; my heart thuds while I listen.

"Aww, Daddy can't protect them, can he?" one of the intruders speaks sarcastically, more shots follow, and then… silence.

I want to scream, but instead, I remain quiet. The deafening sound, I know, means Dad is gone too. Inside, I'm wailing, the pain cutting my insides apart like a blade slicing through fresh skin.The sound of voices coming toward my bedroom panics me. My whole body trembles with fear.

"Check all the rooms."

What do I do? There's nowhere to hide in my room. I'll be dead sooner rather than later. My closet's tiny, but after scrambling in, I manage to drag my clothes over me for coverage as the voices become even closer. The quivering sounds leaving my mouth will give me away if I can't get a grip. Slapping my hands over my mouth, I keep hushed for what seems like an eternity, but it's seconds. Eventually, the voices and padding of their feet become quieter. Thinking they've left, I cautiously peer out. I'm met with a glimmer of light casting a shine on my door, and I can see a wrist bearing a snake tattoo. My bedroom door bangs shut, the sound ricocheting off the walls. I daren't move, in fear they may come back. I've watched enough movies to know how this plays out. After waiting for what seems like forever, I emerge from the closet, shuddering fiercely, not knowing who's where. What greets me is a frightening quiet. Chills course through me like icicles.

In the darkness, I shakily creep toward my door and listen. There's nothing. No voices, no footsteps, just blackness and an eerie silence. I open my door, but before I'm able to take a calming breath, my wrist is snatched, and I'm dragged forward. I fight against the force holding me, but I'm weak compared to this powerful hold. The snake-printed hand holds a gun to my face and forces me down to the floor.

The intruder straddles me and keeps the gun pointed at me. I'm too scared now to open my eyes. But panic sets in, and I kick and throw my arms around so he restrains them by the wrist. Cool air whispers across my body as he rips open my pajama top. I chant to myself—*oh my God, oh my God, please don't let this happen.*

His calloused hands grab at my bare skin from my stomach toward my breasts. They're rough like sandpaper, and it hurts like he's scratching me with intent. Sirens sound in the distance, causing the other intruder to yell. "Shit. We have to go. The cops are coming."

My attacker quickly gets up. "'Til next time, sweetness."

And then he's gone.

He didn't kill me. Why?

I gasp for air but can't move. Fear has me frozen. By the time I get up, all is still. Unwillingly, I'm dragging myself down the hallway. Terror takes over my thoughts, and what I'm faced with, it's indescribable. I scream as I run toward my father, who's lying in a pool of blood, but then more horror greets me. Greetings should be positive, pleasant. This is all but that. My heart shatters into tiny fragments as I take in the scene before me. My mother and brother also surrounded by pools of blood on the floor, gunshots through their heads.

My whole family, taken.

I grab at my chest. The tightness feels like my heart is in a vice and it's getting tighter and tighter, to the point of combustion. It hurts so, so much. My breathing is fast-paced, and dizziness overwhelms me until my knees buckle, then the blackness takes me.

# Chapter One

Fourteen months have passed since the day I lost my family. I'm floating, and I feel like I don't belong anywhere. The only people I have are my Aunt Beth in England, my best friend, Nyla, and my friend Jase. That one night changed my life in the evilest way possible. How the hell does anyone get over losing their family in such a way? To be told it was a robbery gone wrong, and that we were just victims in this tragedy doesn't sit well with me.

Another hammer to my heart is that the intruders have never been traced. Where is our justice? I'm the only family member to have survived, so everything they owned has been left to me. But all I really want is them back, not their belongings. I should have died with them.

My parents were good, honest people, and they also had

rules, no matter your age. I didn't always agree with them, and this didn't always go down well, but I did try to honor them most of the time. I'm twenty-six, for crying out loud. I need to act my age and not like a kid, which Nyla would often say to me.

*"Es, tell your parents you're staying at mine and then we're going to that club, Dilemmas."*

*"Nyla, you're going to get me in trouble one day, but hell, I'm in!"*

This would often be the conversation between me and Nyla. Es is her nickname for me. It has been since second grade, and it's stuck ever since. Nyla and I are best friends and complete opposites, but we clicked straight away. She took me under her wing. Ny is a fiery redhead who loves to dress up. She also doesn't take any bullshit from anyone. If she wants something, she goes out and gets it. Nothing stops her from trying. I'm more laid back. I like to follow the rules, thanks to my parents, but deep inside, there is a wild side wanting to break free. Being in my jeans, t-shirt, and Converse are when I'm most comfy, but I do love a beautiful dress. My mom would always say I got my looks from her side of the family. I'm five feet six with mousy brown hair and a figure most women would die for. My mom would always remind me of that each time I ate a donut.

I love my parents and always will. They made me who I am. Believing in fairy tales and happily ever afters were always in their stories, and I wanted my own fairy tale with the happy ending. Now I've stopped believing in them, because where is their happily ever after? That right was taken away. Their upbringing and over-protection of me has made the young lady I am a very naïve one. They weren't religious, but they did believe in doing things correctly, like their rules. These included curfews, acting a certain way, and not being a slut, as my dad would so abruptly put it. I like to think I made them proud and was mostly a good girl. I followed their rules, unless it was to have a little fun, and for a woman of my age, who could blame me?

I'd had one previous boyfriend, and they liked him. He was a good guy. He couldn't do enough for me. I wanted more, though, but he thought he was everything my parents wanted for me, and he was, kind of, until he ruined it and betrayed me. Sleeping with his co-worker in our home was unforgivable.

You'd think living in New York and the noise from it all would drown out my thoughts, the gut-wrenching sorrow, but no. The noise creates other issues. Every car door closing, every loud noise makes me jumpy and fearful of what may come my way. I'm scared and uneasy in the city I grew up in. Guys walking with their hoods up now have me thinking the worst. I shouldn't be fearful like this. I always knew of robberies and murders, but never did I think it would happen in my own home, to me. It always happens to someone else.

I've been staying with Nyla and her boyfriend, Russell, as facing my home holds too many memories. They are mainly happy ones of growing up, but then I think of the horror, and it has me feeling violently sick to my core. I've finally decided I'm selling up, and I want to find somewhere to rent. Today, I'm venturing out of the four walls of Nyla's home. A place that's been my safety net. I need to begin moving on with my life, but it's also one without my family. First on my list is to find a property with security—safety is a priority considering what I've been through. Plus, thanks to my parents and their savings, I can afford to do just that. Fourteen months seems too soon to be moving on with my life, but I've been brought up to be strong. It's not quite moving on yet, it's just the start of the stepping stones to rebuilding my life.

Nyla comes apartment hunting with me, because, well, let's face it, I don't have a clue what I'm doing. Twenty-six years old, and had the tragedy not happened, I'd still be living at home. It's true what they say; living in New York City is very expensive.

It's a glorious sunny Friday afternoon, and we've seen three apartments. All had fantastic security and were spacious, which is just what I'm looking for. The one with the gym across the road is keeping my attention, though. The doorman told us there's no trouble because of the gym. The guys in there look out for the area. This is the one.

"Are you foolish? Look at the area, Es," Nyla utters.

"Nyla, did you not listen to what the doorman said? I need the security, especially living alone."

She looks at me with sad eyes because she's worried about me and she doesn't want me leaving her place. But for the first time, it's me making decisions for myself.

Eventually, I persuade my best friend that this apartment is the one for me. It's in Brooklyn, and near the subway, so commuting will be so much easier. I talk with the agent and sign there and then. No point hanging around—it's time to start my new beginning. Once done, we go furniture shopping and buy everything I need. I kept a few sentimental items from my parents' home, but decided that I want a fresh start. The money from the sale of my parents' house will give me the opportunity to buy my new apartment if I like it there, but for now, I'm leasing it.

The past week seems to have dragged. I've been counting the days to moving day, and now it's here. Nyla and Jase, our friend from work, are helping me, and they're just as excited as I am.

"Esme, let me place your bedroom things, okay? You know I have an eye for where everything should go," Jase says, standing with his hands on his hips, grinning at me.

"No. You can help Nyla with the sitting area. The bedroom is off limits."

He huffs at me but agrees.

"Come on. Let's go grab more boxes from the van. The quicker we're done, the quicker I can settle."

During the unloading, some movement outside the gym catches my eye. Nyla and Jase realize I'm not picking up boxes and stop to see what has my attention.

"What you looking at?" says Nyla, then cranes her head outside the van to see.

There are a couple of guys talking, and like they know I'm watching, they look across to me and stare. I swiftly turn away, but as I glance back, one of them smiles at me.

He's well built, about six feet two, and God, he's handsome.

I turn away, grab some boxes, and head back inside. The unpacking won't do itself, and I'm due back at work a week from Monday. That gives me just over a week to get my shit sorted.

So, after Nyla and Jase have left, I spend the night settling in. While putting away some kitchenware, I drop a cup. It smashes, and it happens…

*It's dark, and I hear my dad but can't do anything. I'm scared. I know something is wrong, but I'm so frightened.*

*Gunshots, screams.*

There's a pop and I realize I'm no longer there, I'm in my apartment. It was just another flashback. The pop was nothing more than a car backfiring outside. I touch my fingers to my cheeks, which are wet with tears. These flashbacks have started to happen on and off, and I feel like they're trying to tell me something, but I don't know what that something is.

I wake to a glorious Saturday morning and look around my apartment. I know this will be good for me, although I'm still full of fear of the unknown and being alone. It's time Esme Lewis grew up and stood on her own two feet. Starting by making the apartment my own and putting pictures on the walls. It has two bedrooms, and then there's an open space which combines a living and kitchen area. It's cozy, but big enough for me. My favorite is the window bench, which I absolutely love, and I can just sit there watching the world go by.

I glance out of the window and see the guys from outside the gym yesterday. The guy who smiled at me disappears inside my building.

My phone is constantly buzzing. I know it's Nyla, harassing me about going to some new club that's opening next week. She saw it advertised and hasn't stopped going on about it.

"Hey, what's up?" I say, chuckling down the phone to her.

"We're going out next weekend. It's been too long. I promise I will look after you, okay? Plus, it's opening night and there will be freebies, and you know how we love freebies. So, get your best dress on. We are going out."

I agree, just to stop her nagging me, but the thought terrifies me.

I decide to spend the morning shopping for something new to wear and ask Jase to come with me as we haven't spent much time together lately.

"So, what are your specifics for this outfit, Esme?"

"Oh, erm, let me think. Right, I know, something that doesn't scream 'preacher's daughter,' Does that help?"

My parents never really liked my dress sense. They always complained my dresses were too short, or my tops didn't cover enough. I mean, they weren't always that bad, but sometimes I wanted to say, 'Please just say I look nice for a change, instead of criticizing me.'

While walking around, we come across a boutique that's off the main street, hidden away. I'm really curious.

This isn't the type of store I would normally go in. I'm your typical bargain shopper, your jeans and t-shirt girl. We're browsing through a rack of dresses when something catches my eye. It's a beautiful dress, but not over the top. Lined with a lace top, a mixture of creams and black, and a tight skirt, with the material ending above the knee. It's a lot shorter than I usually go for, but it's perfect.

"Get your ass in there and let me see you in it, lady."

"Okay, then."

It fits beautifully, and when I look at the price tag, I'm floored. I would have considered paying full price for it as I love it so much, but it's been reduced twice, which means the dress is going to be mine.

# Chapter Two

I've barely been in the apartment for ten minutes, and the phone's ringing. I answer to Lance the doorman saying there's a young lady to see me but needs to be on my approved list to be let up automatically. It's Nyla, so I explain who she is and to add her.

"You aren't kidding about the security, Es," she says as I open the door to her. "It's a pain, but you're safe here."

I'm pleased she finally understands my choice now. I will always be on my guard and will probably never feel one hundred percent safe, but hopefully, over time, the fear and panic will pass.

We decide to go for a late afternoon drink and try the coffee shop across from my building. It's a chance for me to get out and see my surroundings. I say hi to Lance on the way out and introduce him to Nyla.

"Hey, Lance, this is Nyla."

"Miss Lewis. Yes, we met when she arrived. I've now added her to your list as requested."

"How silly of me. Of course, you met when she arrived." I try to make a little joke of it, but I think I'm failing. Damn, I'm lame at this sort of thing.

"Lance, please forgive my friend. She's still in the learning stages of what we call banter." They both share a chuckle, and I feel like I've missed the joke, but I grab Nyla by the arm and drag her out of the building.

"You are a terrible friend, Nyla Stewart!"

"Es, come on. It was a bit of mockery, and he knew you were making a joke. Stop over-thinking and let's get coffee and watch the eye candy, okay?"

When I follow her fixed gaze, I see muscles galore walking in and out of the gym.

We perch ourselves at a table by the window so we can see everything that's happening around us, and I mean everything. From the old guy walking by picking his nose, to the young couple all loved up and holding hands. It's those sights that make me sigh and think I'm going to like it here.

Nyla and I are chatting about me getting back to work when a darkness blocks our light in the window.

"Has night come and we've missed some hours?" Nyla sarcastically says.

I giggle because I love her more than anything, and she knows how to make me laugh just when I need it. We both look out at the reason for the darkness, and we no longer have a perfect view of the street. The guy I saw staring at me on moving day is right there. Up close and personal with nothing but a thin pane of glass between us.

"Es, darling, you're drooling."

"I am not. Stop being dramatic."

"Esme Lewis, there is no shame in drooling. Just own it, for God's sake."

I'm about to carry on defending myself when Nyla's attention is focused elsewhere, and it's not on our conversation. She's practically frothing at the mouth over this one dude who's just walked in, and he's matching her lustful eyes, too.

"Oi, you're taken, remember? Behave yourself and drink your coffee."

"Well, Muscles there hasn't stopped staring at you, either. Did you not notice, or are you blind?"

"Not blind at all."

That's not a lie, either, I can't stop lusting over him; he's pure perfection. *Pull yourself together.* It's probably my emotions being all over the place causing such conflicting behavior. Yep, I'll go with that. I look back up and he's still staring at me, but now he knows he has my attention, he gives me a smile. There is something magnetic about him that makes me do the opposite to what I want. Like now, he waves while walking away, and I return the gesture.

"Esme, you're flirting."

"No, I am not."

"Yes, you are. You're allowed to flirt, Es. It's not wrong, you know, and don't let me hear you say it's too soon, either."

"Well, it is too soon. It's been fourteen months now, but Jesus, Nyla. I keep expecting them to show up and start telling me how the apartment is all wrong and to get back home. It still seems surreal. How am I supposed to move on and act like they were never here?"

I try not to let the tears fall, but they do every time I talk or think about them.

"No one expects that. You'll always act like they're there. It's how you operate, Es."

I know she's right.

I will always be thinking about them in decisions I make, even when I know they would probably not agree. It's good to know I can still think about what they would think, as one day, their advice may be what I need.

"Okay, fine. You're right. Now, can you shut up about him, please?"

Nyla shuts up, and we finish our coffees in a comfortable silence.

The rest of the week comes and goes quickly with no issues. I've worked out my route via the subway for work, and even though I've always taken public transport, right now, I'm a little apprehensive. I know it will pass, eventually. I don't want to keep feeling like this, but until they find the bastards that killed my family, I don't think this fearful, jumpy feeling will rest.  Over the past week, I've finished unpacking, except for a few shelves that need putting up. Lance informed me the guy who owns the building is quite the handyman and is always happy to help residents. I decide to wait a little longer for those; there's no rush. It's Friday morning and I need a few items from the store, so I quickly run over there as it's a few units down from the coffee shop. I can't be bothered to get changed, so my fat pants it is. I look like your typical bed-head mess, but I don't care. This is me, unless I'm going out or to work. I run down the stairs for a change to burn off the calories I've been binging on lately. I round the corner, slamming straight into the muscles from the gym. I jump back on instinct and apologize profusely.

"Oh, God. Sorry, I wasn't looking where I was going." I look into his eyes, and butterflies form within my tummy. He really is beautiful. I'm brought back to reality with what I can only describe as arrogance and totally not what I expected.

"Okay, well, maybe slow down a little on the stairs. You could seriously injure someone at that speed!" He looks me up and down, and I'm unsure if he's appalled at my dress sense or if he's checking me out. Looking back into his eyes, I see a glimmer of heat, but it's gone so fast that maybe I wished it. He starts to brush past me, but I think fast this time.

"Wow," I mumble under my breath, a little taken aback at his sharpness. "It was an accident, but point taken." I walk by, shaking my head to myself. I thought he might have been a nice guy.

When I walk back in, he's in the foyer, talking to Lance. I curse under my breath and make sure to avoid eye contact as I walk toward the elevator. But no, it's not going to be that easy.

"Hey, you okay after our bump?" I don't know if he's

concerned or being sarcastic. The elevator doors open, and I step inside then turn to face him.

"Yes, thank you," I reply and the doors close, but the fiery look in his eyes doesn't go amiss. I'm quite proud that I didn't give him a chance to reply, but my body is tingling, and these feelings are alien to me. I'd never felt anything like this with my previous boyfriend Lucas, so why him, a total stranger?

The rest of the day passes quickly and then Nyla arrives. She helps me with my hair, and it looks amazing. It's gone from its usual dowdy brown straight look to natural loose curls.

"Nyla, it's fantastic! I love it. Your talents are wasted."

"Oh, please stop. I love my job, you know that." She winks at me.

I laugh because I know exactly what she means. She's incorrigible. It's why I love her. She's also the yang to my yin. We're more like sisters than best friends. If I need her, she's there, and vice versa.

"You ready to go, Nyla?" She seems to be taking forever in the bathroom.

"Yep, I'm coming. Just finishing my lipstick."

And out she comes, looking stunning as usual with her flowing red curls. God, I'd love to have her hair. My brunette color seems bland compared to hers.

We walk to the club since it's only two blocks away, and Nyla notices I'm clutching her hand tightly.

"Hey, it's okay. I promise," she whispers.

I know she believes we're safe, but I scan every person I see to make sure they aren't heading our way or giving off bad vibes.

"Thanks," I say, squeezing her hand.

The fresh night air helps to calm my nerves as we walk. Just before we get to the club, a fight breaks out between two guys outside a shop. Panic swells inside me and it's almost overwhelming, so I turn to head back home.

Nyla tugs me back. "Calm down. It's fine, look…" And as I look, the guys are fist bumping each other.

"I'm sorry, Nyla. I don't think this is a good idea, after all. It's too soon. I'm a bag of nerves. Just look at my hands."

"I will not give up on you, okay? I get that it seems too soon, but you're strong, Es. Besides, what are you gonna do at home? Oh, that's right, you'd sit there watching Netflix shit and stuffing crap down your throat. No. Not happening on my watch, lady."

"Nyla."

She holds her hand to my face, as if to say *shush.* "I want my best friend to find peace, and I believe she will eventually move on without feeling guilty. So, here's a compromise. If you give it a try and you want to leave later, then fine, but give the place a try first, okay?"

I wrap my arms around her and kiss her cheek. "Okay, I'll try. I promise."

I can hear the loud chatter as we round the corner from the line of people waiting to get in. I'm confused as Nyla walks on past the line to the doorman. He smiles and lets us straight through. This doesn't go down well with the other partygoers who are waiting, especially the females, whose snide comments I hear as we enter.

"She's obviously sleeping with him if they get to walk in without waiting," one says, so I turn to see exactly who she is. She talks trash and looks like it too. She gives me a look that could kill, but I just give her a smile and follow Nyla into the club.

The club is amazing. It's dressed in exquisite reds and blacks, and the glass dance floor is huge. I look around and notice there are two floors, but it must be private upstairs as there is security at both ends of each stairwell.

"I wonder what's up there that's so private," Nyla says.

"Oh, no. Forget whatever idea you have. We're here to enjoy ourselves, not get kicked out within the first five minutes."

She laughs at me. "Calm down. I'll be good, I promise." I look at her and decide to get a drink before she wanders off on a mission of her own. I grab her hand, and we make our way to the bar. I jump every time I hear a glass bottle being thrown away by the bartenders.

"Hey, you okay, Es?" Nyla asks, looking concerned.

"Yeah." I look over to her, but she knows me too well.

She entwines her fingers with mine and squeezes them. It's her way of saying, *I'm here. You're safe.*

The bartender comes over to us and looks Nyla up and down. "What can I get you beautiful ladies this evening?"

So, in her best southern drawl, which she uses when she wants something, Nyla replies, "What's on offer this evening?"

"It's right in front of you, honey," he replies with a

smirk.

Nyla leans over to him and whispers in his ear, then he quickly disappears.

"What are you saying to him?"

She gives me a wink. "Trust me. The drinks are coming."

I wonder what she said to him, but when I think about it, I actually don't want to know.

He's soon back with two cocktails. "These are on me, ladies," he says, before giving Nyla a wink and scurrying away. We find a table to stand at and take in the surroundings while sipping our cocktails. There are lots of groups of giggling girls who aren't wearing much and are leering over men when they pass.

Nyla looks at me disapprovingly. "You're judging again. Your eyebrows are raised and your lips are slightly puckered."

"Moi? Never," I tell her, chuckling.

Nyla drags me to the dance floor as our favorite song, The Pussycat Dolls' *Don't Cha* comes on, and we dance as if we're teenagers again.

Half an hour later, we're still dancing when I see a group of men laughing. I realize it's gym guy—whom I've decided to name 'Smiler'—and his friends. I turn to Nyla and point to the ladies' room, letting her know I need a break. We go freshen up, and I see Smiler has disappeared. On route to the restroom, I bump into someone, and I'm knocked straight on my ass.

"Shit," I mutter. When I catch my breath and look up, it's him again.

My cheeks flush with embarrassment, and I try getting

up to no avail. He puts his hand out, and I look at him for a second before I finally get to my feet. He has a smirk on his face, so I fire at him, "Well, you could have apologized for knocking me over."

He just looks at me with that damn smirk. "Maybe you should look where you're walking instead of staring down at the floor, then perhaps you won't find yourself on your butt. Although, I've got to say, it was a great view from up here."

His friend approaches and slaps him on the back. "Easy, Reid. It was an accident. Let's go."

What the hell? First in the stairwell. Granted, that was my fault, and I apologized, but this time, he can take ownership. I look at him, unsure if I want to scream at him for his arrogance and rude comments, or kiss his gorgeous lips, which would be so inappropriate. Damn, what is wrong with me? My hormones really are doing a number on me. So, I do what I do best and walk away.

Nyla pulls at my arm and whirls around towards my ass bruiser.

"You're a real jackass, you know that?" She berates him before dragging me along to the restroom. "That asshole. Who does he think he is, speaking to you like that?"

I stand there, flushed, and it then dawns on Nyla.

"You like him, don't you? I knew it."

"I don't even know him. How can you say that? But he is freakin' hot, and have you seen his muscles?"

She bursts out laughing. "Well, when you look at it like that, yeah, he is, but he's fucking rude and arrogant."

Maybe that's what's drawing me to him. The bad boy

image.

We dance for another two hours, then I decide it's enough. It's only one a.m. and Nyla thinks I'm being a lightweight. She comes up to my apartment with me, making sure I'm okay.

"I'm proud of you, Es. Going out there tonight and moving here is a step forward in your recovery. You got this."

I'm still unsure about being alone, so when Nyla leaves, I get locked up for the night. I'm nervous, but I have to keep doing this.

# Chapter Three

I hear a commotion outside and whisk the covers over me in the hope they'll protect me. My body is trembling from head to toe. Pulling back the covers slightly, I hear the disturbance is still going. I remember one of the apartments having some sort of party when I arrived back. Maybe it's that I hear. I walk into the sitting area where voices are louder; there's something about one of the voices. My chest tightens with fear because I'm wondering, how the hell did anyone get inside past security?

When I've determined that the noise isn't in my apartment, the trembling and tightness starts to subside enough for me to get my bearings again. Grabbing the nearest thing to hand, which happens to be a slipper, I make my way to my apartment door. I look through the peephole, and I see Smiler with a couple of teenage boys who I know live in this block. They're having a heated discussion. I unashamedly listen.

"Jesus, I said no parties, not in this building, especially when you're all underage drinking,"

"Sorry, Reid. We just wanted a bit of fun while the folks were away. You know how it is, right?"

"I don't care. You know the rules, now go pack it up." And they scurry off into an apartment opposite mine.

Curiosity has got the better of me, and I open my door a little and peek out. He spins around on hearing the door creak and gives me his signature smirk.

"Go back inside. There's nothing to see."

I move out from behind the door a little. "It didn't seem like nothing."

Feeling his scrutiny reminds me I'm wearing very thin pajama shorts and shirt; they don't leave much to the imagination. I quickly move back behind the door, and my nipples harden at the thought of him. I notice his eyes are not on my face.

"Is it really necessary to stand there and ogle me?" I ask him.

He chuckles. "What's a man supposed to do when it's in front of him? Look, you're right, I am ogling, but would it help my defense if I told you I'm mesmerized by your beauty?"

I'm floored by his words. Has Mr. Arrogant got a nice side to him after all?

"These kids were partying, and we try to keep the building a safe place, so I'm sorry if they disturbed you."

"Erm, okay. Well, thanks for that."

This is turning out to be a weird conversation.

"Night. Esme." And with that, he's gone.

It's Sunday morning, and my last day off to sort the rest of my crap before I have to go back to work. Then I remember that I need to tackle the laundry room in the basement. It creeps me out having to go down there. Firstly, I need my favorite caffeine rush to wake me up. I enter the coffee shop and order my usual vanilla latte. The barista calls my drink out. I grab it then, as I'm leaving, he walks in. Like a gent, he holds the door open for me and waits for me to pass. But in true Esme style, I'm too taken by his looks, so instead of looking where I'm going, I forget there's a step and start to fall to my fate. Damn this man and the unexplainable effect he has on me. I can't even say why. He's not my usual type at all. I mean, he's so full of himself. But these butterflies in my stomach keep coming each time he's around. Smiler reaches for me, but in doing so, he manages to grab my wrist and pulls me back up before I hit the floor.

"Easy, tiger. You okay?"

I tug my wrist from his grasp, but it's too late. The flashback has started.

*Visions of the tattooed wrist on my bedroom door handle, and then being dragged into my room.*

*"NO. NO!"* I scream out.

Only, I'm yelling out loud in the coffee shop. I look around. The faces staring at me are confused by my outburst. I flee from the coffee shop real quick, my latte splashing to the floor as I escape to my apartment. Running as fast as I can, I fumble with my keys to get in. I bolt all the locks when I'm safely inside. My body slides down the wall then succumbs to rocking back and forth, trembling all over. Uncontrollable tears flow, followed by the pain of memories that refuse to leave.

*Gunshots. Screams. Blood.*

Constantly on repeat over and over in my head.

I don't know how much time has passed when I hear knocking at my door. I'm frozen to the spot. The knocking carries on for a few minutes, then whoever it was stops.

My phone immediately rings, and it's Nyla. I continue to let my phone ring off over and over again until I see I have fifteen missed calls, and I can't ignore them any longer. I pick up, but words don't form in my mouth.

"I'm coming. Hold on, Es."

She knocks, but I hear more than her voice outside. I crack open the door slightly, and she's there with Smiler. This time, I'm not greeted with his signature smile. He looks concerned. I turn away, embarrassed. He must think I'm one hell of a lunatic.

Nyla senses the atmosphere. "Look, she'll be fine. Thanks for coming by and checking on her."

She walks over to me, wraps her arms tightly around me and rocks with me. I can't help it. I melt down all over again. Divulging everything that happened doesn't make me feel better. I know what she's thinking when I get a look of sympathy.

"I don't want a damn counselor, Nyla. It's just a blip.

I'll be fine."

Deep down, she knows I'm lying, but doesn't question me.

I've shut down again, and she knows it. Nyla is used to my ways and knows when to push and when not to. She stays, we eat pizza, watch girly movies until we realize it's late and tomorrow's a work day.

"You going to be okay for work tomorrow?"

"I've been slowly getting better for a few months now. Today was a glitch, and tomorrow's a new day." I smile at her, and she hugs me hard.

"Nyla, I can't breathe. Let go of me, damn it."

"Sorry. I just needed to hug you. You're my best friend, and I'm so damn proud of you and how you've handled everything these past fourteen months. I'm always here for you, whatever happens, okay? Don't ever be afraid to ask for help."

I nod after hugging her back.

Once she's gone, I check the locks and go to bed, hoping for a dreamless night. I've forgotten what those are since the trauma. I know I'll never get away from reliving that awful night.

My alarm is blaring, and rolling over, I see it's 6 a.m. Ugh, Monday morning. I walk to the kitchen and switch the coffee machine on. Once I've woken up properly, I start what is to be my daily routine. Shower, dry, hair, then slide into my navy pencil skirt and quickly button up my cream blouse. There's no set uniform at the store, but they do say smart attire and to stick to navy and cream, so we may as well wear a uniform.

I slip on my navy heels and then grab my bagel and cream cheese that I prepared before my shower. By the time I've eaten, it's 7:45 and I need to leave, as it'll take me roughly sixty minutes in rush hour to get across the city. I head down to the lobby, passing Lance on my way out.

"Bye, Lance."

"Bye, Miss Lewis. Have a good day."

As I step out on the sidewalk, I see Smiler and another guy are putting up a sign outside the gym. He notices me and jogs over. I don't really want to deal with him after yesterday's fiasco, so I turn and walk away in the opposite direction. Unfortunately, it doesn't stop him.

"Hey, Esme! Wait up."

I know he's close, so I brace myself, thinking he'll grab my wrist again. He doesn't. Instead, he puts himself in front of me, and I bump straight into him.

"What the hell?"

"Hey. I'm sorry."

It's actually not his fault, but I can't bring myself to look at him. Maybe I'm embarrassed about yesterday, but he puts his finger under my chin then gently tucks my hair behind my ear. This sends chills down my spine, but not bad ones. And those damn butterflies are back again.

"Hey, it's okay," he says reassuringly. I look into his eyes, and instead of seeing his usual smirk, I see concern. "I'm sorry about yesterday. I didn't mean to scare you like that."

I push his hand from my face as it's distracting. "It's

okay. I overreacted."

"May I ask why?"

I look at him, contemplating how to reply. I'm not ready to divulge that part of my life to a stranger just yet.

"Sorry, it's none of my business. I'm just worried about you."

Damn, he really can be a nice guy when he wants to be.

"I have to go to work." I turn and walk away, but I can feel his eyes burning into my back as I go. As I round the corner, I take a quick glance over my shoulder, and I wasn't wrong; he's still watching me.

My first day back goes quickly and smoothly, but that's because Ruby, our boss, lets me go at my own pace. She's even gone as far as to offer to pay for my counseling, which was generous of her.

"Esme, please, if you need anything, my door is always open. Do not hesitate to come see me, all right?"

"Thank you for being so understanding, Ruby. I promise I will."

I decide not to deal with clients today. I'm not quite ready for that, so I work more out back, sorting and stocking up the new travel brochures that are getting ready to be released. That's the joy of working in a travel store. You can always work out back should you need to. I've been there for five years, and one day, I want to run my own store. Making people's holiday dreams come true gives me a fuzzy feeling inside. One day, I dream of traveling more myself and heading for Australia.

Walking past the gym by my apartment, I notice a poster

advertising self-defense classes. The first session is tonight, and it's free. It's exactly what I need, so I sign up then head back home.

While getting ready, my nerves start getting the better of me, but I push past them.

I decide on leggings and a t-shirt, and I throw my hair up into a messy bun. I don't eat until later, as the last thing I want is to over-exert myself and vomit.

I head outside and stand across the street from the gym, staring at the door.

*You can do this, Esme. You can do this.*

I take a deep breath and head over.

It's so quiet in here. I don't know why, but I expected it to be noisy. I approach the young girl at reception, who tells me to go straight through the double doors. As I do, I'm blown away with the noise hitting me. Men are everywhere. Some are using punch bags and doing push-ups. Many are on machines, their feet slapping hard on the treadmills, and there's a huge boxing ring in the center. I look to my left and see a couple of women gawking, a bit like myself, really. I mean, these men are all sweat and muscle. Who wouldn't stand and stare at them? Someone shouts, and I flinch. It must be the noise and my non-familiar surroundings making me edgy.

There's a calling for all those here to attend the class to follow the instructor.

We file into a room and find a space. The guy who I assume is the instructor for the class has his back to us and is chatting to someone. He then turns to face us, and it's

Smiler. I don't want him to notice me as I don't want to explain why I am taking these classes. I try to hide behind another member and keep my head down, but that isn't going to work. I just pray he stays professional throughout the class.

I've survived the first half, and so far, so good, but he will come over, I just know it. I'm talking to a couple next to me. The guy, Jake, thought it was a good idea for his girlfriend, Sophie, to know some self-defense, and she agreed to go if he went too.

Goosebumps prickle my skin, and I know someone is standing behind me. Jake looks over my shoulder, and when I turn my head, there he is. Smiler.

"Is everything okay? Anything you need help with?" he asks.

Jake quickly replies, "No, we're all good." He grabs Sophie, continuing with what we've been shown so far.

I stand, staring. It's like my feet are frozen solid.

"You got a partner?" he asks me.

"No," I tell him.

I can't seem to take my eyes off his body. It doesn't help that he's only wearing gym shorts. His body is well-defined, something I've only ever dreamed about and never seen up close. He laughs deeply, which infuriates me, making me blush. I instinctively turn on my heel and storm toward the changing rooms.

"Hey, where are you going?" he calls out from behind me.

"Home!"

"Why? You were doing so well in there. Just because

you were checking me out and I caught you, doesn't mean you gotta leave." I stop dead.

"Who said I was checking you out?"

"Well, do you always stand there looking at a guy all glassy-eyed like you wanna eat him?"

This guy really is a cocky bastard. Who am I kidding? I was so checking him out. He has abs to die for, and I wanna see what's underneath those shorts, but to just come out and say it is a different matter entirely. I've never had these tingling feelings before. It's obviously his doing, and I want more. I turn to walk away, but he blocks me, and before I can register anything, he leans down and kisses me. His soft lips are pressed to mine while his hand caresses gently through my hair. I feel like I'm walking on air.

The kiss is rough, but also gentle, and after my initial shock wears off, I kiss him back. A fire explodes through my body, one I haven't felt in a very long time, and I become breathless. He slows the kiss down then pulls back slightly and looks down at me.

"You okay?" he asks.

All I can do is nod because I'm lost for words as his body pins mine against the wall. I know the kiss must have affected him too as he looks at his crotch then back at me.

"I've wanted to do that since I first saw you outside the apartment."

I giggle, unsure of what to say. He stands back to look at me, and it's like he is looking into my soul. He can't stop staring at me.

"You're beautiful, you know that?"

I'm confused because I've only ever seen the cocky,

arrogant side of this guy. I've only seen this soft side maybe once, and right now, he appears to be gentle, kind, and sincere.

"Smiler, what's your name?"

"Smiler? Hmm, why the nickname?"

"Well, if you must know, every time I see you, you give me a signature smile, or should I say, a smirk."

He starts with that same deep laugh again. "Reid Taylor is my name, and I can't help that every time I see you, sweetheart, I want to smile."

I blush at his comment, but I don't know what to say. I know he won't let me leave, so I duck under his arm and walk back to the class.

The rest of the class flies by, and once finished, I gather my things and plan on leaving quickly. Trying to concentrate after that kiss is impossible and having to watch him up front is so damn distracting. I need to get home and grab a cold shower. I'm pretty sure the kiss between us was a normal occurrence in his life. I mean, I've seen the way women flirt with him in the gym. He could have his pick, so why settle for me? He'd told me he'd wanted to kiss me since he first saw me, and now he's got it out of his system.

Walking out, I see him disappear towards the shower area with another female, and that tells me all I need to know.

# Chapter Four

The next day at work, I tell Nyla everything. She gets more excited over the events than I do.

"Jesus, I let a man I don't know kiss the ever-living shit out of me!"

"What's so wrong with that?"

I stand there with my mouth hanging open, then laugh. "I gotta admit, Nyla, that man can damn well kiss, and damn, he has a fine body."

"So, what's your problem? It's not like you slept with him. It was just a kiss. It's good to let loose a little."

I know I have to let loose and have some fun, but I don't do fooling around or one-night stands. I'm pretty much a good girl, or I like to think I am most of the time, anyway.

My parents were strict where I was concerned. Being

the only girl, I had to follow their rules. I even had a curfew unless I was staying at Nyla's or with other friends. Then I felt a bit of a rebel. My parents pretty much kept me in line, but now I don't have to follow that line or their rules. I can do what I want, but I'm not quite sure what that is or how to go about it. This isn't the way it was supposed to be.

Since seeing Reid, I was having thoughts and feelings like never before. My body was mixed up, let alone my head.

"Earth to Es. You okay over there? You're looking a bit flushed. Oh my God, you're having dirty thoughts about him, aren't you? Naughty girl! Do not deny it!"

I look away, my face flushing red with embarrassment. I don't know what's happening, but since that kiss, I'm having feelings beyond my control, but I'm also angry because I saw him with another girl. Now I can't stop thinking how hot he is and how his kiss made my panties so wet that I know I came there and then. It's been a long time since I've been with anyone, and boy, could I use the release. Damn it, I need to stop thinking like this. He's a cocky player, and I was just a target he needed to hit. He hit me all right, but never again.

"Es, tell me… what's going on in your head?"

"What's going on in my head, Nyla, is that I will not be going there again."

"You are so going there again. Life is for living! Have some fun. If anyone deserves some, it's you. Plus, if he kisses you again, are you telling me you're going to just push him away?" She grins. "No, I didn't think so. Just take him by the balls and have the ride of your life."

Jase walks into the break room, narrowing his eyes on both of us.

"What on Earth are you doing in here? It had better be something good to keep you both gone this long." He looks between us, and I blush.

"*Oh my God!* You were doing the deed, weren't you? I knew it, I knew it—"

"You would love that, wouldn't you, Jase? Sorry to burst your bubble. Es here was getting it on last night with her gym buddy, and now I'm going to make sure she has more fun with him, and you're going to help me."

My eardrums nearly burst as Jase squeals like a girl. He is mine and Ny's gay best friend and has been trying for months to get me to lighten up and have more fun, in and out of the bedroom. Now I'm in trouble, because once Nyla fills Jase in on last night's antics at the gym, he isn't going to let it go. In fact, I wouldn't put it past him to start attending the damn classes with me now.

"Esme, I want details, babe. The nitty-gritty. Was it hot, sweaty, and pulsating? What's his body like? I need to know everything."

Looking at Jase, you would think Christmas had come early, he was that excited. I can't let him down now, can I?

I chuckle and sit down. He drops down next to me, and Nyla closes the door—this is something I don't want others in the building to be privy to. By the time I'm done, Jase is fanning his face.

"My God, Esme. I need to see this guy that has you all wet and tingly."

"He does not have me wet and tingly."

"Erm, those were your words, not mine. Every time you talk about him you get redder and redder, and you haven't actually complained about what he did. In fact, by my guess, you enjoyed it. Thoroughly enjoyed it. Esme Lewis wants more. The only problem you have is the other woman you saw him with. That could mean anything or nothing. You gotta ask him, girl."

Jase is right. I was annoyed at seeing him walk away with someone else but really didn't have any right to be annoyed. I can't help how I feel. But damn it, I want to feel those lips on me again. The way he kissed me had me soaking in seconds and how his body reacted to the kiss meant I affected him too. But I know I can't just let it happen again. Random hook-ups and kissing guys I don't know? Nope, definitely not me. Getting to know guys first before I go on dates is me, but when I look back at how that's worked out, I laugh because it hasn't worked out at all. I'm twenty-six years old and have had only one serious relationship that lasted all of six months.

My parents made sure they intervened. My boyfriend knew I was a good girl and that there was no sex before marriage. They even asked his intentions for the future regarding me. Lucas seemed keen at the way my parents were interested in my future until he decided to cheat on me after six months. So, after that, I met guys at Nyla's place to avoid my parents and the embarrassment of them again, but I still didn't want to do hook-ups til I got to know them, which never happened. I always felt there was something wrong with me. There must be, as I never seem to get anywhere with guys, so why would Reid be any different? When he finds out that I freak out over noises and random things, he will run for the hills, thinking I'm a crazy bitch.

Nyla thinks I just need to loosen up a bit and not over think everything when I'm out with a guy, so when Reid kissed me last night, I suppose that was me not over thinking. But it scared me. What if we hadn't stopped? How far would someone like him go? I mean, how far would I have gone? It was like he had me under a spell. I just melted into him, and it felt right, but it shouldn't have. He was a stranger, for God's sake, and I didn't even flinch. I know I could easily get hurt. I saw how quickly he moved from me to another in a matter of minutes, and I won't become another notch on his bedpost.

"Okay, Jase. Yes, I enjoyed it. It felt good to be spontaneous for once and let my guard down. But it also scared me, and I didn't like that because I won't be another one of his pawns."

Jase laughs at me. "Have you heard yourself? You make it sound like from a kiss you'll start tearing each other's clothes off and have mad passionate sex exactly where you're standing. *Oh my God!* That's exactly what you want, you filthy girl. You want to get down and dirty with fighter boy."

I feel anger building because I know, deep down, he is right, but I don't want to admit that.

"No, Jase. You're wrong. What I want is to get back work. Now, come on, before we all get into trouble for being missing off the store floor." I walk out of the room, leaving Nyla and Jase lost for words.

The rest of the day goes by without another word mentioned about Reid, which suits me just fine. But in the back of my mind, I can't stop thinking of that damn kiss and what I wanted to happen, and why he walked away so easily with another woman minutes later.

"Jackass," I mumble under my breath.

When we leave work, the weather outside has really picked up, and it's a lovely warm evening.

"Who wants to grab some ice cream before heading home? It's been a while since we've done that."

Nyla seems hesitant about heading home. When I query her about it, she just shrugs me off, so for now, I leave it. The three of us head to Angelo's as he has the best ice cream around, and we sit outside as it's so warm. Nyla hasn't really joined in the conversation, and most of her ice cream has melted.

"Spill, lady. I know something is up. What's going on?"

"I think Russell is having an affair," she blurts out.

I don't know what to say, and she doesn't look upset, she just seems angry.

"Nyla, you and Russell have been together for two years, why do you think that? Talk to me, please."

Nyla just looks at me with a cold smile.

"Things between me and Russell haven't been right for a while now, and I've been kidding myself that they were. I just didn't think he would actually have an affair behind my back. I knew he could be a fucking asshole, I just hoped I was wrong.

Nyla is getting angrier, and when Nyla gets angry, shit

happens.

"I always thought we were upfront with each other. We agreed ages ago that if things ever got to this point in our relationship, then one of us would leave and not have a goddamn affair. How could he do this to me?"

"Nyla, darling, breathe," Jase says softly.

She looks at Jase. Her eyes have started to bulge, and he looks at me as if to say *help*.

"Each time his phone goes off, he's really secretive about it, and he deletes everything. He never used to delete anything. I always had to remind him to do it as his phone was always full."

I look at Nyla with concern. "So, you've been checking his phone? Does he know?" "No. He no longer leaves his phone lying around like he used to. I have to look for his phone when he's out of the room or in the shower." She lets out a big sigh, and her eyes are heavy with sadness.

I take Nyla's hands. "Look at me," I tell her softly, and her eyes meet mine. "What you're doing is only what any sane girlfriend would do in this situation. If Russell is up to something, then you have a right to know. You made an agreement, and he should've stuck to it."

I can see her anger rising again, just when I thought she may be calming down a little.

"If I find out he's definitely cheating on me, I'll be having the party of all parties at my place, and his belongings will be the main focus."

"Well, I'm in. I love a good old smash-and-wreck-it party." Jase and Nyla high five each other.

I put my head in my hands and groan, and they both

laugh at me. Nyla has calmed down some, and it's time we left.

"Why don't you come back with me, and we'll have some girlie time?" I ask.

"Thanks, but I need to face the music and try to find out what's going on, guys."

As we get up, Jase grins while looking at something up street. I turn to see what's caught his attention, and walking towards us is Reid. He's looking straight at me but doesn't look too happy. Jase looks at me and then back to Reid.

"Ooh, who is that?? He's delicious."

Nyla and I chuckle.

"Erm, he doesn't look too happy. Actually, if steam could come out of his ears, I bet it would be right about now."

I stop laughing and look back up in Reid's direction to find he is right by us, and boy, does he look angry. Before my lips move, he speaks, but not to me.

"Who the hell are you?"

He's aiming those words to Jase. Who the hell does he think he is invading our conversation and space? I'm about to speak when Nyla steps up, and with the mood she's already in, I wouldn't like to be in his shoes.

"*He* is our friend, not that it's any of your business."

Without taking his eyes off Jase, he responds to Nyla. "Oh, I'm making it my business, sweetheart."

This just makes Nyla worse tempered, and I step back because I know shit is gonna fly. Nyla gets between Jase and Reid pushes him hard on his chest.

"Excuse me, but we," she waggles her finger between me and Jase, "were having ice cream together, and it's you who has bulldozed your way into our conversation all hot-headed, demanding things when you have no right to. Who the hell do you think you are, caveman?" Before Reid can say anything, Nyla carries on wagging her finger right in his face and continues her rant at him. "You may be all muscles and tall, but you don't intimidate me. How dare you barge in here and demand to know who he is while staring at Esme like you own her?"

By now, everyone has gone quiet.

"Have you finished, sweetheart?"

"My name is *Nyla*."

"Whatever. She won't be long." He grabs me around the waist, about to haul off with me when Jase and Nyla both step in his path.

"I don't think so, caveman. You're taking her nowhere." Nyla frowns at him then Jase pipes up.

"Esme, are you okay going with him? Be honest with us." I look between them both, and I know how worried they must be, thinking of how I'm feeling.

"Guys, it's fine. I will be feet from you, I promise, and what's he going to do with my two bodyguards right here?"

Nyla doesn't look convinced, but I know she trusts my judgement. Within a split second, Reid is carrying me around the corner out of sight of Jase and Nyla.

# Chapter Five

I can't believe he just hauled me up like that in front of my friends. What the fuck does he think he's doing? He releases me, but I'm pinned against the wall of the ice-cream parlor with his arms on either side of my head. He still looks pissed, but his features have started to soften. I go to speak, but he beats me to it.

"Who is he? A boyfriend? A lover? Because I don't share, princess. I'm warning you."

I'm stunned. Since when does he have any right to ask who any man is to me, let alone Jase? I'm so confused. We had a kiss in the heat of the moment during a fucking gym class, and now he's going on like I'm his property. I need to slow him down right now and put a stop to it. I look up at him, and there are those damn butterflies again.

"Reid, look, we had one kiss in the heat of the moment. That does not mean you own me. Jase is my friend, and by the way, he's gay, not that it matters. But you have no right taking me off like you did, and you certainly have no damn right telling me you don't share when we're not even together."

He growls at me. I mean, really growls. It's kinda sexy, but it also gets me pissed with him as he's being more stupid than I thought.

"Esme, that kiss may have been in the heat of the moment, but now I've had it, there's no going back. You're mine." He raises his knuckles to the side of my face and very gently runs them down my cheek, not taking his eyes off mine. In that moment, I'm lost to him. He leans down to kiss me when I move back, remembering why we're here.

"You're delusional. One kiss does not mean I'm yours. Now, if you don't mind, I need to get back to my friends."

I duck beneath his arm and walk away, back toward my friends. I round the corner, but not before looking back at him. His eyes are trained on me, and they're dark and filled with lust.

"You're mine, Esme," he calls out, then he storms away.

I get back to my friends who are looking at me with huge grins on their faces.

"What?"

Nyla speaks first. "Well, damn. That was hot. He sure as hell has it bad for you. Why didn't you say how hot things were between you?"

"There's nothing to tell. The man is fucking deluded. I mean, it was one kiss, and he goes all barbarian on me. He's a player, obviously. As soon as he thought I was gone, he moved onto the next woman in the gym, remember? I saw it with my own eyes."

Jase has amusement dancing in his eyes.

"Jase, why are you looking at me like that?"

"Because I think you're wrong. That ain't no man who plays around. That was 'this is my woman, and you better stay away or else.'"

"Come on, you two. I'm not his woman. There was a moment of weakness last night at the gym, and yes, it was good. Well, actually, it was more than good, but that's all it was. We don't know each other, and under no circumstances does he have any right to make a claim on me, so can we please drop the subject?"

"Fine," Jase says. "I will let it go, but don't think this is the end of it if the look he was giving you was anything to go by. I think you will be seeing him again real soon."

Nyla laughs and links her arm in mine to make our way to the subway station.

Walking into my apartment building, I say hi to Lance. He's in his fifties and a genuinely nice man. He waves back as I'm getting into the elevator, but then I hear him say, "Hi, Reid."

I quickly press the button for my floor, willing the doors to close real fast. I turn around, our eyes meet, and he walks faster toward the elevator. My heart races as fast as my finger is pressing the button, and luckily, the doors close before he gets in. I will the elevator to hurry up, as I just want to get into my apartment. I can't deal with an overbearing caveman twice in one day. The doors slide open, and I make for my apartment, but just as I get the door open, Reid barrels through the stairwell door and heads straight for me. I slam my door shut before he is toe to toe with me, but he bangs on the door. This guy doesn't know how to take a hint.

I lean against the door, sliding down it until I hit the floor, and then I just sit there.

"Open up, Esme. I just want to talk, please."

His voice sounds so soft. I begin to wonder if it really would hurt to talk to him. But then I remember the gym scene and how it hurt to see him go straight to another girl. It was like a punch to my stomach, but he wouldn't get that. He probably does it a lot. For me, if I kiss someone with the fire that we kissed, then walking off with another guy less than twenty minutes later just would not happen. With that in mind, I go back to being stubborn.

I don't answer him because there's no good guy in what he did. I continue to sit there, then he starts knocking again. His persistent knocking is hurting my damn head.

*Bang, bang, bang.*

"Please, just go away and leave me alone. I have nothing to say to you."

"I'm not going anywhere until you damn well talk to me. So, you have a choice. You can make this easy and just open up now, or I can wait here until you need to go out, but I will make a nuisance of myself and you will only have yourself to blame."

I laugh because I cannot believe the balls this guy has. What does he mean, I will only have myself to blame? Is Jase right, and he really does have it bad for me? *Jesus, Esme. Get a grip, will you?* I decide not to give in to his demands. He can talk through the door. Two can play this game.

"Okay, talk, Smiler." I call out to him. "But I ain't opening the door. Whatever you wanna say, just say it."

There's no response, so I call out his name, and still nothing. He must've got the message and given up. I take a deep breath and jump up off the floor. I need a shower, and then I have plans to veg out on my couch for the rest of the evening. I can hear noises outside on the fire escape, so I walk toward the windows to close them, but don't make it two feet when a huge figure falls through it, causing me to scream. I start running toward my bedroom, but I don't make it. The unknown figure grabs my wrist, and I freeze. I'm numb, and my eyes blur, trying to focus on anything but the memories. Whoever is holding me is talking. I don't hear anything he's saying. All that's running through my mind is that night—the night where everything that mattered was taken from me. Where one of the murderers pinned me to the floor, and had it not been for the sound of the sirens, I'd have been raped. Then darkness closes over my eyes, and I'm out.

"Ain't going nowhere 'til she wakes up," I hear someone growl.

There's a voice I recognize, but I'm not exactly sure what's happening. I must be dreaming. Then I hear Nyla and Reid arguing. I slowly open my eyes, but everything is fuzzy. I realize I'm on my bed, but why are they both here in my apartment, arguing? I try to focus and think. I remember coming into my apartment to get away from Reid, then I remember someone coming in through my window and grabbing me.

I start to panic and knock my lamp off the side, and they obviously heard it because they both race in. Nyla wraps her arms around me and rocks me, telling me it's okay, and Reid is standing there, running his hand through his hair and looking like he's not sure what to do.

Nyla stares at him. "Next time, try using the door."

I'm more confused about what Nyla is talking about. Why is she telling Reid to use the door?

Reid glances at me, and it's not a look I've seen on him before. It's not his usual smiling self. He looks defeated. His eyes are blank, and his head is down.

"What is she talking about? Why'd you have to use the door next time?"

He looks at me and then to Nyla. "I was annoyed when you wouldn't open the door and talk to me, so I climbed up the fire escape to talk to you through the window, but I lost my footing and ended up falling through. The next thing I knew, you were running off, so I grabbed you and, well…"

"Oh my God, *YOU*! You grabbed my wrist!"

"Believe me, Esme, I'm sorry. Especially after the other day. But my brain doesn't always think straight. Dammit, woman. You scared the hell out of me when you blacked out like that. I called Nyla, not knowing how to handle what was happening. Oh, and don't get me started on you not keeping your phone locked."

He paces around my room like an animal. It's like he doesn't know what to do or what to say. And what's with the lecture about my phone?

"I know it doesn't show me in a good light. In fact,

it probably shows me to be more stalker-like. But please know, in my head, I thought I was doing the right thing, I swear. Sometimes I can be a little over-reactive."

"Nyla, give us a minute, will you?" I ask.

She looks at me sympathetically. "Sure. I'll be in the kitchen."

"Thanks."

Looking at Reid right now makes me feel like his nickname, Smiler, doesn't quite fit him. The usual smirk's completely gone, and all I see is a mixture of sadness and torture flooding across his face. All that's fine, but damn, I'm so angry with him. How dare he think it's okay to climb up the side of my apartment and scare me like that? Just because I didn't speak to him. Fuck, he's definitely got issues with behavior and control. He needs to understand this isn't acceptable.

"Reid."

He looks at me then sits on the edge of my bed.

"You called me Reid. I like it when you call me by my first name." He has a smoldering look in his eyes again. It melts me a little, but I'm still pissed, and I'll be damned if he's getting off that lightly.

"You had no right to do what you did. You know that, right?"

The smoldering look has vanished. Now rears his annoyance, but there is no way that's happening. Not this time.

"What you did was irrational. You scared me to the point that I blacked out. Do you even understand that?" By now, I'm standing, and my voice is raised. I don't give him a chance to answer yet. I keep firing at him. "You really have no idea what went through my head when I saw this huge figure barreling through my window. You couldn't give a shit, really, as you don't know me or anything about my life. But let me tell you something, I thought I was about to die all over again, and this time…" I'm an emotional wreck, and Reid has no idea what I'm ranting about. He stands and holds out his hand. I know he's asking for permission to take it, and although I probably shouldn't, I do. He gently pulls me into him, then lifts me onto his lap. Maybe doing this with him right now isn't right, but being in his arms feels good, and I cling to his t-shirt.

"Esme, I've fucked up big time, and if you never forgive me, I'll understand. But I won't give up trying with you. Not yet, anyway. Causing you such heartache wasn't my intention. But will you tell me what caused you to blackout the way you did? Other than me being a tool."

I lean away from him and wipe my face. I'm embarrassed he's seen me this way. I must look a blithering wreck, but this is his fault, after all.

"I blacked out because you decided to be stupid while falling into my apartment. How's that for a reason?" I push off him, needing my space. Nyla walks back in. I know she's been listening to us.

"I think you should leave now."

He looks from Nyla to me. I turn away. It doesn't feel right, telling him about my past and what happened.

"No, not leaving. I may have been the cause of you blacking out, and I regret that deeply, but there's something else that you aren't sharing, and it's scaring you. I care about you, Esme. So, fuck it. I won't leave until you talk to me. Please let me help and try to understand. Give me that, please."

He makes me melt inside once again with his choice of words.

"How can you say you care about me when we hardly know each other?"

He doesn't hesitate to respond. "I have no idea why, but there is something about you that won't leave me. That kiss sent shivers down my spine like nothing I had ever felt before, and it just sealed it for me. The little bumps here and there were meant to be."

And bizarrely enough, what he says is kind of how I've been feeling too. Maybe letting another person in who doesn't really know me may help. I don't know, but it sure can't do any harm, can it?

He must take my silence as a yes. With that, he tries to walk Nyla out of the room. She looks around him at me, waiting for the okay.

"Es, are you sure you want to be left with him? He could be a nutjob, although he did call me in the first instance."

"Yes, Ny. It's all good. I love you."

"I mean it, caveman. Do not hurt her, or I will kill you. That I promise."

"Now, that I believe," Reid says with a smile.

I expected Nyla to barge her way back in and give him hell for manhandling her like that, but all I hear is her chuckling and talking as she walks through my apartment. My guess is that she's called Jase, giving him all the gossip. Those guys are like damn teenagers, but I do love them.

Looking up at Reid, I see questions in his face. Telling someone who isn't close to me will feel like a relief. It's also the only way he will ever understand me. He sits back on the bed, pulling me on to his lap. I go to push myself off, but he holds me in place.

"When you're ready, princess."

I fiddle with the hem of my top and slowly unfold my story. The gunshots. The screaming. The terrifying silence as my family lay dead. My breathing becomes labored as I re-tell the story of that horrific night. Reid holds me tighter and whispers softly in my ear, "I've got you."

I tell him how I hid inside the wardrobe and how I stupidly thought they'd gone as the voices had gone quieter, but I was wrong. So, so wrong. The tears gush down my face. Reid tries his best to calm me, but I need to finish this now, so I keep talking. I know he's struggling to keep it together as his body has become tense.

I'm at the part where the intruder grabbed my wrist and dragged me back into my room, when out of the blue, Reid roars, "Motherfucker!"

I scramble off his lap and claw up the bed fast, scared of what he's going to do. He comes toward me, but I'm curled into a ball, shutting myself off from him.

"God, no. Esme, please don't pull away from me. I'm sorry. I could've handled that better. Shit, I just heard some motherfucker put his hands on you and…"

"I wasn't raped," I blurt out. I have no idea why I felt the need to drop that out.

He stops dead, and you could hear a pin drop.

"You weren't?"

"No, but only because of the sirens. They had no choice but to leave."

This statement doesn't calm him anymore.

I finish telling him how I found my family in a bloodbath and how the darkness took over.

Reid holds both my hands and gently rubs my wrists. "Now, I understand the whole wrist issue." The tears haven't stopped, but I don't really care anymore. It's who I am right now.

I look up at him, scared of what I'm about to say, but he needs to hear this. In fact, I *need* to say this.

"It's just the grabbing of my wrist sends my head and heart right back to that night. It doesn't matter how hard I try, I can't pull myself back to the here and now. I wonder if I'll ever be able to."

He wraps his arms around me tightly and just holds me. I hear him talking to me, but I'm so sleepy that I'm slipping away, then everything is quiet.

# Chapter Six

I wake to a warm, hard body pressed against me and an arm slung over me. Panic tries to set in, but I know who is next to me when that tingling feeling returns. Turning my head, I come face to face with the most intense chocolate eyes ever and the biggest smirk. It's a pleasant sight.

"Morning, sleepy." He's lying in my bed like it's his own.

"Making yourself at home, I see."

"Actually, you fell asleep in my arms last night, and being the gentleman I am, I put you to bed, leaving your dignity intact."

I look down, relieved to see I'm still fully clothed, and so is he.

"Hey, don't get me wrong. I could've happily removed your clothes, but I've put you through enough in the last twelve hours with my stupid behavior."

Wow. He's all protective and caring and owning his stupidity. I think underneath his arrogance and cockiness, there is a soft side to Reid. I'd also be lying if I said I was totally opposed to him taking off my clothes. I jump up from the bed and head to the bathroom to splash my face. I need cooling down and quick before he realizes how his words affected me.

When I return, he's sitting on the edge of the bed, waiting for me. I just stand in the doorway, staring at him. He really is a handsome madman. I wonder how I got a guy like him to notice a girl like me, a nobody with a fucked up past.

"You okay, princess?" I smile at the nickname he's given me. I've never had one before. I'm always known as Es or Esme. I love my name, but a nickname seems more personal.

"Yes, I'm fine. Can I ask, why did you stay the night? And in my bed?"

He walks over and stands before me. "You really think after what you told me and how you reacted from me breaking in that I was going to leave you alone? You really don't know me at all."

I push at his chest, but it's like trying to move a brick wall. I manage to duck underneath his arm and out to the sitting area.

"You're right, I don't know you at all. It's only been just over a week that we've known each other. Yet you've managed to intimidate my friends, manhandle me in the street, and break into my apartment and cause me to blackout." He starts to talk, but I put my hand up to stop him. "Let me finish. I then open up, tell you exactly why I am the way I am, only to wake and find you comfy in my bed. And this has all happened in the space of two days, so please don't dictate to me that I don't know you when it's you who has bulldozed your way into my life and my space."

"You've got me there. I can't deny any of what you said. But even if words haven't always crossed between us, we've exchanged bumps in stairwells and the store, so we have a little history of our paths overlapping. I'd say that's fate, wouldn't you?" He winks at me.

I sit back down, taking the biggest breath ever. Reid has a big smile on his face, but it's not his usual smirk. It's an actual smile this time.

"Why are you smiling at me? Did I say something funny? Because I don't recall anything."

"Actually, you are funny. No one's ever stood up to me and told me exactly what they think before. You're right. I have bulldozed my way into your life, but there was something about you, and after that kiss in the gym, I knew I couldn't just walk away. I knew you needed protecting. Why? I have no idea. It was a hunch. That kiss was like an addiction. Now I've had it, I'll do what I need to get more. This just sealed the deal. Oh, and I protect what's mine. Always. So, you'd better get used to it because I'm not going anywhere."

He sits on the sofa with a longing stare, waiting for my response.

"What if the macho thing isn't what I want, though?

I may want to be wined and dined, go out on dates, and get to know you before I make a commitment or any rash decisions like a relationship."

I knew I was lying to myself because yet again, I feel all mushy inside just from hearing his words about protecting me and saying I'm his. I like his macho ways, even if they are a little over the top, but I'm not about to admit that to him. He needs to work for my affections, and damn am I gonna make him work. How long I can hold out before I crack, only time will tell. This could be fun. If I can last, that is.

He pulls me into his lap and lifts my chin so I'm looking into his eyes.

"Esme, what happened last night and what you told me nearly broke me, so if you need to be wined and dined in order for me to prove my feelings for you, then so be it, and dates it will be."

I look at him wide-eyed. I can't believe he's agreeing to my terms.

We talk some more and agree that I will keep attending the self-defense classes.

"Will you still be teaching the classes?"

"It's usually me or Ash that teaches, but I will always make sure I'm there when it comes to your classes. Don't you worry."

I look up at him with a mischievous grin. "I'm sure I can cope with Ash teaching me, especially as he's as easy on the eye as the other instructor."

Before I know it, I'm on my back on the sofa, and he's hovering over me with those lust-filled chocolate eyes staring straight at me.

"This okay?" he asks, and I nod. "Good. Don't ever tease me where other men are concerned. I don't play nice. You know that." He slams his mouth down on mine, kissing me possessively.

He kisses me just like he did the first time, then he slows it down, and it becomes more passionate. I wrap my arms around his neck and pull him down further. I want more. I need more, but I know we need to take this slow. Things have moved too fast for us already, and that's not my doing. It's all him. I pull away, but I'm breathless, and he knows the effect he's having on me. He gets up and then pulls me to my feet.

"Come on. It's breakfast time, then I need to head out for work. Plus, I know you have somewhere to be too."

He gives me a slap on the ass and a cheeky wink and strides to my kitchenette. I follow him and make us some coffee, and he gets to work on making pancakes.

After we've eaten, I shower and dress, and then we leave my apartment together. I step into the elevator, and he presses the button but then steps back out.

"Hey, you not coming down with me?"

"Sorry. I need to head back to my place and change." Reid leans into me, giving me a deep and meaningful kiss. As I kiss him back, I hear myself moan. I pull back, and there's a huge smile on his face.

"I'll see you later," he says. "Now, go before I change my mind and take you upstairs with me." His voice has turned real husky, and he sounds so sexy. So, before I take him up on his offer, I step back inside the elevator and re-press the button. The doors close, and I sink back against the wall with the biggest grin on my face.

*What am I doing*? I've known this guy for just shy of two weeks, and last night was the first time we'd really spoken. And that was only because he has pushed his way into my life. I've made my feelings known now, and maybe, just maybe, he will calm his caveman ways and let whatever this is between us develop naturally.

"Hi, Miss Lewis. Have a good day," Lance calls over to me as I walk through the foyer.

"Please, Lance, call me Esme. Miss Lewis makes me sound like a schoolteacher." I chuckle.

"Okay, if you're sure."

"I'm sure. Now, I gotta go, or I'll be late. Bye."

"Bye, Esme," he calls out.

When I arrive at work, Nyla and Jase are already waiting outside for me. They come straight for me, so I turn and walk back the other way, but I can hear their footsteps running behind me to catch up.

"Oh, no you don't, missy. Details, now." Jase turns me around by my elbow and frog-marches me into the store we work in and straight into the back room. We're followed by Nyla, who can't stop laughing like the devil as she slams the door shut.

Jase pushes me down into a chair and then grabs one for himself. He sits on it backwards, right in front of me, so I'm pinned between him and the wall.

I laugh because he's desperate to know what happened, so I lean forward and get right in his face. "A lady never kisses and tells, sir."

"You always tell everything, Esme. Now dish the dirt, lady, and dish it fast before Ruby comes in here telling us to start work. I have to know what dirty stuff went down when Nyla got the boot."

We'll need to be on the store floor for when the doors open, so I quickly tell them a condensed version of what happened after Reid forced Nyla out of my bedroom. Both of them sit with their mouths hanging open, and I'm not sure what to make of their expressions.

"Come on, guys. Say something."

"Well, I want details, and I mean everything." Jase. Always the gossip.

"I'm glad things turned out okay for you." Something seems off with Nyla. I expected her to grill me on everything, but her mind seems elsewhere.

"What's wrong? And don't say *nothing* because your whole expression says differently. 'Fess up, Ny."

What she says, I should have seen coming, but Nyla likes to deal with her problems herself, mostly. If she needs you, she'll tell you.

"I broke up with Russell last night. Sorry, Es. I don't mean to make this about me."

"Hey, it's fine, really. What happened?"

"Well, after I left your place, I went home. I tried to be quiet when letting myself in. I didn't want to wake Russell. He can be a moody asshole. I was tiptoeing toward my bedroom when I heard him talking to someone, but he was talking in a sexual way."

"What did he say, Nyla?"

I slap my hand across Jase's arm. "Fuck, Jase. Really?"

"It's fine, honestly. I really couldn't give a shit anymore. His words were, '*Yeah, baby. Spread your juices*'. I pushed the door open, and there he was, cock in his hand, pumping away while video calling with another woman. Can you fucking believe it?"

"You ladies really do lead exciting lives these days. Who needs talk shows when I have you two to follow? Sorry, Nyla. That was insensitive of me. He's an asshole for not treating you like the queen you truly are."

"You're right. What would you do without us girls, eh?"

He chuckles then turns to me. "And Esme, he really does have it bad for you. And whether you like it or not, I think he's staying put, so you'd better get used to it. He may have gone the wrong way about it, but damn, I wish someone would climb my ladder just to get to me."

I can't help but laugh at his use of words. It's typical Jase. He sashays back into the store floor area before Ruby comes looking for us. I look at Nyla to see if she's putting on a brave face for us when I know deep down she's probably falling apart, but there are no outward signs of being depressed or upset. That worries me even more. I put my arms around her and give her the biggest hug.

"Es, I really am okay. I knew something was going on. I just didn't expect to walk in on it."

"Did you know her?"

"No, I don't think so. I couldn't see her properly, and I didn't want to look too hard at the screen." She grimaces. "All I do know is that I'm better off out of that relationship. It's time to move on."

We sit with our arms around one another.

"Where are you going to stay, Nyla? You're more than welcome to move in with me."

She laughs. "I threw him and all his things out. That apartment is mine, not his. So, maybe your caveman has a cave buddy for me." She bats her eyelashes at me.

The rest of the day goes by real slow, and between what happened last night and Nyla's problem, my head doesn't seem to know what to do with itself. I'm sitting at my desk, staring at a blank screen on my computer when my phone beeps. I fish it out of my bag, wondering who would be messaging me as Nyla and Jase are here with me, and I don't have any other friends.

**Reid**: Hey, princess. How's your day going?

I look over toward Nyla and she's busy with a customer, so I can't ask her if she gave him my number, but I know she wouldn't have done that. He must have done it himself when I was sleeping. It's the only logical explanation. I start tapping a reply back to him, but it's not the reply he will be expecting.

**Me**: Don't you *princess* me. How dare you go in my phone and invade my privacy? What gives you the right, Smiler?"

I sit and wait for his reply because I know one is coming. He won't let it go now I've pushed his ego.

**Reid**: I'm just checking you're okay I told you I care about you. Oh, we're back to Smiler now, are we?

I thought we'd gotten somewhere this morning with our talk, but it was obviously short fucking lived.

**Me**: Fuck you!

Why, oh why did I send that? I know exactly what reply I will get, and I deserve it. My phone pings instantly.

**Reid**: I intend to very soon.

I slam my phone down on my desk and grunt, "Fucker." But I must have said it louder than I realized because, as I look up, everyone is looking at me, colleagues and customers.

"Oh my God, I'm so sorry." I retreat to the back room to calm down and busy myself sorting through some magazines. Fifteen minutes later, I quickly grab my coat and bag as it's nearly five p.m., plus I'm so embarrassed over my outburst.

Nyla's finished with her customer and walks out with me.

"Spill it. What has you so wound up that you felt the need to share it with everyone back there?"

"Reid went into my phone while I was sleeping and put his number in it, and now the fucker is messaging me."

Nyla bends over with laughter. "Sorry, but you must have seen this coming. The guy is a tad crazy where you're concerned, and he's made it clear how protective he is of you. Plus, when will you learn to lock your damn phone?"

"Oh, not you as well. It shouldn't matter if my phone is locked or not. He invaded my privacy."

Plus, he's done this without asking. It doesn't sit well with me.

"Okay, you're right, but you've just got to be firm with him about it."

We both burst out laughing at her statement, because…

like that is ever going to happen.

What I do know is that I really need to learn to put a pin on my phone. If he thinks for one second he's getting away with it, then he's got another think coming.

We make our way to Nyla's. We're going out tonight to let loose. Nyla needed girl time, and dancing and drinking is her way of doing that. Man, could I do with some of that too.

# Chapter Seven

My phone's been blowing up with texts since I arrived at Nyla's, and they're all from Reid. I'm refusing to reply to any of them. I'm still annoyed with him for going into my phone and taking my number while I was sleeping, and him thinking it was okay to do so without my consent. We're just finishing the last touches to our make-up before heading out when my phone pings again, and Nyla grabs it.

"He really isn't giving up, is he? Why don't you just reply, and maybe your phone will get a break." She busts out laughing as she knows damn well that's not happening.

**Reid**: Where are you?

**Me**: None of your business. Now back off.

I feel quite proud of myself. I'm actually standing up to him. Yes, it may be over text, but I'm telling him, and I feel elated.

My phone pings again.

**Reid**: I'll find out eventually, and when I do, so help me God!

I stumble back on to the bed, shocked. Holy shit, what an asshole! I show Ny the message.

"Wow, that man's got it bad. But for tonight, ignore him, because it's a girls' night, and we are out to have fun."

I start to giggle, but then I get serious.

"What am I going to do, Nyla? He is so over the top, and we've only known each other just shy of two weeks."

She sits down next to me, and holds my hands like she always does when we're having a heart to heart. "Honey, it's about time you had someone who can look out for you, and if there are benefits alongside it, then what harm can it do? Yes, he is a little overprotective. Actually, extremely overprotective. But you are a strong-willed woman when you want to be, and if you put your mind to it, you can handle him."

"Really? You think I can handle Reid?"

We both drop back on the bed, and Nyla continues talking about how she thinks it's about time I had some fun and male attention. If he wants to protect me in the meantime, then it may just help bring my confidence back and help me to move on. I was strong once, but I let my parents rule everything about me, even when I became of age for drinking and sex. Nyla's right. It's time for me to take back control.

I think about what she said, and I know I've been over

analyzing things, but I want to have some fun with Reid. I think, deep down, beyond his macho ways, there's a guy who'll look after me in every aspect. I shoot him a quick message.

**Me**: I'm out. Will see you tomorrow, then we'll talk.

He responds straight away, which doesn't surprise me in the slightest.

Reid: Fine, I'll do it your way. Can I know where you are? Just wanna know you're safe.

Have I got him wrong? It's a bit much in such a short space of time. He has warned me often enough of his dramatic ways.

**Me**: Okay, we're going to Good Room. Now stop hassling me. I'll speak to you tomorrow.

All remains quiet from him, so I'm guessing my last message has heeded him. So, we head out for a fun night.

We're ordering cocktails whilst the club's slowly filling up to the pumping music. We grab our drinks then head for a high table on the edge of the dance floor. We're sitting there when we hear voices behind us. We turn to see Jase, with his twin sisters, Melody, and Macie. Nyla gives me a smirk. She knew they were coming. It was all planned. So much for our girly night out, but I'm not annoyed. The more, the merrier. Jase is more of a girl, anyway. The twins are stunning, with long blonde hair and legs that seem to go on forever. They're good girls, but they've just turned twenty-one, and now Jase has his hands full keeping an eye on them. He's very protective, as any big brother would be.

It's time for some dancing when *Shout Out To My Ex*

starts playing. I grab Nyla and the twins, and we mingle with the crowd, dancing our asses off. I'm not sure how many songs have passed, but the twins have gained the attention of a group of guys.

Two guys make a beeline for Nyla and me. We've have had a few cocktails by now, and we're feeling playful. I should behave considering everything I've been through, but my body is telling me to let loose. What harm can it do to dance with them? They come up behind us, and I feel some large hands grip my hips. I freeze, and then I remove them from my body.

Then he whispers in my ear. "Just relax and dance."

He's a little close, but his hands are now being kept to himself.

So, I'm swaying, and as the music gets further along, I look over to Nyla and notice she now has her arms wrapped around a guy's neck.  I'm not stopping her, as she needs to have fun after everything Russell has put her through lately. It couldn't do any harm. It's been a while since we had some fun like this.

The guy who has his hands on my hips takes the lead, and we carry on dancing. He turns to face me, but he's become way too close for comfort. I put my hands on his chest to push him away, but he's too close. Then, without warning, he grabs my ass, pinning us together. Grabbing hold of his biceps, I struggle to get him to move back. Even as I try to back away, he has a firm hold of me. Now I'm scared. Why won't he let me go?

"Get off me, please."

But he doesn't budge.

I look at him, about to plead again when I see his dry lips are all puckered up and heading for mine.

Oh, shit, no. I start to turn away when I feel him let me go.

"I believe the lady said get off." Puckered lips has been pulled away. Now, I'm face to face with Reid. An unhappy Reid.

The guy has scuttled off somewhere, but I'm more focused on the fact that Reid is here.

"Thank you for saving me." I say.

He lowers his mouth to my ear and growls. "No one gets to put their hands on what's mine, and in case you didn't understand the first time, hear this. You're most definitely mine."

His tone is one of deep anger, but he also looks wounded. Fuck, is this my doing? This isn't fair on either of us, and I'm tired. He's not exactly given me much choice about how it will be, but I think he's proved he isn't going anywhere fast. I need to pull up my big girl pants, take a chance, or say *adios* once and for all.

"I'm sorry. Nyla and I just wanted to have some fun dancing. I never expected that." He still hasn't said anything, so I try something else. "Will you dance with me?"

He doesn't have to be asked twice. I'm pulled into him, and we start swaying together.

Life is about chances, and I'm taking this one. I'm tired of being a good girl. Life's been really cruel these last few months. Maybe Reid is the medicine needed. Hot, sexy, and a whole lotta fun in between. The protective stance is a big plus with how jittery I am. It also has its advantages as he's my own personal bodyguard.

I snicker to myself, but then realize I was doing so out loud. The alcohol in my system doesn't help. Now Reid's looking at me like I'm crazy, which is probably true.

"Care to share what's so funny?"

I stay quiet, staring up at him, then I reach up on my tiptoes and wrap my arms around his neck. I wrench his lips towards mine and kiss him with all the passion I can muster. He kisses me back just as fiercely, and that's when I have a brave moment and jump into his arms. We're making out like wild animals while dancing. His arm grips me tight round my ass, the other is in my hair while he growls like a beast in the middle of devouring my mouth.

I'm certain by this point that I want him. I whisper in his ear.

"I need you. Please take me home."

He swoops me up into his arms and heads out of the club. He gets me to hold his phone to his ear while he chats to Ash, I presume.

"Ash is taking Nyla home. He'll take good care of her, I promise."

It's like he can read my mind and knew what was going through it without me speaking. It took all my worry away about my best friend.

I'll still have words with him about him invading my phone. There are boundaries, and he's crossed them. But right now, my body hungers for everything that's Reid.

We jump in a cab, and once inside, Reid wastes no time in pulling me on to his lap so I can straddle him. Damn, I'm feeling bold now. His hands are roaming everywhere, and it feels electric.

"Your skin feels so soft, like silk," he pants.

His touch is soft but rough at the same time, and it's setting sparks off all over my body in places I never knew were sensitive. I want, need, and crave so much more.

I'm dry humping Reid. These firsts just keep coming, and I hope they don't stop. We're becoming more sexually heated as the cab ride goes on. He tries adjusting his bulging erection; it looks uncomfortable in his jeans. We arrive within minutes at the apartment building. Reid rapidly exits the car then clutches my hand to help me out.

"Who would have thought you could be a real gentleman underneath that rough exterior?"

Reid gives me a devilish look, and then I'm slung over his shoulder, only to be waltzed through the foyer, squealing like a child.

"Oh, a gentleman I can be. But right now, I want you upstairs in my bed, so I can worship you like the royalty that you are, okay?"

A grunt sounds, signaling that Lance heard everything Reid said. I drop my head in shame on Reid's back as I'm hanging over his shoulder.

"Lance," Reid says, striding towards the elevators.

"Reid," Lance replies. I look up and mouth *sorry*, only to see the biggest grin on his face, which he cheekily follows with a thumbs-up sign.

Even Lance is happy about this. The door slides shut on the elevator. Reid slides me down, but pins me against the wall to continue his sexual torture on me. Who am I to complain? His kiss is an addiction, and I will always need more. It's like I can't let him go. This is what he meant when he said pretty much those words to me too.

From our first kiss, I was hooked. I dreamt of all the naughty and dirty places those lips could go, and don't get me started on what he could do with that mouth of his. His hands travel down my neck and then along my shoulders. He grabs hold of the straps of my dress, ripping it open and baring my breasts.

"What the fuck?"

He growls like a beast, and I can't help but look into those mesmerizing chocolate eyes of his. I don't get a chance as he latches on to my nipple with his mouth, and the sensations that spark through my body are like nothing I've ever experienced.

His other hand slowly maneuvers across the other breast then slides over my hip until it reaches the hem of my dress. My panting has become heavy, and lasting doesn't look good. When the elevator pings and the doors slam open, I gasp because I expect to see someone waiting to enter. Luckily, there isn't, and we've reached Reid's floor where he tugs me out, not letting me cover up. I begin to protest when he opens a door and swoops me into a bedroom so fast I hardly have time to catch my breath.

Standing in front of me as Reid is right now, it's like looking at a god. He's pure perfection. His eyes are filled with lust, and I know his cock will do things to blow my mind as it's struggling to stay inside his pants. He strips off his top and pants and remains only in his boxers, then he steps closer to me, brushing my hair behind my ear before gently kissing me again. He drops gentle kisses to my cheek then my neck while slowly removing what's left of my dress from my body. It feels different than when we were in the elevator, and true to his word, he is slowly worshipping me. Eventually, my tattered dress drops to the floor, and I'm left in my lace panties. He wraps his fist around them, and with a quick tug, they're gone. Being exposed so suddenly, I gasp.

"I will replace them," he says with a grin. "In fact, it may be best if you don't wear any again, princess."

I don't know what to say to that. No one has ever spoken to me with such words before, and while I still think he is a caveman with issues, I'm hugely turned on by it and too busy thinking of my soaked panties that he ripped off.

"Really!"

"Sshh. Just follow my lead and trust me."

I am now completely naked and at his mercy. My body is craving his more than it should, but it's been too long since I've had sex, and Reid is sparking things within me that no man has ever done before. I don't know how long I can last before that first orgasm ricochets through me. If I'm naked, then he should be too. I want to see every part of this beast in front of me. Bending down, I hook my fingers into his boxers waistband, pulling them down until his cock springs free and juts upwards towards his stomach.

I gulp loudly. Massive is an understatement. His package is what the ladies were gawping at in the gym, and I can't blame them, but it's all mine now.

I must've been observing a little too long as I'm being

lifted up. I use this chance to wrap my legs around his waist. Looking into his lustful chocolate irises hypnotizes me. It's like his eyes draw me to what's underneath that rugged exterior of his. He's staring at me now with such hunger and passion, I know there's no going back, and I'm done fighting it.

Reid kisses me and consumes me with his caresses. He places me gently on the bed, leaning over me and kissing my earlobes. I move my hand to feel his cock, and he groans loudly as I take it in my hand and slowly stroke him. He strokes his index finger across my now throbbing clit, and my breathy pants become more and more erratic. I need Reid Taylor more and more, and I'm eager for him to make love to me.

"Please, Reid," I beg.

He thrusts his fingers inside me and his thumb rubs over my clit. The sensations that are building within my stomach are so powerful it's like I'm about to combust.

"Holy fuck. ARRGGHH!"

Reid whispers in my ear, "Scream the building down, princess. Go for it."

He doesn't relent on the thrusting. His fingers are pushing in and out of me so fast that the orgasm building within me is on the brink of detonating.

"I need to taste you."

This is a new concept for me. Previous boyfriends never got that far; it wasn't something I felt comfortable with. With Reid, it's different, but he must sense my hesitancy because concern crosses his beautiful face.

"First time?" I just nod in reply. "I'll be gentle, I

promise."

He slides my legs apart and groans. Then he licks upward over my clit and sucks. Gripping the bedsheets with my fists and digging my heels into the bed, I try to control the orgasm tearing through me like a freight train at a hundred miles per hour. No orgasm has ever done this before.

"Jesus Christ, Reid," I cry out as my body spasms out of control. He keeps up the assault until my body lapses slightly. He then peppers kisses up my torso until he reaches my lips. I turn my face away, because kissing a guy after that seems wrong, but he isn't letting me off that easily.

"Never before?" he asks, and I shake my head. "I promise you'll like it. Do you trust me?"

I nod, and he kisses me gently. It's not like I thought at all; it's quite sweet.

Before we get too carried away, Reid stands and walks over to his bedside unit. I'm unsure what he's doing when I hear a foil packet being ripped open. In the next instant, he's at the foot of the bed, rolling the condom over his swollen cock. It's fucking beautiful. My desire for him is so hot, and I need him filling me faster than a speeding car on a race track. I gulp because his cock seems to have swelled even more while I've been admiring it. But before I can think any more, I'm pulled down the bed, and Reid gently slides himself inside me.

"I need to know if I hurt you, okay?"

I look up at him and the alpha male that I'm used to seeing is still there, but this guy is all about caring for me right now. While I love it and want to take things slow, my hormones and body tell me otherwise, and I want my alpha Reid right now.

"Yes, now can you please fuck me hard, Smiler?"

The nickname is all it takes; he grabs me by my hips, pulls back, and thrusts inside me, repeating it over and over again like a savage animal. He pushes my legs up onto his shoulders, then his hands are on my breasts, pinching at my nipples. From the deepness his cock is taking and the pain his hands are causing on my breasts, I feel another orgasm building, and I know this one is going to rip me apart.

I run my hands up and down Reid's back, but the sensations running through me are becoming too much, so I grab the side of the bed as his thrusts become wilder.

"I can't hold on, Reid! I'm coming."

"Go for it," he growls as he pours himself into me with an almighty roar.

"Fuuuck."

My whole body is trembling from the most intense orgasm that has ever ripped through me. I'm on a high. My limbs feel like they're floating, and I can see stars floating above my head. My whole body feels ravished. Reid gently takes my legs down from his shoulders, then crosses the room, removes the condom, and disappears into the bathroom.

# Chapter Eight

What just happened? Why'd he go straight to the bathroom after what was the best sex of my life? Deciding I'm not going to hang around and be made a fool of, I grab my things off the floor and run for the apartment door.

"Going somewhere?" I halt but can't bring myself to turn and face him. There's anger flowing from me, but I feel vulnerable, and I won't let him see that. He comes up behind me then turns me around so we're chest to chest. Well, nearly. He's taller than me, after all. He places his finger gently under my chin and tilts my head up, so I have to look at him.

"Did I do something wrong?"

How can he act like he did nothing wrong? Leaving me there after pulling out of me made me feel like a whore.

Then he goes off, getting dressed like nothing happened. I thought I meant something to him. My temper is getting the better of me, and out of nowhere, I slap him hard across the face, which stuns us both.

"What the fuck was that for?" He rubs his cheek.

"Are you fucking kidding me? Did you think you'd get to fuck me and then walk away when you were done? Wrong again. I won't let you humiliate me a second time."

I turn to walk out the door, but he picks me up and takes me back to the bedroom. I'm kicking and screaming when he puts me down on the vanity unit in the bathroom.

"Just so we're clear, I came in here to start running the water for the shower. Damn thing takes time to heat up, and I didn't want to put you in a cold shower."

It's then I notice the steam in the bathroom, and the shower is running.

"And just to clarify, do I look like I'm dressed?"

Very awkwardly, I look down and there, in all his glory, is Reid's naked form.

"Eyes up here, or there will be more than a shower happening."

"Hmm." I sigh.

"Why would you think I would do that to you? Have I not made my feelings clear enough?"

Now I'm the guilty one. I misjudged what he was doing, when in fact, he was looking after me. I'm so used to looking after myself that having someone look out for me is now a foreign concept.

"I'm sorry. I jumped to the wrong conclusions and assumed you were done with me. I couldn't bear to be humiliated like that and be another notch on your bedpost."

"Hey, I'll admit, I've had my fair share of women. I can't change that. But you, you're different, and I said I will do whatever needs to be done to make you mine."

Wrapping my arms around his neck, I kiss him fiercely. I've fucked up, and I have to show him I'm sorry.

"Come on, princess. Shower now. There you can show me how sorry you are."

He lifts me off the counter but then slaps my ass, and boy, did that feel painfully good.

We wash each other in the shower from head to toe, taking our time, which only works us up. I'm so ready and panting. I desperately need his cock to fill me. It's swollen again already.

"I hope you're ready for this." He doesn't give me a chance to answer. He lifts me up and slides me down on his cock. "Christ, how can you be so tight?"

My legs are wrapped around him, and my heels dig in just under his buttocks. He pushes my back against the shower wall with a little force, but it doesn't hurt me. Then he's pounding into me relentlessly, and I can't get enough. It feels different this time. My sensitivities are more heightened, and it feels amazing. My orgasm is ready to explode. Nothing is stopping it, and just as it releases, Reid comes with me too in another powerful but beautiful explosion.

He holds me and his arms tighten around me. Reid kisses me softly, and it's the most beautiful, loving kiss so far. When he finally pulls away, he carefully puts me back down. Reid looks down, and I see he's not happy when he growls.

"Shit. I didn't use a condom." He then steps out of the shower and grabs us both towels, and walks into the bedroom.

Unsure what the hell happened, I quickly wrap the towel around me and follow him. I stand before him, placing my hands on his chest to calm him.

"Hey, why are you so mad?"

His eyebrows are slanting inwards, creasing his forehead. That's how I know he's annoyed, but I think it's more with himself than anything.

"Esme, I'm sorry. I'm never this careless. Using a condom is a priority, but I got carried away in the moment and, well, fuck."

I look down and realize we just had unprotected sex. He is really beating himself up over this. While I'm a little freaked out as I'm always so careful too, we need to talk about it calmly.

"Reid, look at me."

He looks at me, and his eyes are full of guilt. It's killing me to see him like this. It's not just his fault; we were both foolish.

"Hey, I was as much to blame. I could have stopped it at any time, and I didn't."

"But I should know better."

"Why should you? We're both adults, and we both knew what we were doing."

"I'm the guy. We're supposed to protect and be sensible. I've just done the opposite by being stupid and careless. Fuck. Careful is my middle name, but being with you sends all my rational thinking out the window."

I laugh because, when he says it like that, he makes it sound ridiculous. Him, irrational? Really?

"Oh my God, you're actually being serious, aren't you?"

"Princess, you and your friends call me a caveman, but that's how I feel. I feel protective of you all the time. I want to take you away from everything and keep you safe. Knowing what you've been through already makes my irrational thinking worse. I won't let anything like that happen again."

I can't think of a response, so I try to address the fact that we've just had unprotected sex and deal with that issue first.

"Listen to me. While it wasn't very clever of us, I can't say it didn't feel right, Reid. In fact, it felt more than right. You know I felt things I've never felt before, because it was with you."

"Don't try to dress up my fuck up, please."

He's so dramatic sometimes. He should be called princess.

"Look, I'm clean and on the pill, and as long as you're clean, I think we're going to be okay." He obviously likes this news since he pulls me onto the bed. He towers over me and looks at me with so much lust in his eyes that the intensity is back, and I know whatever I said was the right thing.

"Yes, I'm clean. I get checked regularly, and you can come with me next time if it makes you happy. Oh, and bare sex it is for future reference. I'm throwing all the condoms out if that's okay with you? Now, get up here."

"So fine with me."

And I am on my way to another mind-blowing orgasm.

The rest of the evening is spent wrapped around each other. It feels right being here with him. But in the back of my mind, I know something will go wrong. It's the way my luck runs.

I wake up with Reid and his huge arm wrapped over me like he's afraid I'm going to disappear. I manage to remove his arm and roll over, and I just lie there staring at him, admiring his body as the sheet is just covering him from his junk down. He has the most perfect abs and a few tattoos. I presume the one across the top of his right arm is about someone he lost. It's two hands in the prayer position with a cross dangling over them and then the saying 'IN GOD'S HANDS'. He also has the words *brothers* tattooed on his left arm. It's two fists wrapped around a sword with roses. It's beautiful, and I know this is about his bond with Ash. Maybe one day I'll be brave and get one.

"Enjoying the view?"

Such an arrogant ass, but he is right. I was definitely enjoying the view, and now I need more from him.

What has he done to me? I'm always a good girl. Sex before him was usually plain missionary style, and there was never any foreplay. Being with Reid makes me want to explore new things, but I'm afraid if he knows exactly how inexperienced I really am, he will kick me to the curb.

"The view is okay, I suppose."

He quickly dives over me and pins me beneath his strong, hard body. He strokes his hand down the side of my face. "You're so beautiful, you know that?"

I shy away from him, and he turns my face back towards him.

"Hey, why do you do that?"

"Being spoken to with such kind words… I'm not used to it."

He leans back slightly, like he's studying me, then it's like a lightbulb goes off in his head. He leans toward me and kisses me slowly and passionately. But then my lips are left wanting more when he whispers in my ear, "You really are a good girl, aren't you? You're a bit like the preacher's daughter. You wanna play but haven't met the right guy to play with, am I right?"

I look up at him. My eyes must be bulging. I am so busted now. I don't know which way to look. I act like I know what I'm doing, but I'm a novice to a man like Reid, who must've had a string of women. Why would he want a woman who is practically a virgin?

I try to get up, but he doesn't budge. He keeps me pinned to the bed with his naked form.

"Hey, I didn't mean to upset you."

"Yeah, well, you're right. That's me. I haven't had the experience you've had. My parents were strict, hence my lack of experience, so I guess our time is up now?"

He looks like I've just sucker-punched him, but it soon disappears and is replaced with his smirk. Shit. Here we go again. He grinds his cock against my entrance and then thrusts inside me without any warning. He lifts me up, so we're sitting face to face, and I have to wrap my arms around his neck to hold on as he picks up the pace.

The position we're in makes it feel so intimate. As he thrusts within me, he's hitting a point that I can only describe as pure ecstasy. I feel the need to rise against him, so I flatten my palms on his shoulders and push myself up, which gives me the leverage to slide my pussy up his cock, and then I guide it back down real quick. I match his thrusts, and anyone watching would think we were competing for a race. Each thrust becomes more powerful. The sweat is pouring off his forehead and he becomes more animalistic as he growls. In a quick flip, I'm turned over, then he rams into me from behind, grabbing my hip with one hand and bunching my hair in his fist with the other. He powers into me like he's drilling me and doesn't know how to stop. I have never felt anything like this before. It's raw and harsh. Nothing about it is gentle, and I love it. I feel my orgasm building.

"Oh my God, Reid, please don't stop."

"Now, princess. Come for me!"

And boy, do I come. It's like a lightbulb that shatters after being switched on, and I explode into a million pieces. I grip the bedsheets, and the scream that leaves my throat is like nothing ever to leave me before. Reid has the sexiest growl ever, and he is still gripping onto me as he lets the last of his cum pour into me.

We lie down, facing each other, and it's like seeing him for the first time. Maybe he looks different because he looks happy and carefree. Every time I've seen him he's been angry, or there's been some sort of confrontation between us. Right now, it's just calm. He starts talking and jolts me from my trance.

"Just so we're clear, I don't care about experience, and all that crap you were saying. You are what I care about, and you should always remember that."

"Reid, there are things you're gonna expect of me that I probably haven't heard of, let alone done. Remember, I've led a sheltered life compared to yours."

He cups my face between his soft, strong palms and stares straight into my eyes.

"Exactly what kind of life do you think I've led, Esme? I'm intrigued to know."

Shit. Me and my big mouth. I don't really know anything about him. I'm just speculating based on what's happened so far, and that's me seeing women throwing themselves at him in the gym and the roving eyes that follow him on the streets when he walks past.

Dammit. What exactly am I going to say now? I don't really have anything to back up my theory. I get up off the bed and start gathering what's left of my torn clothes.

"The life of a typical fighter boy. Trains all day in the gym, women fawning over them all of the time. I mean, come on, I saw it with my own eyes at self-defense class. Oh, and don't forget the woman who followed you into the back after class. You had the time at the night club, and the way you spoke to me. If you speak that way to all women, I bet there is always one that gives you what you want. A quick fuck here and there."

His smile has dropped. He sits up on the edge of the bed and slips his sweat pants on. He won't make eye contact with me, so I know I've either annoyed or upset him. But he has to understand, he has a past like I do, and it's something we're both going to have to work with. This is going to be harder than I thought.

"I'm sorry. I don't mean to sound so negative. You asked, and I told. What am I supposed to say, that you're an angel?" I start to giggle, but he just growls at me. I stop and stare at him.

"I've slept with women, yes. Lots of them, and lots of them, I can't remember their names. Have I treated women disrespectfully? Yes, and I'm sorry about that. Well, for some of them, anyway."

"Reid, you can't go around treating any woman disrespectfully."

"Don't go there."

I've obviously hit a nerve. There is more to this, to him, and it's something that needs addressing if he really wants us to be together. But for now, I'll leave it as he's fidgety, and he keeps looking at his hands.

"I can't help who I was," he says. "You are who I want. You make me feel things I've never felt before. My heart feels alive for the first time in years, and that's all you."

Damn him and his words. Tears prick the backs of my eyes. But is what he is saying too soon?

"For someone who doesn't have experience, you sure as hell rocked my world. I think someone's been keeping things to herself."

I walk toward him, tears still in my eyes, and stand between his legs.

"I'm so sorry for saying what I did. We all have a past, and I have no right to judge you for yours."

"Stop saying sorry. You were just being honest with me,

and although this talking and being honest thing is a first for me too, it's all good. Never be sorry for being you."

"You really are a beautiful gentleman, Reid Taylor. Through your cocky, bossy, and over-protectiveness, there is a good guy underneath."

"Easy, princess. I have an image to maintain, you know." We both burst out laughing, and it's good to see him this way.

He wraps his arms around my waist and buries his head against my stomach while I run my hands through his hair.

"What you said doesn't matter, but from now on, things are changing, okay? I'm yours, and vice versa."

Right now, I couldn't be happier.

# Chapter Nine

Nyla has been bugging me ever since I arrived at work. She wants to know every detail of what happened, so I dish. We've never had secrets, and I need my best friend to tell me I'm doing the right thing, considering it's all been overwhelming and fast-paced. I have to know that she's okay, too, especially as things are still so raw after what happened between her and Russell.

"Es, I'm fine. I was escorted home by the delectable Ash last night, who, happens to be single, by the way. Did you know?" All the travel magazines I'm carrying crash to the floor as I stand there gawking at her with a huge grin on my face.

"What the hell? You have a weird look on your face."

"You like him, don't you?"

"We're just friends. Nothing more, and to be honest,

I'm not looking for anything. Well, maybe a little fun wouldn't do any harm. You think?"

She starts belly laughing, and that's when I know Nyla has something up her sleeve, and she won't leave well alone until she gets what she wants.

"So, Reid rocked your world good and proper last night? Well, it looks good on you. You're glowing, missy."

"Oh my God, Ny, be quiet. I don't want everyone to hear about my night. But you're right, he did more than rock my world. He woke the woman in me, and now she's out, she intends to have lots of fun."

"It's about time she came out. But if he hurts you, so help me God, I'll strip him of his balls, you hear me?"

"I hear you. He's a good guy underneath, just misunderstood. Do you think it's all happening too soon?"

"Yes, it's happened fast, but sometimes that's how insta-love works. We cannot control who we fall for, and if it feels right, then who are we to deny ourselves happiness? The best things usually come to those who least expect it."

"Thanks, Ny." Maybe she's right, and I should just enjoy and be happy with what's happening right now.

"Okay, time to stop thinking and to start having fun. This weekend we're going out. Oh, FYI, it's not a typical night out. Ash told me about a fight that's going on, and I said we would go."

I'm a little shocked to think Nyla would be into that kind of stuff.

"A fight? Really? It's not your thing, nor mine."

"Yeah, I know. Ash said the guys at the gym train there for these fights sometimes, and I was a little apprehensive when he first mentioned it, but I'm excited to go watch now."

"I've seen them briefly at the gym training. Maybe a boxing match would be okay to go see."

"It's not a boxing match. It's mixed martial arts."

"What the hell is that?"

"Ash told me it's a fight without gloves. He also said it gets real rowdy in there, but we will be fine with him." She flashes her begging eyes.

Shocked is an understatement as violence is not my thing at all, but I find myself wanting to go. I agree, and she shoots Ash a text telling him we're in.

The following Saturday evening comes around, and I'm looking forward to the fight. Reid and I have been texting and calling each other. I've seen him during our gym session and in passing, but he's been busy with work and training. He assured me he would come to see me after he was done on Sunday. I'm frustrated. Quick moments here and there and texting are not the same as spending time together. I know I'm developing feelings for him faster than I wanted too, but there's something about him. I haven't felt like this about a man before, and it's scary.

We meet Ash at the gym, but it's all locked up, and there's no sign of Reid anywhere.

"Hey, Ash. Where's Reid?"

"He's meeting us at the fight. He had a few errands to run and said he'll see us there. Sorry, Esme." Something seems off with Ash's tone, but I can tell he doesn't want to say anything more. His attention is all on Nyla, so I just have to suck it up and wait until we get to the fight so I can see Reid for myself and maybe get some answers.

"Hey, firecracker. You wanna sit up front with me?" Ash asks Nyla.

"Sure." She nods at me to make sure all is okay, and I nod back.

We get into Ash's truck, and he takes us across the city to what looks like an abandoned warehouse, but there are numerous cars everywhere, so this is obviously a huge fight that's taking place. Nyla senses I'm not comfortable with my surroundings. I'm jumpy and cringing at the loudness of the cars beeping and their music blaring all around us. Nyla takes hold of my hand and grips it for reassurance.

"It's going to be fine."

Ash, also sensing my nervousness, is at my other side in an instant.

I grip Nyla's hand real tight because, although we have Ash right by our sides, and he isn't someone I would mess with, I still don't feel comfortable. The looks some of the guys are giving us here gives me the creeps. Maybe I was wrong to agree to this.

One guy shouts across to us. "Hey, Ash! How are you doing?"

"Hey, Colt! It's been a while."

"Ladies, nice to meet you. They both yours?"

"You're real funny. No, they're just friends."

"Okay. First time here?"

"Yes," Nyla and I say in unison.

"Well, enjoy the fights. Ash, drinks soon?"

"Yeah, sure. See you soon." They bump fists, and Colt

walks away.

Maybe it's not as bad here as I first thought. We get inside, and the first thing I notice is the smell. It's a mixture of sweat and must; it's unpleasant. We make our way past the burly guys who don't smile even a tiny bit. I presume they are the security, and I don't let go of Nyla's hand. She holds Ash's hand, and he's practically pulling her along toward a huge cage in the center of this wide-open space. Someone grabs my shoulder and tries to pull me backward, making me lose the grip of Nyla's hand. I freeze, not knowing what I'm about to face behind me. The thought is tightening my chest, and my hands start to shake, when I'm spun around to be face-to-face with a guy who has a huge scar across his cheek, and a bald head. He caresses my cheek with his hand, and I don't move. I can't. This guy is tall and hideous-looking. I try to move, but his other hand is still pushing down on my shoulder. He's strong, and I'm not moving.

"Hey, sugar. You wanna see what a good time feels like?" I'm frozen with fear, and inside, I'm trembling. Before he can say or do anything else, Ash appears with Nyla.

"I suggest you remove those hands right now, Linc, if you know what's good for you."

Linc, as I now know him, drops his hands straight away. I feel relief, but I wish Reid were with me, as I know I would be a lot safer.

I look between the two guys. They obviously know each other, and the grin on Linc's face is not a good sign. There seems to be a history between them from their tones.

"Well, well, well. If it isn't Ace. She yours, is she?

Because if I'm right, you don't do girlfriends. Plus, she looks pretty fine where she is, so if you don't mind, beat it." He goes to caress the side of my face again.

By now, my eyes are wide. Where in the hell does this jerk get off telling Ash that I'm fine right where I am? My fear hasn't gone, but I seem to have gained some balls out of nowhere, and one hell of a temper, which is starting to flare inside of me. Knowing where we are, it's probably not the best place to start a raging war with a guy I don't know, especially when I have no idea what he's capable of. But I just don't know when to stay quiet. I seem to be taking lessons from Nyla in that department.

I manage to whack his hand away from my face, and he laughs, which pisses me off even more. I'm pissed that he thinks it's okay to touch me again, but he isn't concentrating, and that's when I take my opportunity.

"Does this feel fine?" I step forward and lift my right knee straight into his groin as hard as I can. He grunts in pain, but his hands move from me, and it gives me the space to step away from his grasp. He shoots his fist toward me, and I hold my breath, waiting for the blow. But it's blocked by Ash, who grabs me and pulls me behind him.

"You've really got a death wish, Linc. I think she gave you her answer, but just so you know, she isn't mine. I'll give you one guess who she does belong to, and when he finds out you had your filthy hands on her, you'd better watch out."

Ash doesn't give him a chance to answer as he turns and walks away, pushing us towards the cage at the front of this so-called arena where there are people already hanging around. We're standing ringside, and the commotion is deafening. We can hardly hear each other above all the cheering and chanting.

"This isn't your normal boxing fight, Esme. Nyla explained it to you, didn't she?"

I just nod. "I'm still pretty clueless though, if I'm honest."

"Okay, well, it's basically a mixture of combat fighting and mixed martial arts, hence no gloves. But be warned, there's going to be a lot of blood. You all right with that?" I hesitate at first, then from somewhere, I pull up my big girl pants and decide yes.

"I think so.."

"I will be here the whole time. If you want to leave, just say, and we'll go, I promise."

I'm grateful Ash is being considerate.

"Esme, there's something else. This type of fighting isn't legal, hence the rundown warehouse. The rules are different here. It's fight until someone taps out, or until someone is KO'd…"

Ash just looks at me, and I know what he's trying to say. Nyla gasps beside me, and she's shooting daggers at Ash. When they organized this night out, he obviously kept those rules out of the conversation.

"Listen, we can leave if you're not happy being here, Nyla." Then the commotion gets louder, and I look into the ring

The fight that was happening finishes abruptly, and there is a guy completely out of it on the ring floor. The security comes in and helps him out, and the poor guy has a bloody nose. There is still no sign of Reid. I'm beginning to think he isn't going to show.

Nyla looks at Ash, and he is about to say something when the announcer calls the next two fighters. The music that starts to play is so loud I can barely hear the first fighter's name, but I just capture it and Nyla and I start to laugh as it sounds so pathetic. I mean, who calls themself Pretty Boy? He comes out to the song, *One and Only* by Chesney Hawkes. By now, Nyla and I are belly laughing. Ash tells us to behave, and we try to control ourselves.

The guy they call Pretty Boy is far from a pretty boy. He has huge muscles and must be about six feet tall. He has shaved hair at the sides, but the top is longer and is tied back with a hair tie. The announcer calls out his opponent's name, Thunder. Now that's more like a fighter name. He strolls out to the music *Thunderstruck* by AC/DC with a hood up so you can't see him clearly. Everyone is cheering for this guy, so he is obviously popular here.

He climbs into the cage and has his back to us, then he removes his top, and the ref calls both fighters to the center. That's when I realize who Thunder is. I know those tattoos. It's Reid. I turn to Nyla for some answers, as I'm confused.

"Did you know? Is that why you and Ash brought me here?" Nyla looks across at Ash, and the exchange they share tells me that she did know. I am livid they kept this a secret, and the fact that Reid didn't even tell me what was going on makes it worse. I feel like they've all been keeping secrets from me. Some friends they are.

"Listen, Es, I did know he was going to be fighting tonight, and it was supposed to be a surprise for you.

Obviously not a good one going by your reaction. I honestly thought that once you saw him up there you might become excited. I'm sorry."

"I don't know if I'm ready to watch him beat on someone, or him take a battering for that matter." Ash laughs. "It's not funny, Ash."

"Sorry, but you haven't seen him fight yet, and you're worried about him. He can handle himself."

I look back at the cage, and the fight is about to start.

"So, tell me, Ash, why didn't he tell me what he was doing? Is this why I haven't seen him all week, aside from at the gym?"

"Maybe to protect you, but he has been working on top of training at the gym. You should also know he doesn't realize you're here tonight."

"What? Why would you bring me here without him knowing?"

Ash drops his eyes from mine, looking anywhere but at me. He's hiding something and I want to know what's going on, so I continue to stare at him until he caves.

"Fine. I happened to let it slip about the fight when Nyla and I were talking, and she convinced me to bring you along to see him fight." He looks down then back up at me. "I didn't tell him because I knew he would go insane over it, and I didn't want to let Nyla down either. So, I kept quiet."

Wow, he's truly taken with her.

The crowd roars as the fight starts, pulling my attention away from the conversation. Reid is slightly taller than Pretty Boy at six feet two, but otherwise, they are pretty much even. Reid is quick as Pretty Boy comes at him a few times, but Reid dodges the advances, and Pretty Boy stumbles, hitting the cage. Reid then goes in with an uppercut to his jaw, and Pretty Boy's head swings to the side. That's when Reid sees us. He stares at me, and my breath is stolen from my chest when I realize Pretty Boy is about to hit him from behind. I scream at him and he moves, but not in time, and Pretty Boy manages to get him in a chokehold, taking him down to the floor. I scramble toward the cage, but Ash pulls me back.

"Don't!" he warns me. "Reid knows what he's doing, okay?"

"Really, Ash? He's choking him. I caused that distraction, and it's thanks to you."

"He can handle it, trust me."

I look back at the cage, and Reid is now beating down on Pretty Boy like some kind of mad man. It's like someone has unleashed the beast within him, and he can't stop. Watching him defend himself when I thought he was going to be the one being beaten, I find myself chanting his name along with everyone else.

Pretty Boy is no match for Thunder, and finally, in round two, he taps out. The ref runs in and grabs Thunder's hand, raising it in the air and declaring him the winner. Both opponents are bloodied, but more so is Pretty Boy. My guy has some pretty beat up knuckles that need attending to, and a small gash on his cheek. I think his ego may be a little bruised from being taken down while distracted, but other than that, he looks okay.

There is a lot of shouting and music blaring again as the night is drawing to an end. We go to walk toward Reid when I see him standing at the edge of the cage just staring at me. He is all sweaty and bleeding, and boy, is he pissed. He storms forward.

*Here we go.*

"What the fuck is she doing here, Ash?" Reid makes a grab for Ash, but I move quickly and stand between them.

He grabs me by the hand and pulls me past the cage and down a small corridor into a room, slamming the door shut behind us. He runs his hands through his hair, growling through gritted teeth. Then, he starts punching the wall, and I'm annoyed with him when I should be scared.

Walking behind him, I place my hands on his back and start to rub, hoping it will calm him. Big mistake. He is totally wound up, and he turns around so fast I don't have time to register what he's doing. He picks me up, slams me against the door without hurting me, then kisses me so hard I can't breathe. Eventually, he pulls back, but our foreheads remain touching and his arms have me caged in against the door.

"Why are you here? You shouldn't be here. It's no place for you." He gently runs his hand over my face and then holds my chin. "Fuck, this place. It's too dangerous for you to be here."

I maneuver my hands over his sweaty chest and up to his face. I cup his face and make him look at me.

"Please, shut up. I haven't seen you all week, and it's been torture, so just freaking kiss me."

"That I can do."

He lifts me and I wrap my legs around him,as he kisses me with everything he has.He finally puts me down and rests his forehead to mine, staring into my eyes like he's looking deep into my soul.

"I mean it. You don't belong here. It's far too dangerous, and I don't want you here."

I get the need to protect me, and after earlier, I understand why. But he can't just dictate to me and think I'll follow his orders without some real explanation, other than it's dangerous. I know it's dangerous, but I should be okay if I'm with him or Ash.

"I'm a big girl, Reid. I think I can handle a few obnoxious guys, like I did earlier." I realize then I made a mistake as the hard look returns to his face.

"What do you mean *like earlier*?"

Damn, I need to learn to keep my mouth shut.

"It was nothing, really. Can we just focus on the here and now, please?"

I drop my gaze, but he puts his finger under my chin and lifts my face to him again. There is no way he will let this lie, but if I tell him, it will either be Ash getting it, or that guy, Linc. Either way, someone will pay for it.

"It doesn't matter," I tell him.

"Fine. Wait here and don't leave this room, you hear me?" And he's out the door, slamming it behind him. I jump back at the sound of the door whacking into the frame.

Oh, like hell am I going to stay here while he goes on a rampage, causing a thunderstorm. I follow him down the corridor. He's fast, and I run to try and catch him, but he's reached Nyla and Ash before I'm even at the end of the corridor. I race over to them as Reid grabs hold of Ash, but Ash can hold his own and he manages to knock Reid off him.

"What the fuck? What is wrong with you, Reid?"

"Tell me what happened with Esme earlier. I mean it, Ash. What the fuck happened?"

"It was nothing, just a misunderstanding."

"Man, just tell me what the fuck happened." He's losing his shit real quick now. Ash looks at me, and he knows I don't want Reid to know.

"I dealt with it. They know now who she's with. Leave it, for Esme's sake. Just go home."

Ash understands I don't want to see Reid get into any trouble, but unfortunately, I think my best friend forgot the memo because she decides he should be told.

"His name was Linc, and he manhandled her until she kneed him in the balls."

Truth be told, I think she was just standing by Ash and not letting him take the flack for what Linc did. If that wasn't bad enough, Linc walks by and can't keep his mouth shut.

"Hey, sugar. Did you enjoy the fight? Oh, and I'm ready now if you are…"

He winks, and that's all it takes. Reid dives on Linc, leaning into his face. He says something to him and then punches him square in the face over and over until Ash and a few others pull him off and get Linc out the way. Some women are screaming, and others are fawning over Reid, which starts to piss me off.

"You broke my nose, you bastard."

"You're lucky these guys pulled me away when they did because if I had my way, I'd have buried you." The security has taken Linc away to stop anymore shit happening, but I've had enough. I look at Nyla.

"I want to leave now," Nyla tells Ash, and he starts to escort us towards the exit.

"Esme!" Reid shouts to me, but I ignore him and carry on walking out. He catches up to us, stopping in front of me.

"I'll bring her back, bro. You take Nyla."

"I said I'm going back with them, not you." And just like that, I'm over his shoulder and being carried away.

"Put me down! I can walk."

"If that were the case, you would have done so straight away, so suck it up."

# Chapter Ten

Again, he slams the door shut, but this time he locks it. He's angry. He lets me down, and I go to punch his chest, but he blocks me with his palm.

"What is it with you and throwing me over your shoulder?"

"Easiest way to get you where I need you. Now it's my turn for questions. Why didn't you tell me what that dick did to you, and why did you want to leave with Ash and Nyla and not me?"

"You know what, Reid, violence isn't always the answer to every problem. My feelings on this subject are strong after what I went through losing my family. I lost them to violence, and it scares me. I don't need you hitting everyone that makes a pass at me. Plus, you totally acted like a goon."

His shoulders slump. "Understood. But, fuck, you're

stubborn. Did you ever think there may be a reason I lost it? Linc attacked a young girl. The girl happened to be the girlfriend of my best friend, Jack. She was only eighteen at the time, and it scarred her for life and resulted in her suffering psychological issues." He looks shattered telling me all of this, and I can see the torment behind his eyes. "It was because of Jack and me that she was here at the underground. She followed us one night, unbeknown to us, and like tonight, Linc saw her before we did." He sits down next to me. "Linc, being the strong guy he is, overpowered her, and she didn't stand a chance. Someone saw what was going on, but it was too late. The damage had already been done. She went home and the police were called, but as it was an illegal place, there were no signs of people around once they arrived back there. The case was closed eventually because they had no leads, and she didn't know his name. Jack struggled with the guilt until it became too much, and he committed suicide."

Tears fall freely down my cheeks, and Reid tries to wipe them away. Now I understand why he was hell-bent on teaching Linc a lesson. Knowing what sort of a person he is now, let's just say he deserved all he got tonight and more.

I straddle his legs, and he grabs my ass, pulling me into his lap, then he wraps his arms tightly around me. We sit there for what seems like ages, just holding each other while he calms down, and eventually he starts talking again.

"You don't belong here, princess. This world is a dangerous one, and full of men and women who would kill if the need came."

I understand what he's saying, but if it's dangerous for

me, then it's also the same for him. So why does he continue to come here? I feel the urge to tell him that as much as I hate violence, seeing him up there tonight fighting was a huge turn on. Yes, I was screaming, but what Nyla and Ash didn't realize was that I was screaming for Reid, or Thunder, or whatever he was called. The adrenaline that started to run through me toward the end of the fight was something I had never felt before.

"Hey, look at me," I say softly, and when his eyes meet mine, there's so much guilt there.

"I never chose to come here tonight, but I also didn't say no. Granted, I had no idea you were fighting, but even so, I still came."

He leans his head back in surprise at my words. "Ash never told you I would be fighting tonight?"

"No. He just said you were running some errands and were meeting us here. Anyway, when I saw you up there, yes, I was shocked, scared even, but seeing you fight like that with all that power and rawness, it showed me a side of you I have never seen. It was beautiful."

I give him a grin and remove my top before stepping back, kicking off my pumps, and shimmying out of my jeans. Now, standing before him in just my pink lace bra and panties, I'm practically quivering with delight. I don't seem to be able to control myself around him, and watching him fight was an even bigger turn on. He's looking at me like he wants to eat me, and I can see it's taking all he has to keep his control.

"You wanna keep those?" he growls, his eyes fixated on my underwear.

He doesn't wait for an answer before yanking them off me. He turns me to face the wall and unclasps my bra.

"Put your hands on the wall, princess, and show me that ass." He groans, caressing my neck, then down my back until he gets to my ass.

"That side of me you saw tonight, Esme, does it make you want to run?"

I move one of my hands from the wall and guide it between us, seeking his cock. He has removed his shorts and is fully naked now. As I rub my thumb over the tip of his dick, smoothing around the bead of precum, he groans.

"Does it look like I want to run, Thunder?"

Hearing me call him by his cage name must have flicked a switch inside of him as he slams my hand back to the wall, spreads my legs apart, and then slides straight into me. He wraps my hair around his fist and starts thrusting in and out of me painfully fast. He pulls my hair, which pulls my head back, and kisses the side of my neck. It feels amazing, but then he starts to slow down, and I'm panting for more.

"Don't stop Reid. Give me everything you have and give it to me now."

I don't know what's come over me, but I can't have him slowing down. I was just reaching a mind-blowing orgasm when he slowed. He has picked his pace back up and he's drilling into me like a jackhammer.

"Jesus, Esme. You're so fuckin' amazing."

He reaches around to my clit and starts rubbing in slow, delicious circles. He picks up the pace and then grunts. God, is it sexy. It tips me right over the edge, and I come so hard my legs give out from under me, and Reid has to hold me up.

"I got you. I got you." He wraps his hard, warm body around mine and caresses my hair until I can feel my legs again.

We get cleaned up, and then he carries me back to the bench. That's when I notice the gash on his cheek is bleeding again. I brush my thumb gently around it trying to clean away the blood, but there's too much of it. He hands me a first aid pack from his bag, and I tend to his cut carefully.

"Thank you," he says softly, wrapping his arms around my waist and pulling me into him to rest his head against my stomach. "We need to get out of here. They will be locking up."

I pull back a little, and he goes to reach for me, but I'm too quick for him. I grab my clothes and rush to get them on. We need to leave. It all seems real quiet outside, so I guess everyone has gone by now, and I don't like the idea of being locked in here. Reid starts to dress too, when someone bangs on the door, startling me, I let out a squeal.

"Thunder, we're locking down now. Time's up."

"Come on, princess. Let's get you home."

He grabs his bag, and my hand and we head on out. We make our way down the corridor the way we came, but we stop outside an open door where a guy is stuffing money in a bag. He's flanked by two burly-looking guys.

"Hey, Reid, great fight tonight, although…."

"Don't say it. I know I nearly fucked up out there. I can assure you it won't happen again. Dave." I start to walk out of the room and leave them to it, but I'm soon pulled back.

"Not me that has to worry, dude, but I'm guessing the

reason is right here. Nice to meet you...?"

Oh, he's talking to me.

"I'm Esme. Nice to meet you, Dave." He takes my hand and kisses it. Reid growls beside me, and I laugh. Dave gives him his cash, and then we leave.

Outside, the air is now cool and I didn't bring a coat. As my ride has left already, I'm wondering how long before a cab comes. The neighborhood here isn't exactly somewhere you want to be waiting around. Reid walks us toward a bike, and then he pulls out his helmet from his bag and passes it to me.

"You never been on a bike before?" he says when I hesitate to take it from him.

I shake my head at him, while lost for words. He looks hot as fuck on this bike. I have always had a fear of bikes and just stand there staring at it. He must sense my anxiety because he pulls me toward him slowly and whispers in my ear, "Trust me."

I nod and follow his instructions.

"Put your foot on the bar and lift your right leg over the seat." His hand is under my thigh, gently lifting my leg, and it feels so sensual. He knows what he's doing to me. His fingertips run up and down my leg, sparking sensations. He's then behind me, telling me to shuffle forward, but all I feel is his manhood pushing into my ass. How much longer does he think I'll resist?

"I think I got it, now can we get going, because my restraint for you is non-existent."

"You got it, princess." And he's on his bike so fast I missed it. "Get your ass up here. I need that body against mine."

I slide forward until my front melds into his back. He sighs when I do this and then tells me how good it feels having my arms wrapped around his waist.

"Having your arms wrapped around me on my bike is the best feeling ever. It feels right."

We finally arrive back at the apartment complex and pull into the underground garage, but we don't park where all the other cars are. We pull into a secure area on the far side which has its own doors. I gasp when we pull in. There is one sports car, two four-wheel drives, and a Harley Davidson.

Reid turns off the bike and helps me off. "You okay there?"

I look at him, unsure of what to say. I open my mouth to speak, but nothing comes out.

"They're not all mine. One of the trucks and the Harley is Ash's. We share this garage."

"Does Ash live in the apartments too?

"Yeah. We live on the same floor. There are only our two apartments on my floor, so it's pretty quiet up there, just how we like it—unless it's us partying, that is."

We walk out and over to the lift, and Reid presses the button for his floor once we're inside.

"So, we're going to your apartment then?"

He grips my hand and lifts it to his lips, kissing it gently. "I just wanna have you near me tonight, Esme. No funny business. I just need you close. Can we do that?"

I smile and squeeze his hand. "Sure, Reid. We can have a quiet night in."

We spend some of the night cuddling on the sofa, talking about random stuff.

"Tell me, princess, what's your job like?" I never expected this type of conversation from him.

"I love my job. Ruby is real good to me and very understanding. You'd like her."

He kisses my head. "That's good to hear. So, have you traveled far in your job?

"No, not really. I always turned it down because my parents disagreed with my job choice. I think they wanted me to be a doctor or something."

We both chuckled at that thought.

"What about you? What was your dream job?"

"It's never crossed my mind to do any other job. Being at the gym is somewhere I have been since I was fifteen, so I thought, why not work there too?"

The conversation continues, and we find out more about one another before we fall into bed at about two a.m.

I give up trying to sleep for more than an hour at a time eventually. Seven a.m. So much for having a Sunday sleep in.

I go to make some coffee, but Reid doesn't have any, and damn, I need a coffee fix first thing in the morning. I know I don't have any at my apartment as I need to get groceries, so I run out to the coffee shop. I look at Reid from the bedroom door and decide to leave him a note if he does wake. Previous incidents have proved exactly how he will react if he can't find me, and it doesn't bear thinking about.

The early morning air is warm, and it's starting to look like it might be a beautiful day. I find myself daydreaming about what we can do together today, when I slam into someone.

"Dumb bitch. Look where you're fucking going."

I'm floored. I mean, jeez, it was an accident, and who the hell is he to speak to me like that? I look at the guy in question and realize there are three of them: two young guys and a young girl. None of them can be older than nineteen or twenty. They start to walk away, but I seem to have gained some courage lately, and I let them have it.

"Really? Do you always speak to people with such disgust? It was an accident. Get over yourself."

They all stop and turn, and the taller of the two guys walks back toward me. The look on his face has me thinking *what the hell have I done?* I'm alone, and there are three of them. He walks right up to me, and it's then I notice a nasty scar on his face. He gets right in my face and says, "Listen, bitch, look where you're going in future and keep your trashy mouth shut, you hear me?"

I'm too scared to speak. The situation feels really wrong. The three of them have now gone, but my head is having some sort of party of its own, and my chest has gone real tight. I think I'm having a panic attack again. There is so much going on, and I feel like it's going to burst. I know this is something to do with those guys, but why?

I manage to calm myself down and my head returns to normal. I'm outside the coffee shop, so I take a breath and go inside to order my usual vanilla latte and an Americano for Reid. I sit down while I'm waiting. I must have slipped into a daze or something because I'm being nudged by the barista, Lucy, who hands me the coffees.

“Thanks,” I mumble, before taking them back over to the apartment. But the whole way, my head is still not right. I try to shake it off as just some jumped-up kids, but it’s like my brain wants to tell me something, and it’s stuck.

Reid is sitting on the sofa when I get back, in just his pants. I can’t help but lean against the door frame and take in the sight before me. He has the most perfectly sculpted body, with muscles men would die for. I have to pinch myself that it’s all mine.

“Hey, handsome. I thought you would still be in bed.” I sit down beside him and pass him the coffee.

“I couldn’t sleep when I felt a cold spot next to me. I thought you’d left until I saw your note. I take it I’ve run out of coffee again?”

I snuggle up to him and relish in his warmth, and the feeling of security being near him gives me.

“You okay?” He knows when something is wrong. Don’t ask me how he knows, but he does.

“I’m fine. What are your plans for today?”

“I have a few lessons, but after that, I’m all yours. What do you feel like doing?”

“I’d like some extra defense lessons.”

“Sure. Whatever you want.”

When he leaves for work, I go back to my apartment, clean up, then grab a good book for some me-time. I’m sitting in my snuggle seat in my window, a smoothie and a book in hand, when I happen to look up out the window. I see those guys again from earlier, minus the girl this time, and they head into the gym. My head is doing the same thing again and is buzzing with something. It’s like a mixture of voices and noises, but it's all muffled. It's like whatever wants to be heard can't get out. Curiosity gets the better of me and I throw on my gym clothes, and head over there.

It's manic when I enter. I slip past the reception area and go work on the treadmill for a while. But as I walk across the gym, I see Reid talking to the two guys I bumped into outside the coffee shop. He obviously knows them, and they are all laughing, so they must be friends. I don't want a confrontation in front of him, so I walk away, but he spots me and calls me over.

Damn it, my nerves really can't cope with this. I pretend I haven't heard him, and keep walking.

I get to the treadmill, put my earphones on, and get to it. I keep my gaze down, but as I'm working up a sweat, my eyes drift, and the guys are still talking. One of them looks my way. I don't like the way he looks at me. It's a look I can feel in the pit of my stomach. I start to feel dizzy, so I hop off and make quick work of heading to the ladies locker rooms. I sit on the benches, and grab my water, and eventually everything starts to ease, but when the door opens, my skin prickles. I feel someone standing behind me, but I can't bring myself to turn around. I know it's the guy from the cafe incident earlier, and also the one who looked at me while talking to Reid. He bends down to my ear and starts talking.

"So, you're my bro's new piece then. I must say, you're not his usual type, but he never was fussy, to be honest."

He leans further into me so his front is pushing against my back and moves my hair to the side. I'm frozen to the bench and praying someone walks in.

"Now, there's something about you that's niggling at me, sweetheart, and I just can't seem to put my finger on it. But rest assured, I will find that something out, and I will come find you when I do, I promise."

I look down to where his hands are pressed against the bench on either side of me, and I see his wrist. My breathing becomes labored. I try to stand, but all I can hear are screams and gunshots. I try to make my way to the door, but I have no idea where the guy has gone, or if he is still here. My head can't take what's happening.

I see my parents lying in a pool of blood, a man trying to rape me. I hear voices, screams. Everything is happening at the same time, then in the midst of it all, I hear Ash's voice, but I don't know how. It's like he's in the distance, but I can hear him telling me it's okay.

"It's okay, Esme. I got you. Shhhh." He has me cocooned in his arms on the floor of the ladies' locker room and the sobs are slowly subsiding.

"Where's the guy that was just here with me?" I ask. Ash looks around the locker room, shaking his head.

"There was no one in here when I came in. I heard you screaming and crying from outside."

"I don't understand. There was a guy in here with me just now. How did you not see him?"

I push away from Ash once I've calmed down, and we sit back on the benches. From the look he's giving me, I know he knows about my past.

"I guess Nyla told you about my parents, then?"

"She told me briefly, and for what it's worth, I'm sorry

you had to go through that."

"Ash, there was a guy in here before you came in. He said he was Reid's brother."

"I didn't see anyone, but his brother was in the gym talking to him earlier. His name is Declan. He likes to be called Dec, though. Has him being here got something to do with you having that attack just then?"

God, I don't know. My head is spinning all over the place. Could it be true? That tattoo on his wrist was the same as on the guy in my parents' apartment the night they were killed. Surely, this cannot be a coincidence. Their voices outside the coffee shop were so familiar. It would explain why I freaked out. But I can't be one hundred percent sure. Also, how is Reid going to react when I tell him I think his brother may have killed my family?

"No, it was nothing to do with him. I just remember someone coming in and introducing himself as Reid's brother, and then I had my meltdown. I wondered if he had seen me, but he must have left before."

I think Ash buys my story, but for how long, I don't know. I need to speak with Nyla and fast. I have no idea what to do, but this situation could turn nasty if it is them, and they realize who I am.

"Ash, would you mind letting me out the back door, please? I just need some fresh air."

"Yeah, sure. You want me to wait with you?"

"No, you go back inside. I just need a few minutes to myself."

"Okay. Make sure you close the door when you come back in."

"Will do."

And then I'm alone. I make my escape quickly, and once I'm back in my apartment, I call Nyla and tell her I'm on my way over.

# Chapter Eleven

**M**e: Gone out with Nyla. See you later x

I turn my phone off as I arrive at Nyla's because I know Reid will be blowing it up looking for me, but I just need some time to work out what's going on. My head is all fuzzy, and I can't seem to place everything that's running through it since this morning's encounter with Reid's brother and his friends. And then the gym incident.

"Es, talk to me. You haven't said a word in the last hour since you arrived, and you're as white as a sheet. This isn't like you." She wraps her arms around me and pulls me down, so my head is laid in her lap.

"This morning, I ran into some guys and a girl outside the coffee shop, and it got a bit heated. But there was something about their voices that made my head hurt, and it scared me."

"It's probably just some thugs. Stop overthinking."

But then I tell her I decided to go to the gym.

"The guys were chatting and laughing with Reid in the gym. So I walked straight on by. But later, in the locker room, there was a guy behind me. I didn't hear him come in."

She tenses. "What happened?"

I sit up and take in her worried expression. "He said there's something about me that's bothering him, and he will find that something out, then come find me."

"Ny." My voice is shaking with fear now. "He had a snake tattoo on his wrist."

Nyla's eyes are wide, which tells me what I already knew deep down. Declan, Reid's brother, murdered my family. Nyla's phone starts ringing, and I automatically assume it's him, but it's Ash. He knew something was wrong at the gym.

"Listen, firecracker, Reid is going nuts wanting to know where she is. Tell me where you both are so we can come check on you, okay?"

"Oh, no. She doesn't need him here right now. Her head is a mess."

"Why? Has this got something to do with her meltdown in the locker room?"

"I can't say. Please leave it, okay?"

"Listen, I cannot unsee what I saw from Esme earlier. She looked tortured, and no one should feel like that. If I can help, let me, please."

"Fine, but only if you promise to come alone and don't tell Reid. Not yet, anyway." I nod in agreement. I could use his help.

"Dammit, woman. You're asking me to lie to my brother. My best friend." He sighs.

"I'll explain why. Trust me, you'll understand."

"Okay, I will come alone. Give me the address."

Twenty minutes later, there's loud thumping at the door, just how Reid knocks. I knew he'd tell him.

"I knew we shouldn't have trusted Ash." Nyla goes to look through the peep-hole when a voice booms through the door.

"It's me, Ash."

Nyla swings the door open and drags him inside. "Hey, thanks for coming and helping Esme when she needed it earlier today."

"You're welcome, although Reid is pissed at me." He looks my way. "How are you doing, Esme?" They sit on either side of me on the couch. "He is going out of his mind not knowing where you are, and turning your phone off is making his neurotic mind ten times worse. He thinks you've left him."

Tears are brimming, and I feel the first one fall down my face. Ash wipes it away gently with his thumb.

"Esme, I know something happened in that locker room, but we can't help you if you don't tell us."

"God, this is such a mess, but it's my mess, and I have to deal with it. I just know people are going to get hurt." Ash embraces me in a hug, and it's so tight I think he's going to crush me. But I hug him back because I need this. When he finds out what Reid's brother has done, who knows whose side he will take. I mean, they're family, brothers, best friends. I am just a nobody, really.

"As much as Reid charges about, he cares about you, Esme. He will help you through this, whatever this is."

"He won't help me, Ash. He will hate me because I'll be tearing his world apart."

"How, Esme? Explain it to me."

I take a deep breath and tell him everything. I can't make this decision on my own, and Ash is his best friend. I need his help.

"Shit, Esme, are you sure? He rubs his hand through his hair. He gets up and starts pacing around.

"I'm pretty sure it's him. The tattoo, what he said in the locker room, outside the coffee shop… there are too many coincidences."

I can't get the voices from that night out of my head now. The tears are back, and he comes back to me and embraces me.

"Hey, it's going to be okay. Reid will fix this. We both will, I promise." I just shake my head against his chest. "Declan and Reid are real close, but he has been hanging with the wrong crowd, and Reid doesn't like it."

"So, what would you do?" I want to hear what he thinks.

"If you tell him, yes, it will break him. But he will also stop him before he does any more damage." He holds my hands. "Please, Esme, I'll be there when you tell him if it helps, but he needs to know before you make any rash decisions."

I push him away, angry at his words. "What rash decisions do you think I'd be making, Ash? Would that be, oh, let me guess, maybe doing the right thing and going to the police? He murdered my family! I lost everything that night, everything that meant the world to me. Do you know what it felt like to hear them screaming and then to see them lying there in their own blood when there was nothing I could do?"

I sob with the memories and the pain.

"I should have died with them."

"Don't you ever talk like that, Esme. Never, you hear me, girl?" Nyla wraps her arms around me, hugging me closely.

Ash gets up and walks to the door. "All I'm saying is give him the benefit of the doubt. Let him try to help you." With that, he walks out of the apartment.

I stare at the door wondering if Ash will tell him or keep this to himself.

"He won't divulge anything unless you say so. It's your call. Whatever you decide to do, I will stand by you."

"Is it okay to stay here tonight? I can't go back, Nyla. I need time away from him to think."

"Sure, no problem. Take as long as you need."

It's 2 a.m. and Nyla is fast asleep. I feel such a jumble of emotions. My head is saying do one thing, and my heart is saying the opposite. I'm so confused. I know Reid needs to know, but I also know he will want to deal with it himself. How could he even deal with something that huge? He and his thugs committed murder and took everything from me that night, and they need to pay. I get dressed and leave the apartment quietly.

It's so quiet outside, no cars to be heard, no one walking

the streets, just the glow from the streetlamps. Before I know it, I'm standing outside the police precinct.

"You okay, Miss?"

An officer is standing beside me, but I can't seem to form any words. I'm just staring at the entrance. The officer waits patiently for my reply, but I look around me, trying to find the words that don't seem to want to come. The hairs stand up on the back of my neck as I see *him* across the road in the shadows, leaning against the building, watching me. He smirks, and I gasp and grip the officer next to me.

"Miss, are you okay?" the officer asks me.

I manage to point across to where I saw him, but he's gone. I feel my legs give out under me, but the officer has a hold of me and carries me into the station.

I'm in a private room. The officer, whose name I have learned is Jenkins, has sent someone to get me a drink. He hasn't asked me anything yet, but he will want to know what happened.

"Listen, you came here because something is bothering you, and whatever it is scared you enough to collapse out there."

I want to speak out. This is eating me up inside, and my emotions are completely screwed up. I have no idea what to do for the best, but just now, seeing that face and that smirk… How did he know where I was? My head is a mess of what-ifs, but what I do know is that he has worked out who I am, and now I'm in danger. Real danger.

Jenkins has called Nyla for me. I haven't said anything yet other than to give her name and number. I'm lying on a bench in the room when she comes storming in like a whirlwind and wraps her arms around me.

"Why don't you answer your phone, Es?"

"It's dead."

"Jesus. I woke up, and you were gone, and you wouldn't answer your phone. And shit. I am so, so sorry. Please forgive me."

"Ny, why do I need to forgive you?"

I don't get to finish that sentence as there is so much chaos going on outside. I get up and open the door to hear a voice I know only too well. Reid. I whip around to look at Ny, and she holds her hands up in her defense.

"Don't you dare look at me like that. You're my best friend, Es. To wake and find you gone after today's antics, I had every right to be worried. I thought something had happened to you. I called Ash to help, and he called Reid, and… you can guess the rest." By now, she has tears streaming down her face.

"It's fine. He was bound to find out eventually. You can't keep anything from him and I'm sorry for not telling you I was leaving."

I explain everything. Why I left and what happened outside when I saw him, and Nyla is just as scared as I am now. We work out that he must have followed me to Nyla's to be able to follow me here. So why didn't he do anything while I was alone and vulnerable?

"You need help. You have to tell Reid and Ash."

I know she is right, so she gets the guys. It's now or never. I need their help, and only they can protect me.

Nyla walks back into the room followed by Officer

Jenkins and Ash, but Reid stays at the door. He's looking at me all over like he's searching for something, but I have no idea what.

"Officer, do you mind?" He checks it's okay with me then leaves begrudgingly.

"If you need me, I will be down the hall, Esme, okay?"

"Thank you." I reply.

Reid starts pacing the room. His fists are clenched. Knowing his brother is responsible for my family's death must be tearing him apart. Dec is all he has; Ash told me so.

"Why, princess? Why?" He starts towards me, then stops midway. It's like he wants to come, but he isn't sure anymore. "This is all so fucked up. You must have it wrong. Are you sure? I mean, really sure? You haven't just gotten it wrong?"

"Get him out, Ash. Please." The tears are falling more than ever now. I knew it would be hard for him to hear the truth, but he's pretty adamant that I have it all wrong. I should have known. Let's face it, how long have we known each other? Just over two weeks, and that's not even properly. He's known his brother all his life, through the bad and the good.

"Just leave her alone, Reid. I think you've made it clear what you believe. Leave with Ash now." Nyla is standing in front of him with her arms crossed and looking fierce as Reid looks at me over her shoulder. He seems torn, but I can't help him. I need to look after me.

"Have you made a report to the police yet?" Reid asks me.

"No, but I have to now." I look down at my feet. I can't

bear to see his face anymore.

"Please let me help. He has no idea that you're the girl from that night. Let me try to put this right. I promise you're safe with me."

I laugh out loud. I have no idea where it comes from, and everyone is just staring at me like I've gone mad. Rage swirls inside me like hot lava. The fear has really gotten to me once and for all, and I pour it all out.

"You really have no clue how I'm feeling, none of you! That night I was sleeping, my family was alive, and I woke to their screams and deafening gunshots. Then I found them dead in a pool of their own blood. I was also nearly raped by the guy with a tattoo on his wrist, and yes, that was your brother, Reid. So forgive me if being here upsets you, but none of this is about you or how you feel." Everyone stares at me, stunned.

"Nyla, please go get Officer Jenkins." She nods and squeezes my shoulder as she walks out.

I fall back onto the bench. I am so tired now, but I want to get this over with. Reid kneels in front of me and reaches for my hands, but I pull them away.

"Please, just go."

"Princess… I can't walk away from you like this."

"I need their help and protection. Your brother is dangerous."

Reid lifts my face to look at him, and Ash steps forward too.

"What do you mean, Esme?"

"When I was outside earlier, he was watching me. It was frightening how he looked at me."

I didn't realize Nyla and Officer Jenkins had walked back into the room.

Reid leaves without even looking at me. It's like I don't exist.

Officer Jenkins has also brought in a female officer to take down my statement. He also has the case files with him, back from my family's murder, to clarify some finer details.

I make my statement to Jenkins and Evans. They tell me that counseling will be provided should I want it, and that a safe house is being provided for me as Declan is affiliated with a known gang.

"I don't want a safe house. What I want is to go home, please. You can protect me from there, surely?"

I feel like my life is spiraling out of control, and I have no clue what to do anymore. They reluctantly agree and inform me of everything I need to know, but the one person I need by my side to protect me can't do that because his loyalties lie elsewhere.

Nyla and I step outside the station to a crisp early morning. I need to get home and get ready for work. I thought they would stop that too, but having police protection means hopefully not everything has to change. I look around, wondering who is protecting me when Officer Evans appears at our side.

"You won't even know they're there," Officer Evans tells me.

"So they will be, like, in the shadows?"

He smiles at me and nods, then walks back inside.

"Esme, you don't have to go to work today. Ruby will

understand, I'm sure."

"No. I need normality. Something to keep me occupied."

The day seems to pass by in a blur. Ruby has been great about everything and said anytime I need to step out, or if there is an issue, to let her know. Jase and Nyla tried to smother me at first, but I have to put my foot down with them both.

"Please stop, both of you. You're too much. You're suffocating me. I get that you're worried about me, but what I need is normal, okay?"

Jase grabs my hand and has a huge grin on his face. "Ruby, I'm taking Esme and Nyla to lunch, okay?"

She laughs and waves him off.

We're sitting in a quaint little café around the corner from work, and Jase orders pancakes with all the toppings. When it arrives—one huge plate, three spoons— it's huge, but between the three of us, we dive in, and the mess we make is unbelievable. We laugh and talk about Jase and his latest hook-up, and it feels good. It feels normal.

It's five p.m., and Ruby is closing up.

"Es, do you want to stay with me tonight?" I love her fiercely, but I decline. Knowing I have protection makes me feel a lot easier now.

"Sorry, Nyla. I just want to go home tonight."

"Hey, it's your call. Just remember, I'm here, always." God, she is always thinking of me.

I call Officer Evans just to make sure I'm not alone

before Nyla leaves me. She tells me to look across the street at the guy in the baseball cap, and there is Officer Jenkins. He turns so as not to give himself away.

"Hey. You can go now. I'm going to be fine." Nyla goes to look around when I stop her. "Don't give anything away. I'm fine. I'll see you tomorrow."

My phone has been quiet all day. I haven't had a text or a call from Reid. He must know by now that the police are looking for his brother, so I guess he has chosen his side. I thought we had something, but how can I compete with blood?

Before going back home, I remember to grab some coffee from the local 7 Eleven. I need that first thing in the morning. I arrive home shortly after, but can't stop thinking about Officer Jenkins out there, protecting me. I didn't see a vehicle as he followed me, so he must be on foot too. I make the dto offer him a drink as it will be a long night for him. As I open my door, he is already standing outside.

"Oh, hey. Would you like a drink?" What am I doing? The guy is undercover, and here I am asking him to come into my apartment. Nope, he won't come in. He'll think I'm crazy.

"Thanks, that would be great." He just stares at me.

"Oh, sorry. Come on in." I move aside to let him in, and in doing so, I see Reid standing in the door of the stairwell. His lips are pressed together and his eyes are bulging, but I don't have time for him and his shit right now, so I go in and shut the door.

# Chapter Twelve

I offer Jenkins some coffee, and he kindly accepts.

"Esme, I've read the report from your family's murder. It must have been horrific. We will find Declan Taylor. He is key to all this, but we're hitting a brick wall finding him."

I get the impression Jenkins thinks I know more about Declan than I'm letting on, but I don't know why.

"If you're asking me where he is, then don't. I have no idea where to find him, and why would I? I didn't even know his name until a friend told me."

"Is that friend Reid Taylor, by any chance?" His sarcasm toward Reid doesn't go unnoticed.

"Actually, no. It wasn't him who told me, but I get the impression from your tone there is something about Reid you don't like."

"Let's just say there is history. How are you and Reid

acquainted, may I ask?"

He continues to stare at me, but I get the feeling he isn't asking me the questions in a professional manner. In fact, I'm starting to feel a little uncomfortable. As I look at him, I catch something in his eyes, a glimmer of heat. I try to distract him.

"Go take a seat, Officer Jenkins."

"Please, call me Leo."

Not personal at all. This doesn't feel right, using first names. I grab the mugs from the cupboard.

"I'll bring it over. You must be tired after all that walking around earlier."

He smiles, and it seems to be the most genuine smile I have seen in a long time. I sit down on the opposite couch and listen to him talk about his day whilst we drink our coffees.

"It hasn't been too bad, to be honest. I sat in the coffee shop on the corner by your work, and every now and then I would take a walk to check the perimeter. Plus, I wasn't the only one watching you today. There were other officers."

While I'm relieved the police are holding up their end and protecting me until they find Declan and question him, these officers must have families too, and I'm taking them away from them.

"What are you thinking, Esme?"

I tuck my feet up underneath me on the couch. "You must have your own families to go home to, and here you all are, out watching me because of a verbal accusation I made. I just feel…"

"It's all part of the job. We are here to protect our country and all who live in it."

It's then I really look at him and notice just how good-looking he is. I wouldn't say he'd be what I'd go for, but back when my parents had a say, then he would be exactly the type I'd end up with. Good job, clean-shaven, and from what I can see, no tattoos. Just chatting with him in my apartment and listening to him say how important it is to keep me safe has me really looking at him. I realize I'm gazing at him, and he's returning it with the same lustful look he had earlier when he was talking about Reid.

"Shit," I hiss.

Leo's eyes widen. "Is everything okay?"

I need to find my phone. I was angry with Reid over what happened at the station this morning, and we haven't spoken all day, and then he sees me letting a guy into my apartment. I get that he's picked his side, but I'm not like him. I have a conscience, and I need to get it off my chest.

"Esme, what's wrong?"

"Erm, I just need to let a friend know that I'm okay."

"Is that someone a gym owner?"

Now I'm more confused. Who is he talking about? "Care to enlighten me? Because I don't know any gym owners."

I go to grab my phone from the kitchen, and Leo follows.

"Sorry. I thought from what happened at the station earlier you were really close friends. I mean, the way he blew up in reception at the station, I would say it was more than friends."

He's talking about Reid. He owns a gym? My temper is rising now with all his cryptic shit. So much for being a nice guy. Maybe I got him wrong too.

"Yes, that someone is him, but it's none of your business!" I snap.

He steps back. "Sorry, Esme. I've no right to make a judgment. I'm just concerned about you. Reid's brother is out there on the loose and dangerous. He knows about you, and we can only guess that his gang does too. It's more dangerous than you think."

"You said that Reid owns the gym, but that can't be true. He just works there as an instructor."

I'm staring at Officer Jenkins, dumbfounded, thinking everything he just said is wrong, but he confirms it.

"Sorry, Esme. He owns Fortitude."

I feel stupid for not knowing, but at the same time, why would he tell me?

"Yeah, well it doesn't matter. It's not like I should know. We're only friends."

Leo sits back on the couch, and I go sit back on the other one.

"Sorry. I didn't mean to snap, but all these questions about Reid are making me uneasy. Is there a reason you're so inquisitive about him?"

"I'm sorry if I came across as abrupt, but I'll be honest with you. It's the least you deserve after what you've been through." He gives me a smile, which I'm sure is supposed to be reassuring. "As I said, there's a history between us, and it's not all pretty. Be careful and don't believe or trust everything that he tells you. Blood is thicker than water, as they say. "He doesn't divulge any more to me, he just stands up. "Thanks for the coffee, Esme." He smiles, walking to the door.

"There will be another officer on shift tonight. Again, you won't know he's there, and for what it's worth, I am sorry if I crossed the line tonight." He nods and slips out of the door, and I'm left even more confused than before.

I have no idea what to do with the information given to me. What did he mean 'blood is thicker than water'? He definitely crossed the line for professionalism, and I am pretty sure what he said tonight was unorthodox.

I have had enough thinking for one day. I lock up, but as I'm closing the drapes, I notice a figure across the road in the darkness, covered by the buildings. As quickly as I see him, he is gone, leaving icy chills down my spine.

I have never been so afraid of being alone in my apartment, but I feel like a burden on my friends lately. I let the police know I'd seen a figure outside, and they immediately looked into it, but there is no trace of him. I just need to go to sleep. Tomorrow is a new day.

I wake the next morning to my phone ringing. It eventually stops, only to start again. I roll over to grab it and see it's Jase calling me.

"Hey, Jase."

"Esme, were you still sleeping, hun?"

"Erm, yeah, you woke me, but it's okay. I need to get up and get ready for work."

The line goes quiet, and for a second, I think he's gone. Then there's banging at my door.

"Who the hell is banging on my door?"

"It's probably Nyla." I get out of bed and walk through the apartment to the persistent banging.

"Why would Nyla be here, and how do you know that?"

"Just open the door and she will explain." I open the door and Nyla practically falls through it.

"Thank God you're okay."

"Why would I not be okay, and why are you here so damn early pounding my door down?"

"Look at the time. It's ten a.m. No one could get hold of you. We thought something had happened!"

In the background, I hear a voice, and I realize Jase is still on the line.

"Sorry, Jase. Can I call you back later?" He says it's fine, as long as I'm okay.

I hang up and deal with my crazy best friend, who looks like she ran a marathon with the way she's puffing.

"Well, I need a new alarm. The damn thing never went off." I check my phone alarm and see it actually did go off. I must have slept straight through it.

"Really, Es. I thought you'd been killed, you idiot! Never do that to me again."

"Sorry. Oh, crap. Ruby is going to kill me."

"Look, don't panic. Ruby is all good. Honestly, she's surprised you're still coming to work with everything that's going on."

"Erm, shit. Sorry about that. How the hell have I slept in, Nyla? I'm never late for work. What the hell is wrong with me?"

"You've been through hell in the last twenty-four hours. Your body is running on fumes. Just rest, okay?" She walks me back to my bedroom and makes sure I get back in bed, then leaves.

"Fine. See you later."

I'm lying in bed, but I can't sleep now, so I take a long, hot shower and contemplate the discussion last night with Leo about Reid and the gym. Then I start to think all kinds of stupid scenarios as to why he should and shouldn't have told me.

"Arrrgghh!" I grumble to myself. I'm driving myself insane thinking this way.

I go to make some coffee and realize I still need to get some groceries.

I slip on some sweats and throw my hair up into a messy bun. Grabbing my purse and phone, I fling open the door, but I freeze.

Reid and Ash are standing literally outside my door. I haven't heard a thing from Reid since Monday morning at the police station. He just up and left, not a word since. It hurts knowing he knew it was his brother that killed my family and nearly raped me, and even knowing all this, he still chose to walk away and leave me vulnerable. I can't forgive that. I needed him, and he left.

"Esme, are you okay?" Ash asks.

I really can't talk right now. Seeing him has my emotions fucked up. I want to scream at Reid for what his brother has taken from me, but I'm also on the brink of breaking the dam as I miss him. I miss his persistent and bossy ways and the way he made me feel safe all the time. But when I look at him, I see Declan, then I see blood and the faces of those no longer here, and it's killing me.

"I'm good, thanks, but I need to go. Excuse me."

I skirt around them both and press the button for the lift. I know he's right behind me and all I want to do is lean back into him, but I can't. So, I move my body toward the lift doors. His arms cage me in when he puts them on either side of the lift, but he isn't touching me.

"Esme, we need to talk to you, please. It's important," he whispers.

"Talk to me about what?"

I still can't look at him.

"I need to know what you said to the police about Declan. I need to know what I'm dealing with."

The doors to the lift open. I step inside then turn around to face him.

"You really are a piece of shit. You want to know what was said? ask them yourself. And just so we're clear, stay away from me, do you understand? I never want to see you again."

The doors close. I slump against the back wall, and the dam breaks once again.

I ask Lance to call me a cab and decide to go to Jase's apartment. I need to be away from here and him. I send both Jase and Nyla texts, letting them know where I'm heading, then I tell the officer I clocked outside too.

By the time I get there, Jase had already arrived to let me in.

"Hey, Esme. Are you okay? What happened?" I bury my head into his shoulder.

"Why did I have to fall for the wrong guy, Jase?" Pulling my head back gently, he gives me a sympathetic look.

"Esme, you haven't fallen for the wrong guy at all. It's just a messed up situation. Now, I want to hear what happened, but Ruby is expecting me back at work. Nyla and I will be back here real soon, and you can tell us everything. Until then, make yourself at home."

"Before you come back, could you go to mine and grab me some things. I kind of left like this." I hand him my keys.

"Yeah, sure. Send me a message with a list." He kisses my forehead and is gone.

I binge watch some TV for a few hours when I hear the door open, and in bounces Nyla and Jase.

"Hey, we got everything you asked for," Jase shouts.

"Thanks, guys. You are the best friends." Nyla looks at Jase, and I know something has happened. "Spill it."

"Okay, when we were in your apartment, Ash knocked on the door. He was shocked to see us. Anyway, he said he was sorry about earlier, and Reid is just a complete mess. He also said he has no idea how to deal with any of this."

"He left me, Nyla. He's had no contact since he found out, and when I needed him, he bolted. And then, when he eventually surfaced, all he wanted was information, so he knows what he's up against. He's a piece of shit." She pulls me into a hug, and then Jase hugs me too. "I needed him. He said he would protect me always. Since we met he's been persistent and bossy, and when I actually need him, where is he? Gone! His brother killed my family. Nothing justifies that."

It's then that I realize I'm really crying. The floodgates have opened and I can't stop them.

"I can't stay there anymore. I don't feel safe in that building or even in this city. What am I going to do?"

"It will all be okay Es, you have us. Nothing is going to happen to you, I promise." If only she believed that. I sense the tension in her when we hug; she's just as scared as I am.

We order Chinese takeout and Jase tells me I can use his spare room for as long as I need to. After a few hours of eating and watching *Legally Blonde*—one and two—I wake to find Nyla and Jase both passed out on the sofas. I pull the throws over them and head to bed, wondering what tomorrow will bring.

# Chapter Thirteen

Another two and a half weeks pass by and life has to carry on as normal. Well, as normal as can be. I'm constantly looking over my shoulder as the police have no leads on Declan's whereabouts, and I still haven't heard from Reid since our encounter by the elevator. I miss him and his stubborn, crazy ways, and I wonder how he's been, too. I'm still staying at Jase's, but I need to go home. Nyla has offered to come stay with me. Jase needs his place back as I'm cock blocking him. Not that he actually used those words, but for a guy who enjoys male company, he sure has been celibate these past couple weeks. It's time for me to go.

I'm at work when my phone pings for a message. It's from Reid, but there is no text, just an attachment.

We finish work and I grab a cab home because of the bags I

have. I put my earplugs in and open the attachment. It's an audio. He sent me a song by Meat Loaf -*I'd Do Anything for Love*. The tears are silently streaming down my cheeks as we travel back towards my apartment. It's pouring outside when I pull up, and I have no coat. I grab what I can from the trunk of the cab, but as I turn, I slip. I let out a squeal, but there are two huge arms to catch me, and I know right away who it is.

"Thank you." I'm frozen to the spot just staring at him and thinking of that song he sent me. My God, I've missed him. He has about a week's worth of stubble growing, and he looks like he hasn't slept at all, but he still looks irresistible. I pick my bags back up and try heaving them into the foyer area, but they are way too heavy.

"Here, let me help you." He doesn't move, and I realize he's waiting for a reply. We're both getting soaked to the bone because I keep staring at him. I think it's because I can't believe he's actually here.

"Esme."

"Oh, yes. Just take them to Lance. He can help me take them up."

I move inside, and press the button for the elevator, and as I step inside and turn around, he is stepping inside too, with the rest of my stuff.

"Don't say anything, please. Just let me bring these up for you. It's the least I can do."

I close my mouth, which was hanging open, and look away. If I don't, I know I will want to touch him, kiss him, hug him, because that's the pull he has on me. He came into my life like a tornado and then disappeared just as quickly. My heart is fractured and only he can fix it, but how and when, I don't know.

I walk into my apartment and he follows me in. He drops my bags by the couch while I go put the coffee maker on. I grab us both towels as we're soaked from the rain, but he takes mine and starts to dry my hair. It feels so good having him caress my hair the way he is that I moan.

"Esme." I open my eyes and he is just about to kiss me, but I back off.

"What the hell are you doing, Reid? Jesus, is this why you helped me, to get back in my pants?"

"What? No. Fuck, princess. You've got it all wrong."

"Don't call me that. I am not your princess. Not anymore."

And that's all it takes. The hurt and pain on his face is like someone has died. I know that look because it was the look I held when I lost my family. And with that, he turns on his heel and strides away, slamming my door behind him. No words, no fight, just gone.

Reid Taylor is not the man I thought he was. The rough-looking, strong, and over-protective alpha. No. He's actually a coward who runs at the first sign of trouble, and I have to ask myself, do I really need a man so weak in my life?

I'm about to hop into the shower when my door flies open, and Reid barrels through. He picks me up and throws me over his shoulder and takes me up to his apartment. I'm kicking and screaming, but he won't let up, and deep inside, I'm happy dancing because this is the Reid I know. The fighter, the man who doesn't give up and doesn't take no for an answer. But I am also downright pissed he yet again barged into my apartment un-invited and swooped me up like it was normal.

"What the fuck, Reid? Put me down right now, you piece of shit!"

"Piece of shit, huh? That's a new one. Nope, sorry, not happening."

He storms through his door and straight into his bedroom.

"You're going to hear me out, and you're not leaving until I'm finished. If you still want to leave when I'm done, then fine, but until then you're staying, understood?"

He drops me down on his bed, walks out of the room, and then comes back with two steaming cups of coffee. I notice he has dimmed the lights and placed candles around the room. He must have done all this when he came back up earlier. He isn't wearing the same wet clothes either.

"I'm still wet from the rain. You didn't give me a chance to get changed, Smiler."

This makes him smile and he grabs me one of his t-shirts. I make quick work in removing the wet clothing, and he doesn't take his eyes off me the whole time. I see the lust building in his eyes and I think it's taking all his self-control not to move. I sit back on the bed and he faces me and takes my hands in his.

"My brother is all the family I have left. Our parents died in a car crash when I was eighteen and Declan was eight years old. It was up to me to bring him up and I tried the best I could, but I was still a kid myself and I had no idea what I was doing."

My heart breaks for him as he has lost just as much as me and then had to become a parent when he was still a kid himself. I had no idea he held all this responsibility.

I squeeze his hands, letting him know I'm with him and listening.

"Go on."

"My life had always been about my friends, and I was never really at home. Parties and drinking from the age of fifteen was what we did. And sex," he says the last part quietly, ashamed. "I was out at a warehouse party when the police found me and told me of the accident. Declan was also in the car, but he managed to survive with a few cuts and scrapes, the main being to his face. Dad died instantly, and Mom died on route to the hospital."

"What happened to the other car?"

"It was a drunk driver. He died on impact too. It seems he had just split from his wife, and he couldn't handle it, from what the police said. I tried to do right by Declan, but he wasn't the easiest of kids. He had his own trauma and issues from the accident to deal with, and by the age of eleven, he was getting into trouble with the police, stealing, and then he ended up in juvie at the age of twelve for fighting and attacking people. I didn't help either. My way of dealing with him was to lash out at those he hung out with, and in return, he rebelled even more."

"How long was he in juvie?"

Reid looks defeated. "He spent nearly three years in there. Eventually, he started to settle down. He had a mentor who seemed to take an interest in him, although I never met him. He was never there when I visited, but he managed to help Declan get out on good behavior."

I have no idea what to say to him. I can't imagine how hard it must have been for him at such a young age being left with such a responsibility, but blaming himself for the path his brother chose to take is not his fault.

"Declan seemed to be turning his life around when he got out. He finished school and got a job. He was out most days, and I thought all was good. There were no issues with the police, so I went about my own life and didn't pay attention to what was going on in front of me until it was too late. Declan's mentor inside had set him up with a job when he finished school, and let's just say it wasn't exactly legit work, but he was earning good money. But it was dirty money. I tried to stop it, but he wouldn't have it. Each time I dragged his ass home from the cop station, or stopped him doing something stupid, we ended up having the worst fallouts. He would run away for hours, sometimes even overnight, and he didn't care when I was out all night looking for him. Eventually, he begged me to back off and said he could handle what he was doing and that he actually enjoyed it. I was drained trying to keep up with him, so I let him go and do his thing.""

"But do you think there was nothing more that could have been done, honestly? I get you were drained, but look what he ended up doing, Reid."

"Maybe, but he was turning eighteen, and he made sure I remembered that too. It meant I had no hold on him when that happened."

He takes a sip of his coffee and continues telling his story.

"We agreed to keep out of each other's business, and it was then he asked me to just be his brother and not his parent. I knew he was part of a gang called the Vipers, and they were well known in Brooklyn for some notorious crimes. I was always in the shadows, watching him when he least knew it. Some of what I saw I was ashamed about, but he never killed anyone, Esme… not until your family. I wasn't there to stop him and that kills me."

He really is beating himself up over his brother and I have to ask if anyone has ever considered what he was going through at such a young age also.

"Where were you that night? You said you were normally in the shadows, watching."

"I was at the underground, fighting. I wasn't supposed to be there, but I heard that Declan and his friends were going, and that could only mean one thing. Trouble. I didn't realize until the last fight that they weren't coming, but it was too late. I had signed up to fight so it didn't look like I was there by coincidence. It was a decoy to keep me out of the way. He must have known I'd been watching him."

His brows are frowning and he is clenching his fists, the last thing I need is the caveman to rear his ugly head, so I need to calm him the best way I know how.

"Reid, can you hold me, please?"

I know with him doing that, his focus is solely on me and nothing else.

"You sure?"

"Yes, I'm sure. Please. I need it as much as you do right now."

I don't have to ask again. He pulls me to him and wraps his arms around me, but he isn't doing it tightly like he normally would. He's gentle, and I sob quietly. I'm crying because of everything he's told me, and because of the past two weeks and what we could have been and have lost and have still yet to deal with. I miss this caveman so much, but even though this may be why his brother is the way he is, I still can't let him get away with what he has taken from me. I won't settle until Declan Taylor is behind bars or dead.

Reid pulls back and gives me my coffee.

"I meant what I said earlier. I just want you to hear me out, then if you want to walk away, I won't stand in your way."

"Okay."

"When Ash told me what happened, I was already going out of my mind thinking you had left and had second thoughts about us. That maybe I had pushed you too fast. My head was a mess.

So when he told me about Declan and you, I was devastated. The fact that my brother could even be part of that, but also the fact that it was you he did it to fucked with my head, and I had no idea how to deal with it."

"So, Ash told you everything after Nyla called when she thought I was missing that night?"

"Yeah he did, but he did it for your own safety. You need to know that. He cares about you, too."

He is pacing the room again, but his anger is at bay for now, so I let him continue.

"Killing your parents is one thing, and I'm in total agreement that the police need to deal with him, but I need to find him first before they do, okay? This is something I need to do. Please."

"I get that you want to help your brother and I'm grateful you understand my need to let the police deal with this."

"Stop. Let me make this clear to you." His rage is starting to boil. His brother will always come first, and I can't compete with that. "I will not be helping my brother in any way. He has crossed a line, and it can't be taken back. He needs to pay, and I need to be the one to deal with him. Do you understand me now, Esme?"

I get off the bed and stand behind him. I get it now, and it's time for him to stop beating himself up over his brother. He's been doing this for far too long, and it's time someone stood *with* him and is there *for* him.

"Hey, you wanna stop beating on that wall for a minute?"

I rub my hands over his back and then down his arms as he lowers them from the wall. I grab his hand and he turns. What I see breaks me apart. He is crying so much his face is soaked. This man who everyone assumes should be a protector because of his size and the fact he's a fighter is falling apart in front of me. We sit back on the bed and he goes to speak, but I stop him with my finger on his lips.

"I know. I get it now, and I'm sorry for not listening to you and giving you a chance to explain, but this thing with your brother is not your fault, okay?"

"He messed with something of mine, and that is a line that once crossed there is no going back from. He knows that, Esme. You were mine, and he will be dealt with brother to brother."

I don't like what I'm about to agree to, but I trust him, and I have to believe deep down that he will still protect me if we're together or not.

"Okay. Do what you have to and I won't stand in your way. Just promise me one thing, that's all I ask."

"What's that?"

"If it gets out of control, let the police deal with it. That's my one condition."

"It won't."

"Reid, can you please just give me that one reassurance? If you can't then I'm leaving, I mean it."

I get up and walk toward the door, but he's like lightning, and I'm being carried back to the bedroom before I can even blink.

"We aren't finished talking yet, Esme. But, yes, I agree, you infuriating woman."

Finally, I see a hint of a smile trying to break through, but it soon disappears because the next talk will be about us, so I let him lead.

"I'm new to all this relationship stuff, and I know I haven't handled things right, but you came into my life so unexpectedly and I wasn't ready."

"You weren't ready? Do you think I was ready for a guy that

sped along like a rollercoaster and didn't know where the stop switch was?"

"Ouch, Esme. Don't hold back, will you"

"Sorry, but it's true." He picks up my hand and gently caresses it.

"Don't ever be sorry for being you, Esme. Look, what I'm trying to say is I've never done this before. You… you're different. I can't keep away, and I don't want to. I'm not perfect. I have my faults, but don't we all? But what I can promise and will always promise is that I will be here should you need me. I will care for you always, and I'll protect you with everything I have, if you let me. You've awakened something in me, Esme Lewis, and I'm not willing to let you go without a fight."

And there he is, my bossy overbearing alpha, telling me what's what before I've even agreed to anything.

"Neither of us is perfect, but relationships are about compromise and talking, so if we can do that then maybe we stand a chance at this. But you also said you'd be there last time and you disappeared on me when shit happened. How do I know it won't happen again?"

"Because things have changed now. You are my family, not Declan!"

That statement sends shivers through me.

His tears are drying up. I look at his face, and although he tries cracking a smile, his tired eyes tell me deep down he's sad over his brother and what he's lost.

I really have missed him, and it's about time I showed him how much. I push him back on the bed and straddle him, and his hands immediately go to my waist.

"You sure about this, Esme?"

"Please stop calling me that, and yes."

I don't get to finish as he flips me over and is devouring my mouth. My God, have I missed this.

"Princess, I promise not to let you down again."

We spend the night with each other as he doesn't want me out of his sight while his brother is on the loose and nowhere to be found, and I'm not arguing. Tonight has been hell for us both, and I just want to wrap my arms around him and sleep.

# Chapter Fourteen

I wake to voices and wonder who Reid is talking to. I'm guessing it's Ash. I grab a pair of his sweats, not that they fit me properly as I have to roll them over and over to get them to stay up, but they will work for now. I make my way out to where I hear them in the kitchen and catch his brother's name, but they both stop speaking as soon as they see me.

"Please don't stop on my account."

I grab a cup, but Reid puts a fresh cup of coffee right in front of me and wraps his arms around me.

"Morning, princess. You sleep okay?"

"Yes. I had the best sleep, and it was needed, too. Thank you for letting me stay the night."

"Never thank me for that. You're welcome here anytime you want. If it was up—" He gets interrupted by Ash talking to me, so I have no idea what he was about to say.

"Morning, Esme."

"Hey, Ash. I will see you both later. I really need to sort my apartment out before it thinks I've disowned it."

"Can we talk before you go? There are just a few things we need to discuss and go over with you," Reid says.

He looks worried. So does Ash, and this time, I don't argue. I sit at the breakfast bar with them opposite me, staring at me.

"Okay," Ash starts. "Since the police station incident, we have put word out that we're looking for Declan. We've tried all the places he would normally hang out, but it's like he's just completely vanished." He looks at Reid to continue.

"Usually, when I go looking for him, he knows, and he surfaces somewhere, but this time, it's different."

"Do you think something has happened to him?"

Not that I wouldn't welcome that, but I can't voice that in front of Reid. He's still his brother, after all.

"No. I think it's the opposite."

I have no idea what he means by that, and I look between him and Ash, trying to read them both. I sense whatever they think is going on is not good.

"Jesus, just spit it out. I can't deal with any more cryptic shit and everyone keeping secrets from me!"

"Hey, calm down."

"Esme, we heard from an ex-gang member that they're not finished with you…"

"What the hell is that supposed to mean? Are they planning on doing to me what they did to my family? Is that it?" I get up and start for the door.

Reid grabs me and whispers, "Hear us out, please, and

then I will take you downstairs."

"Just tell me one thing. Do I need to run?"

The tears flow freely once again. I have no idea what to do anymore. The police can't find him, Reid and Ash can't find him, and now I'm a target. I break down against him, and he steers me to the couch, but he places me on his lap and holds me tight. The next thing I know, Ash is right there too, holding my hand.

"Esme, because you now recognize them from the robbery, in their eyes, you need to be dealt with."

"What does *dealt with* mean, Ash? They're going to kill me, aren't they?"

"Pretty much," Reid says, stroking his hand up and down my back to somehow try to make this okay. "But listen to me, it's never going to happen. Not on my watch, you understand me?"

"How can you guarantee that though? You can't be with me every minute of every day. You have a life, work, your fights, the gym…"

"None of that is important right now. Keeping you safe comes first, princess. You also have the cops watching you too, so you're safe. I promise."

This is all becoming too much, too fast again. What am I supposed to do? I have a job and a life. I cannot expect people to babysit me, including the police, but what choice do I have? It's that or play Russian roulette with my own life every time I walk out of the door. We talk more about Reid and Ash escorting me to work and back and making sure I have their numbers in my cell phone.

"Thanks, Ash, for everything. And I'm really sorry

you're being dragged into my mess."

He comes to stand in front of me and pulls me into a hug. Reid growls at the side of me, but I just ignore him.

"Esme, please. Reid is the brother I never had, and we've been through some shit together over the years. He is family, and family sticks together in times of need. And just for the record, you mean more to him than he will ever tell you, so I will. You are his everything, which means you're part of this family, like it or not. And we protect our family."

I wrap myself around Ash because no one has said such sweet words to me since I lost my family, and I'm starting to think that maybe there is hope and I can belong again.

Ash leaves, and I go back to my apartment. Nyla is going to join me as Reid needs to head to the gym to take some classes. The music is blasting, so I don't hear the door at first, and when I finally do, I assume Lance has let Nyla up as usual.

When I open the door, I see Declan standing there. I go to shut the door, but he puts his large foot in the way, so I make for my cell. I dart past the couch, and just as I make a beeline for it, he runs at me from the side, knocking me into a cabinet. It knocks the wind out of me, and I hit the floor with a grunt. Declan is well-built like his brother, but Reid is slightly taller and bigger, but not by much. I'm like a twig compared to him, and if I don't have any broken ribs, it's going to be a miracle.

"Looking for something, sweetness? You wanna call someone, maybe?"

"What do you want?"

I need to get to the window so Nyla, or the police if

they're out there, can see that something is wrong, but I can't move. The pain in my ribs is unbearable.

"What I want is what I wanted that night you hid in your wardrobe." He bends down to me and smirks. "Yes, I knew you were in there. I was just biding my time, waiting so I could fuck you while you screamed."

He strokes his hand up my bare thigh, and I only have on shorts and a tank top, which makes me panic even more. *Please, God. Don't let this happen. Not now.*

I try to move and push him off me, but he's so strong that I don't stand a chance. How the hell did he get up here? And where are the police?

"Get the fuck off me, you murdering bastard!" I knew the minute the words had slipped out of my mouth, I shouldn't have said them, but it's too late. The back of his hand collides with my face so fast that it steals my breath.

"Well, well, well. She's feisty, I like it."

"I know exactly who you are. Declan Taylor, wanted for the murder of my family and attempted rape." I can't seem to keep my mouth shut, but he has opened the pain and anger within me all over again.

"Well, I may as well do the crime if I'm being accused of it. What do you say?"

I need to move fast. I look around me and grab the only thing heavy enough to break through the window; a marble ball ornament. I throw it in the direction of the window, but as I look up, I see Declan's fist, and then everything goes black.

I can hear the sound of beeping and I smell antiseptic,

but my eyes won't open. They seem so heavy. I remember Nyla being in my apartment and then being in an ambulance, but everything is really fuzzy. I try to talk, but nothing seems to be coming out.

Where am I, and what's going on? I try again to talk, but it becomes too much. Closing my eyes is the easier option now.

"Es, it's Nyla."

I start to rouse again, but this time my heavy eyelids move, and a bright light starts to peer through. I immediately lift my arm to shield my eyes.

"Can we have a doctor in here? She's waking up."

"Water. I need water."

Nyla passes me some water and helps me sit up then closes the curtains to shield my eyes from the brightness as they hurt like hell. I finally manage to open my eyes a little more, and I notice I'm in the hospital. I lie back and think about what happened that made me end up here, and then it hits me. Declan!

"Es, you remember, don't you?" I start hyperventilating, and Nyla is quick to sit on the bed and wrap herself around me. "Hey, shh. It's okay. I'm here now. He can't hurt you anymore. I promise you're safe."

"Have they caught him? Please tell me they have him. Please, Nyla."

She gives me a grim look, and I know he got away again.

"What happened?" I ask. "I remember Declan being in my apartment and he attacked me!"

"Calm down. You're okay, I promise."

"Thank God you came when you did," I say between sobs.

"I was just walking toward your building entrance when something came flying down onto the sidewalk. I looked up and noticed your window was smashed, so I ran inside and told Lance to call the police, and I headed up. Probably foolish of me, but my best friend needed me. I heard shouting as I opened the door and I must have startled him, as you were out cold on the floor and he was…"

She stops talking, and I know what she's about to say as he'd already told me before he knocked me out what he was going to do. Thank God Nyla came when she did.

"He told me he was going to rape me, the sick bastard." I start crying again because there is nothing left to do.

"You took a pretty good blow to the head."

"Yeah. My head and eye are pounding right now. Does Reid know?"

"Yeah, he knows. He and Ash went to speak with the police. They'll be back in a minute. Es, you need to know that Declan thought I was his brother coming through the door. In fact, he wanted it to be him."

"Why? I don't understand."

"When I walked in and startled him, his words were, 'You're not my brother. That's a shame. I was so looking forward to letting him see me take what's so precious from him.' Sick bastard."

"What the fuck did he say?" Reid growls from the doorway.

I stare straight into his eyes, but there is hurt and fury behind them, and it's because I know exactly what Declan meant by those words, and so does Reid. His brother may have been eight years old when he was scarred for life, but he has never forgotten or forgiven, and for some reason, he holds Reid responsible.

The police inform us that a call was made, telling them Declan had been seen a few blocks away, so all officers were called away, leaving me with only one officer outside just as he planned. He must have watched Reid leave for the gym and knew I was alone, and then made his move. Lance had no idea the police were looking for him. That's why he let him up, thinking he was going to his brother's place.

There's a knock at my room door, and in walk Officer Jenkins and Officer Evans. The tension in the room thickens, and Reid and Leo cannot take their eyes off one another. In fact, if looks could kill, I would say we were all pretty much doomed. What the hell is their history? I want to know, but I also want to know why they're here.

"Esme, how are you feeling?"

Reid is right beside me like a flash, and the sneer on Leo's face would have been missed if I wasn't looking straight at him when he asked the question.

"How the fuck do you think she is? Have you seen her face?"

At that point I realize I still can't see properly out of one eye, so I ask for a mirror. Nyla grabs me one from her purse. A gasp leaves my mouth when I see my face is pretty beat up and extremely swollen over my right eye. The bruising is already starting to show, so my face isn't going to look pretty for a while.

"Esme, we're sorry this happened and we're doing

everything that we can to find him."

"But you can't find him, can you? It's been over two weeks, and you have no leads as to his whereabouts, and then he manages to lead you all away today to get to me, and it worked. If it hadn't been for my best friend here, God knows what could have happened to me."

"I'm sorry, Esme. We promised to protect you and we let you down. He was very clever in his ploy to divert everyone from your area."

"I think it's time you left, officers. She needs her rest." Reid pushes them out the door, followed by Ash.

I don't know what is said, but I can hear raised voices, then Reid and Ash are back. I'm too tired to ask what was said, but I do need to know how the hell Declan managed to flee my apartment so easily when Nyla walked in on him.

"What happened when he saw you, Ny, other than what he said? Please, I need to know."

"I tried to get my phone out, and he lunged at me, knocking me to ground, and then he ran out through the door. I'm sorry I can't be more help."

"Hey, you have nothing to be sorry for. I'm just grateful you came when you did. I love you, Ny."

"He would have gone down the fire escape stairwell that leads to the back of the building. That's how he did it," Reid informs us.

They all stay with me until the doctor gives them their marching orders. None of them are happy, but there is now an officer outside my door. This suffices for Nyla, but not Reid. He wants to stay, but the doctors are adamant he can't.

"I will be back here first thing, I promise."

"I look forward to it."

The next day, they are all back, waiting for the doctor to give me the all-clear to go home. Nyla has been doing my hair while we wait, and the guys have just been sitting there watching us. They have given me a patch to wear when I go out as the light is still affecting my eye. They reckon it should rectify itself and hopefully go down in time, but right now, I look like I've done twelve rounds in a ring.

It's late afternoon by the time we go, and we all leave in Reid's truck to head home. Ash and Nyla go back to his place, and I'm taken back to Reid's apartment. I'm not complaining one bit. My apartment is the last place I want to be. There are now two officers outside his apartment.

"What do you want to do, princess? Eat or sleep?"

My stomach rumbles and he hears it too, so he grabs the takeout menus and we sit and go through them and decide what we want. The hospital gave me some painkillers, so a glass of wine is a no no for me, even though I could really do with one.

I hear a knock at the door and realize the food has arrived.

"Hey, sleepy. You sure you wanna eat?"

"Sorry. I didn't mean to nod off. It must be the painkillers." My stomach growls, and I know I really need to eat. I try to get up but the pain is excruciating and I hiss. Reid is at my side in flash, and he doesn't look happy at all.

"Damn it, Esme! Will you just sit still and let me look after you?"

"I'm no invalid. Not yet, anyway, so don't treat me like

one."

We eat while watching TV, and as I try to get up again, I cry out as a sharp pain sears through my side. I lift my top to see why it hurts so much and all down my side is starting to turn black from the impact of hitting the cabinet. My body didn't stand a chance, as I'm tiny compared to him.

"I am going to fucking kill him for what he's done."

"Look, I get you're angry, and you have every right to be, but this is what he wants. For some reason, he wants you fired up."

"Yeah, I heard what he said to Nyla, and it's all bullshit that he's spewing. Something didn't add up in what he was saying to her, but I can't figure out what it is." He picks me up and carries me to the bedroom. "Come on. Time for bed. Your eyes are getting heavy again, so don't argue."

I don't. I let him carry me as the pain is too much. He settles me so I'm comfortable and lies close by my side. He falls asleep quickly. He looks so peaceful and content, but I feel like all I've bought is carnage to his life since we met. I wonder if my leaving would be better for both of us. By leaving, I mean getting on a plane and going someplace far, far away. Somewhere Declan and his gang could never find me. Officer Evans told me I needed to go into witness protection, but I didn't see why I should leave my whole life behind because of what Declan Taylor and his crew did.

I grab my phone and send my aunt in England a text. We chat back and forth for a while and I mention that I'm thinking of visiting, and will be in touch. I kiss Reid's cheek, then roll over and go to sleep, but I can't help but wonder what tomorrow and the future holds for him and me, and whether England is the way forward.

I wake feeling like I've been battered. Oh, wait, I was battered. I roll over, trying not to make a sound, but it's so hard when the pain is excruciating. I still can't see properly out of my right eye. I manage to get to the bathroom without waking Reid. I lift my top and take a look at the damage, and I struggle to see anywhere that isn't bruised now. No wonder I'm in so much pain. He must have broken something, but I don't remember the doctor telling me so. I finish up, and as I turn, pain and dizziness take over, and I scream and slump to the floor. The door crashes open hard. I look up, and there stands my protector, all disheveled, but angry as hell and ready to kill.

"Shit, you crazy-ass woman. Why can't you stay put and let me look after you?"

I try to giggle, but the pain is too much, and I hiss at him instead. "I needed the toilet and I didn't want to wake you. You needed the sleep."

"Sleep is overrated," he growls. "You, on the other hand, are precious and need to start doing as you're told."

He lifts me into his arms and just stares at me and then looks at the toilet.

"Erm, do you still need to go, princess?"

He looks so uncomfortable it's laughable. My overbearing alpha doesn't know what to do in a toilet situation. I really try not to laugh because the pain is killing me, but I can't help it.

"Stop laughing at my expense. You're going to hurt yourself then I will be pissed."

I bury my head in his chest, and eventually I stop laughing. "Nope, I'm all done. Now take me to bed."

"That I can do. But rest is all you will be doing."

Pain once again wakes me, and Reid is fast asleep next to me. I manage to grab my phone and see that it's ten a.m. and I have several messages flashing on my screen. I recognize the ones from Nyla and my aunt in England, but there is a message from an unknown number. I open it and start shaking with fear.

*There is no escaping. Your fate is settled. And remember, those protecting you will not be spared.*

I know what needs to be done now. It's going to hurt the people close to me, but it's for them that I need to do this. I send a message and set the wheels in motion.

Jase comes to Reid's apartment that afternoon to stay with me while he goes to the gym to take his class and then he'll be right back. I don't have long before he suspects something.

"Listen to me carefully, pretty boy. If anything seems out of place, or you hear anything weird, you call me right away. Do not hesitate, I mean it," Reid instructs Jase.

"Yes, caveman. I mean, sir. Oops, sorry, Reid. She will be fine. I promise to call should anything happen, okay?"

Reid kisses me softly on the lips and tells me he won't be long then leaves for the gym. As soon as the door is shut, Jase is in motion.

"Okay, everything is packed and ready to go by your door. We just have to be downstairs in five minutes because the cab will be here to take us. So, let's go, before caveman comes back and busts us."

I look around, and although I know this is going to kill him and me, I know I'm doing the right thing. I have to put my safety first and think of my friends and what it's doing to them too. I leave Reid a letter, but I don't tell him where I've gone. The less he knows, the better. Jase has a letter for Nyla, and I just hope she understands why I've done this.

The cab is waiting when we arrive in the lobby and Jase quickly puts my bags in the trunk. I try to walk by Lance as discreetly as possible, but I fail miserably as he shouts my name and asks if I need a cab. I keep walking and just say I'm fine. I get straight into the waiting cab and try to swallow past the huge lump in my throat.

"JFK," Jase tells the driver. I look across at the gym as we pull away and all is quiet outside. I'm silently sobbing, or so I think, and Jase hugs me gently.

I get out at the airport, leaving Jase to go back with the cab, as I couldn't deal with anymore goodbyes. I'm a mess as it is. I gather my case and start toward the door when my phone pings. A message from Reid asking if I'm okay. But before I can reply, something is put over my head, and all I can see is black.

# Chapter Fifteen

## REID

She still hasn't replied to my text, and that idiot friend of hers isn't answering either. I'm close to walking out of this fucking class and spanking her ass, if she wasn't so damn battered, that is. I'm also worried, and she knows how I react when she doesn't answer. So I call Lance to check on her for me.

"Hi, Reid. I'm sorry. Esme and her friend left about an hour ago in a cab."

I slam my fist into the wall. I told her not to go out unless Ash or I were with her. I try her again, but it doesn't even ring, it just goes straight to voicemail. So, I leave her a stern message so she knows I'm pissed. I try Jase again, but he still doesn't pick up. God damn it, what is it with these two? I go in search of Ash to see what he knows. He's with Nyla in the locker room and… Jase.

"Where the hell is Esme, you fucking jerk? You weren't supposed to leave her side. Do you remember those instructions I specifically gave you?" He doesn't have chance to speak because I cross the room and I have my hands around his neck up against the lockers. Nyla is screaming at me to let him go, but I don't see anything but his face, which is turning pale. I let him go and he gasps for air, clutching at his neck. He clambers back up and looks at me, his eyes widened in fear.

"Listen, it wasn't my idea, okay? She's my friend, and she begged me to help her."

"What the hell are you talking about? Where is she?"

Nyla has tears streaming down her face and I fear the worst has happened.

"Reid, she's gone. I'm so sorry."

"What do you mean *gone*?"

"She couldn't carry on looking over her shoulder all the time and fearing what was around the corner waiting for her, and for those she loved."

"She didn't have to fear anything! She had me to protect her, she knew that."

"She was also carrying guilt about dragging us into it, and according to Nyla's letter, she didn't want to be a burden to us all anymore, especially you. She left you this."

He hands me a letter, but I can't bring myself to read it right now. She left me. She took the coward's way out and didn't give me a chance to protect her after everything I promised and told her.

“Where’s she gone, Jase? I need to go and speak to her.”

“Erm...”

“Spit it out, jackass! Where is she?”

“England.”

“What?” everyone says in unison, and we all stare at Jase.

“Why the hell would she go to England?” I ask.

“She has an aunt there and that’s where she’s heading.”

I try her phone again and still nothing.

“Fuck, this can’t be happening. Why didn’t she trust me to protect her?”

I sit down on the bench with my head in my hands. Nyla sits next to me and leans into me, grabbing my hand.

“She cares about you, Reid, more than you know, and for her to just get out of Dodge and leave like this can’t have been an easy decision for her. The Esme I know fights for what she wants. She always has. Something bad has to have happened for her to just give up and leave like this. You started to change her, Reid. You gave her new hope in life. You must have known that.”

I see a smile on Nyla’s face and she knows my princess better than anyone. Deep down, I know there has to be a reason for her to run, but why wouldn’t she tell me and let me help her rather than leave? She thinks leaving makes her safer, but I have no idea what lengths Declan and his crew will go to to find her. Damn it, I need to get on a plane and be with her, or at least bring her home and take her somewhere she will be safe.

We all leave in Ash’s truck for the airport, minus Jase. I can’t blame him for all this, really, but he did piss me off by not letting me know what she was thinking. I make a last attempt, in the hope she answers her phone, but if the timings are right, she'll be in the air now.

"Hello."

What the fuck? That isn't Esme's voice.

"Who the fuck is this, and where the hell is Esme?"

I hear some chatter in the background and my temper is beginning to flare. Why is there a guy answering her phone and who the hell is he?

"Excuse me, sir, my name is Vivienne Green and my colleague passed you to me. I am the manager of Customer Services within JFK airport. But who, may I ask, are you?"

"I'm her boyfriend, dammit, so ex…"

"You're the boyfriend of the owner of this phone, is that correct?"

"Yes, that's right. So do you wanna explain why the hell you have my girlfriend's phone?"

"Sir, unfortunately I cannot answer your questions right now. Please contact the police to further assist you with your enquiries."

I don't have the chance to reply as the bitch hangs up on me.

"Ash, put your foot down. Something is wrong."

Nyla demands to know exactly what was said in that call. But I don't know myself. I have a sick feeling, and I'm getting more worried the longer it takes to get there.

"I don't know anything, Nyla. A woman just answered Esme's phone and told me to contact the police for further help. That's it."

"Okay, well, let's not fear the worst. Not yet, anyway.

Just rein your temper in, Reid. For her sake."

Nyla and Esme are more alike than I realized. She can see through me, just like Esme, asking me to rein it in. I can't. I know something bad has happened. Jase said he dropped her off at the doors and she was fine, so what happened? Ash parks and we all race inside, but I stride ahead of them. I'm looking for the customer service desk when I notice a woman flanked by two security guards. I'm in front of her in seconds.

"Vivienne Green?"

"Sir, how may I help you?"

"You answered my girlfriend's phone. Esme."

"As I already said, sir, I cannot help you. You need to leave."

"Tell me where she is, now." I grab hold of the security guard and raise my fist. I know I'm out of control, but I don't care.

"Sir, please let him go."

Ash is at my side; he's pissed too. "Reid, take it easy, man. Let's hear what she has to say."

"Talk fast."

"Miss Lewis's phone and bags were found outside by the door, and a bystander brought them inside to be handed in. We put a call out through the airport asking for the owner to come forward to claim it, but nothing. That's all I can tell you."

I can't breathe. Everything I promised her wouldn't happen is happening, and there's not a damn thing I can do. My fucking brother and his crew have finally caught up with her, and God only knows if she will survive this. She knows enough to put him in prison for life for murdering her family. She's the key witness, and with her gone, he will be free.

"Ash, we need to see the CCTV. It's the only link to what happened to Esme."

"Agreed, but how the hell do you plan on getting it? There is no way that fucker Jenkins will hand it to us once he has it."

"We can ask, but failing that, I have a plan. Can you keep them busy?"

"Without a doubt."

So, I ask Ms. Green, "Can we see the CCTV footage?"

"I can't allow that, unfortunately. It's now a police investigation, sir."

Like hell am I waiting for the cops. Ash keeps them busy while I disappear and make a quick call to an old friend who works here. Nate is a guy from the underground I know. He works security at the airport. Asking him for a copy of the footage could cost him his job, but he does it anyway when I tell him why. I told him, should he lose his job, to find me at the gym and I'll make it right.He gives me what I need, and we leave. I need to get to the gym fast and watch what happened. Time is ticking and I have no idea how long she has, or if she's even still alive.

We watch the footage and I know for sure it wasn't Dec who took her, but it's his crew. I've watched them enough times.  Nyla wants to know what we're going to do, and right now, I don't know. I'm losing patience, but time is something we don't have. And then, in walks my worst nightmare. Officer Jenkins.

I make my way out of my office and stop him in his tracks. I know he wants the copy of the CCTV I have, but I'll be damned if he's getting it. Not yet, anyway.

"Well, Reid, you never did learn to abide by the law. Explains why your brother chose the path he did."

This fucker just never knows when to keep his mouth shut. This is my turf, and it doesn't go unnoticed that he's not in uniform either.

"What do you want, Jenkins?"

"You interfered in a police investigation and that footage needs to be handed back."

"I have no idea what you're talking about."

He scrunches his face and balls his fists, but he's in the wrong place to pick a fight.

"Don't push it, Taylor. I know you have it. Give me the evidence and I won't arrest you."

I laugh in his face because I know it's pissing him off, and I have every desire right now to make him angry. There is also something about him that just doesn't feel right. He always seems to show up in my business whenever there is trouble. Never any other officer, only him.

"Let's see. You're not in uniform, you're alone, and this is private property, so leave now."

Ash is now by my side, and Nyla is still in my office, but I know she's watching. Jenkins goes to step around us, but Ash blocks his way.

"This is how you want to play it? You know I have a search warrant, right?"

"If that's so, then you also know you need to have your badge, and I wanna see the warrant."

Both Ash and I take our eye off the ball for a second, and he whips around us and heads toward the office. He slams the door to the office open, but its empty, and I wonder where the hell Nyla has gone. I look at Ash and he shrugs. Jenkins has gone straight to the laptop and he growls.

"Where is it, Taylor?"

"I have no idea what you're talking about, and as I've already said, no warrant, no search. So, get off my premises."

"This isn't over, Taylor. If you want to see Esme again, you need to play ball with us."

And with that, he's gone. I look out of my office window, wondering where the hell she is and what they're doing to her, when something below in the alley catches my eye. There's a car with a couple of sly-looking guys getting out and making their way towards the end of the alley. Jenkins walks towards them. Something about all of this has alarm bells ringing, so I quickly make my way out of the gym the back way, and Ash is hot on my heels. I enter the alley and I can see the guys back at the car. Jenkins sees me and quickly disappears back out of the alley. The two guys jump into their vehicle, but I can't see their faces clearly as they have their hoods up. They start driving toward me, and the passenger stares straight at me—it's Declan. The car is gone, and I'm left more worried than ever. How is that fucker Jenkins involved in Esme's disappearance?

"Nyla, where the hell are you?" Ash calls out.

She appears from the ladies' restroom.

"Calm down, boys. The lady is all fine and in one piece. Oh, and so is the evidence, in case you were worried." She waves the memory stick in front of us.

We re-watch the footage, and something about the two guys that took Esme doesn't sit right, so I pause on them and just stare. It's their clothing. Well, one of them…

I think hard and then it hits me. The color must drain from my face, and they know something is seriously wrong.

"Reid, buddy, what's wrong? You're scaring me."

"Ash, how did we miss it? Look at his clothing."

Ash looks and it must hit him too.

"For God's sake, will you tell me? I can take it, you know!"

"Nyla, the guy in the footage is Jenkins."

"It can't be," she says in disbelief. "He's an officer of the law. Why would he want to take my best friend? He was just here wanting the footage to help get her back."

"Come on, both of you. We're going to get some answers," I say.

We leave the gym, go to the police station, and I ask to speak to someone above Jenkins. I tell them what we've worked out, and ask where he is. All we find out is that he has taken a long leave of absence, and that they will look into it. They told me to leave it alone and will be in touch if they need more information. As I leave, I notice a car idling across the street and my gut feeling tells me it's Jenkins. I get into Ash's truck and tell them everything, then I tell Ash to follow the car I saw. This is my woman in danger, and I'll do anything to save her.

"Reid, listen, I got your back whatever happens."

He looks at Nyla and she knows he has something to say to her.

"Spit it out, Ace," she snaps.

"Okay, I think you should get out. I don't want you caught up in whatever happens from here."

"Are you stupid? Don't answer that, I already know." She rolls her eyes. "No. Es is my best friend. No one knows more than me what she has been through these past few weeks. I'll be damned if I'm not going to be there for her now. I've always been there for her."

Her eyes start to well up. This is hitting her harder than I realized. She's tried to be strong for Esme, but deep down, she's hurting and scared.

Jenkins has left Brooklyn and we seem to be heading out to a remote area. It's dark, so I cut the lights. I don't want to make us known. We're following at a safe distance and he turns off down a dirt track. All of a sudden, we're hit with blinding headlights.

"What the fuck, man? I can't see a damn thing."

I realize, nearly too late, that we're about to be hit. I swerve off the track and toward the trees, slamming the brakes on. As I turn to see who the hell was aiming at us, I see Jenkins' car pass by.

"Fuck, he knew it was us, Ash!" I slam my fists into the steering wheel over and over.

"He led us on a wild goose chase. I should have known better, him being a cop."

"Listen, we will find her, I know it. We just need to be cleverer than him." I wish I had Ash's confidence. Everything seems to be against us. I just want her back.

# Chapter Sixteen

My body hasn't even healed from the last beating, and now I've taken another. Luckily, Declan hasn't tried to rape me. Well, not yet, anyway. That could be due to the young girl who keeps coming in to bring me food and water. Her name is Effie, and I get the impression she isn't here by choice. Where the hell am I? I've no idea where we are as my head was covered all the way here. They threw me inside this cold concrete room that seems to echo whenever anyone talks, and left me with my hands bound behind my back.I hear the lock on the door and watch to see who enters. I pray to God it's not him. My body can't take much more.

"Hey, Esme. I've bought you some magazines to read." She really is nice. Not what I was expecting, considering who has me held here.

"Thanks. I'll be turning pages with my feet, but I'm grateful."

She smiles at me and I decide to try and find out more about her. It may backfire on me, but what do I have to lose?

"Why are you here, Effie? You don't seem the type to hang out with the likes of Declan Taylor and his crew."

She turns away from me, and for a while, she's quiet. She gets up from the chair, and as I think she's leaving, she starts talking.

"It's because of my brother that I'm here. I owe him my life."

"Okay. Can I ask why?"

She looks toward the door like she's afraid, but she keeps talking.

"I was attacked ten years ago and the police said that no one would be charged due to the lack of evidence. My brother didn't take it very well."

"What did he do?"

She looks close to tears, and I feel bad for opening up old wounds for her.

"My brother blamed the guy I was seeing at the time because I followed him somewhere I shouldn't have gone. That's where the attack took place." She pauses to take a deep breath and then proceeds. "My brother paid him a visit, and the next thing I heard was that my boyfriend had committed suicide, but I had a feeling it wasn't suicide. I couldn't prove anything, but when I asked him, he denied it. He was so protective of me, and we were always so close, so I truly believe he thought he had done nothing wrong. But without any proof or evidence, there was nothing I could do."

"Effie, what your brother did was wrong. We have police to deal with people who have done wrong. You know that, right?"

"My brother *is* the law."

Well, I wasn't expecting that. She tells me how she adores her brother and how he has looked out for her and not let anyone hurt her since. But I get the impression she feels trapped here at the same time. Her brother is obviously linked to the gang somehow, and I'm becoming more and more scared as to how I'm linked in with all this.

"Effie, I get that you think your brother was probably doing the right thing back then, but it was wrong. Your boyfriend, he didn't attack you, did he? You chose to follow him to wherever it was, so how was it his fault?"

"He blames him because he says he didn't protect me, and he allowed that thug to do what he did to me… him and his friend."

"Friend?"

"Yeah. He was with his friend the night I followed him, but my brother only went after Jack. He said his friend will get his justice very soon."

Why does this story and the name Jack sound familiar to me? I'm about to ask her when the door opens and a guy calls her to leave.

"See you soon, Esme."

"Yeah. Bye, Effie."

Her story has some holes in it, and I feel like she was trying to tell me something without meaning to, but I don't know what that something is. The name Jack is stuck in my head, but I don't know anyone called Jack. The door slams back open, ricocheting off the wall, and in walks my worst nightmare, Declan Taylor.

"Well, hello, sweetness."

The sound of his voice makes me cringe and I can't even look at him.

"Look at me when I speak to you," he booms.

I still can't bring myself to lift my head, and I know I'm on borrowed time where he is concerned. He storms across the room, grabbing my chin and turning my face toward him.

"You will look at me when I speak to you, bitch, or you will suffer the consequences, do you understand? Oh, and I'll have great pleasure in delivering those consequences, every single hour of every single day until you fucking crack."

I slowly lift my head and I know he sees the fear in my eyes. I try to be strong and hide it, but I'm not feeling strong. This man took my family, and he will take my life too, eventually. I just can't understand why he's taking his time to do it. It's like he's tormenting me on purpose.

"Why, Declan? What did my family and I ever do to you?"

"Oh, don't flatter yourself. It wasn't a personal killing. Your family… it was part of the game. They were just unfortunate targets. It's just a shame you chose to hide that night because you'd be with them now and not giving me shit."

I never asked for any of this. He and his crew killed my family for pure fun, in their eyes. They don't give a shit about the consequences. I'm a fucking victim, and it's about time that bastard knew it.

"Me giving you shit? I think it's the other way round, don't you?

"And there she is. Sweetness does have fire in her, after all. I knew my brother saw something else in you other than a good girl."

"You know nothing about me, but I sure know about you. Where should I start? Oh, let's start with you losing your parents to a drunk driver when you were eight years old..."

He has his hands around my throat and slams me up against the wall so hard I see stars. He's re-battered my already bruised and broken body and now my neck is burning from his death grip.

"You ever talk about shit like that again and you won't see tomorrow, do you hear me?"

I'm not getting out of here alive anyway, so I say my piece.

"Asshole, I'm only just getting started. You left juvie and joined the Vipers, and your life has been, let's just say, not what your brother wants for you."

"My brother couldn't give a shit about what I want, and your time is up. I'm done." He shouts to someone outside the door and then slams me down on the cold concrete floor.

"Jasper, get in here now." A greasy-haired kid walks in. He can't be much older than eighteen.

Jasper unfastens my hands and then restrains them above my head, keeping me still. Shit, this is happening. Declan is really going to rape me like this. He yanks my jeans from me and then my panties, then forces my legs wide. I try kicking and screaming, but he is far stronger than I am. He grips the top of my thighs and pushes down on them so I can't move. Fear swirls in my stomach as the realization of what's happening hits me. My breathing accelerates, and all I can hear is the pounding of my heart. I close my eyes as I can't bear to see what happens, and I don't have the energy or the strength to fight him anymore.

"Ah, you have a perfect pussy, sweetness. But by the time I'm finished with it, it'll be far from perfect. I will ruin you for that bastard brother of mine."

Tears are streaming down my cheeks. I try to focus my mind on Reid and everything good we have, but the words Declan is spewing are crashing through me like a tornado, and I know that once he violates me, I will not be the same Esme again.

His rough finger is trailing down my pussy, and then he rams it inside of me with no warning. He is relentless, and I'm sure he's causing damage inside me.

"You're hurting me! Please, stop."

"This is just the start. You have no idea the torture I wish to reign upon your body, now shut the fuck up." He cracks a slap across my face so hard I see stars.

"Please stop," I repeat, hoping he finds his humanity in there somewhere.

I try to release my arms, but the big hellhound behind me isn't budging, and Declan is so strong. I spit in his face, and he becomes more outraged.

I really have pushed him too far now.

"You fucking bitch."

He unbuckles his jeans and pushes them down. His boxers come next, and he then palms his penis, stroking up and down. I turn away and he bellows at me to look, but I won't. I can't.

"You don't want to look? Well, then, you'll choke on it."

I open my eyes, and his penis is brushing my lips. I squeeze my lips tight and he pushes the head hard against them. I start to panic when the door flies open, and a voice booms across the room. Declan jumps off me real quick.

"What the fuck are you doing? I can't leave you alone for a minute, and you're fucking this whole thing up before we have what we want."

I recognize that voice, but I don't want to believe it. Surely he can't be part of this mess. I open my eyes, but he has his back to me. The hellhound has let me go, and I realize the door is open and unoccupied. Declan and the other guy are still talking, so I decide to make a run for it.

Stupid, stupid mistake. I'm grabbed from behind before I've even taken half a dozen steps toward the door, and a hand has covered my mouth.

"Take it easy, Esme. I won't hurt you."

He releases his hand from my mouth and then turns me around. And there stands the man who is supposed to be protecting me and upholding the law; Officer Leo Jenkins.

"Why?"

He laughs. "All in good time. But what I can say is, you're just an added bonus in all of this."

"You're supposed to protect people like me, not, not…"

I can't form words. I feel betrayed by the people I

trusted to protect my life. When, in fact, the one person who would have protected me, I walked away from. Now I will probably never see him again, and it's all my fault. Instinct takes over and I crack a slap across his face, which surprises him. But he just wipes at it and then sneers in my face.

"I'll give you that one, but next time, it's like for like, understood? Oh, and it won't be me giving it out." He looks toward Declan.

My body is dying a slow and painful death. It can't take much more. What the fuck has he done to me?

# Chapter Seventeen

## REID

Ash is driving and we managed to catch Jenkins' tail. We've followed him to an area that's pretty much desolate. He drove up into what I can only describe as a compound of Vipers. It looks like some type of old disused factory. There is no way we can get in and out of here alive, but it doesn't stop me trying to figure out how I can get in knowing my princess is in there somewhere with that psycho.

"Hey, bro. I know what you're thinking… forget it. We aren't getting killed tonight, understood?"

"Understood, but there's no way we can sit on this, Ash. Jenkins is somehow part of all this, and it doesn't sit right."

"We need to get Nyla out of here, and then decide how

to attack this. We will get her back, Reid. I promise."

We're about to leave when I see a woman leaving the compound alone. We follow her car so far before I've had enough. I overtake her to cut her car off. She has no choice, but to stop. I'm out of the truck and rounding her vehicle faster than a lion chasing its prey. I swing open her door only to be met by a swift boot to the stomach, and she winds me. I need some answers from her, and she's going to help us. I lean in, and it's then that everything I wanted to say comes to a halt.

"Effie?"

She looks up at me, anger slowly subsiding from her face when she realizes it's me.

"Reid? What the… oh, God, you need to let me go, now!"

Ash and Nyla are both at the other side of the car, making sure she doesn't try and run for it.

"What the hell is happening here? You both want to shed some fucking light on this shit storm?"

Effie looks scared.

"Nyla, calm down. I know her, and you're scaring her. Ash, deal with her."

"Deal with me? What am I, a pack of fucking cards?"

Effie reaches her hand out to me, and I help her out of the car.

"Reid, I meant what I said. You need to get away from here."

"Why? Shit, Effie, how are you connected with the Vipers, and where's Esme?"

Now she's the one looking stunned.

"Esme? Oh, God. We need to get away from here, and I'll tell you everything I know. But we need to move now before any of the Vipers see us."

Ash takes his truck with Nyla, and I travel with Effie, and we go back to my place. When we arrive, she's reluctant to get out of the car and is looking all around her like someone is about to pounce.

"You're safe here."

She follows me to the elevator, but asks if there are any stairs.

"We're on the top floor, Effie. It's a fair way up." She looks agitated. "Hold my hand, and close your eyes. I promise you'll be there before you can count to ten, all right?"

She nods her head and gives me a weak smile, a smile I remember seeing ten years ago. I have so many questions to ask her, most of them being about Esme, but also about her, and that damn awful night that resulted in my best friend taking his life. A night that's haunted me ever since it happened.

Ash and Nyla are waiting on us when we exit the elevator, and Effie is on edge again. It's not helping that Nyla is giving her the evil eye.

"Nyla, we need her help. And before you start, I know Esme's your best friend, but she's my woman, and that trumps you right now." I unlock the door to my apartment, and we all go inside. "Effie, sit, please."

"Reid, I'm so sorry everything is such a mess." She's gripping at the hem of her top, but she won't look at me.

"I didn't mean for any of this to happen. Following you

and Jack that night was my choice. I know that, regardless of what my brother thinks." She pauses for a second, and I think she's done.

"What does your brother have to do with any of this, Effie? I mean, I get he'd have been angry at the time, but how does he fit in this damn puzzle?"

"I was a shell of myself afterward. I couldn't leave the house, Reid. I flinched at every sound." Her shoulders slump, and I know this must be really hard for her to re-live. "My brother was by my side every day. He had no idea what to do or how to react to my issues. What he did was blame Jack and you for showing me that place."

"Fuck. We had no idea that you knew about it, Effie. You have to believe that. Jack would never have allowed you anywhere near those idiots."

"Reid, I snuck in there. I followed you and stayed in the shadows. I thought he was cheating and needed to find out." She holds her hand up to me to halt me from speaking. "I could hear the fighting and went inside. I knew as soon as I stepped inside it was a mistake, but it was too late."

"Damn it, Effie."

"My brother went to see Jack, and the next I heard he had died, but what concerns me more is that I think my brother was the reason he died."

What the fuck is she talking about? Jack committed suicide. We aren't getting anywhere. I need to know what any of this has to do with Esme.

"Effie, I don't do patience where Esme is concerned, so just tell me, what has she got to do with your brother?"

"Okay, okay. My brother said Jack was dealt with, and

that you would be next. He became a prison officer and then a police officer, and he said first your brother, and now he has the prize, which I know as… Esme."

"No, it can't be… he can't be. Are you telling me that your brother is Leo Jenkins?"

By now, my temper is raging. Effie nods her head, and I can't control myself. Everything starts flying. Anything that can be moved, I fling across the room or smash with my fists. Nyla and Effie run for cover, and Ash fights with me to calm me down. Eventually, he manages to pin me against the wall until I stop and realize that this is because of Effie and what happened, and now Esme is paying the price.

The girls come out once I've calmed down, and they see the state of my place and start tidying up.

"Leave it," I bark.

"Easy. They aren't the enemy," Ash snaps at me.

"Damn right we aren't, and this is nothing compared to what I'll do to you if we don't get her back, you hear me, caveman?"

I belly laugh at her feistiness. Good old Nyla knows how to break the tension. I think Ash's nickname for her is proving spot-on. Firecracker.

"That's better. Now let's clean this shit up and concentrate on who we have to kill to get our girl back, okay?"

Declan's mentor in prison has to have been Jenkins, and he is the connection that got him in with the Vipers—all in the name of revenge. What I can't get my head around is how Esme fits into all this. I never knew her back then, so why?

"Okay, Effie. Explain how Esme fits into all this. No more long stories."

"All right, Reid, listen. Leo was already a police officer and there was an undercover operation at the prison, and he jumped at the chance to do it. He knew Declan was being held there, and it was the perfect way to get to you, as you've worked out, and he then set him up with the Vipers."

"Effie, Esme, now!"

"Okay, okay. After he found out you and Esme hooked up and it was Declan that killed her parents, he knew it was his opportunity to seek the revenge he wanted for what happened to me. But, Reid, he plans on her being bound to him."

"What the fuck does that mean?"

"I don't know. It's just what I overheard between him and Declan. They were always arguing over her and who would claim her."

"Are you fucking kidding me?"

"Please, Reid. I've told you all I know, and if I don't arrive back there soon, they will know something is wrong. Then we will all be in danger."

I need time to think and she's right, holding her here is wrong. She's already on edge, and I can see she wants to run. I can't blame her.

"Dude, you know we have to let her go."

"Yeah, I know. Listen, Effie, I won't keep you here. I just needed answers. I hope you understand."

"Yeah, I know, and I'm sorry. I really am, Reid."

"Hey, you have nothing to be sorry for. You're stuck in the middle of this as much as Esme is, and I'm going to fix it. Please tell Esme that Smiler is coming for her, okay?"

"Yeah." She smiles. "I will make sure she knows." She hugs me.

I wasn't expecting it, but I'll take it, and I think she needs it, too.

I whisper in her ear, "He really did love you, Effie, and what happened broke him. But I promise we will fix everything."

"Please, no empty promises. You have one goal, and that is getting Esme out. I love my brother, Reid, and he has only ever protected me, but he isn't good, and neither are those he has working for him."

Ash coughs and starts talking. "Are you telling us that your brother runs the Vipers?"

"Yes."

"Fuck."

"Ash, we need to move fast. I've seen what these guys do for real, and for fun, and Esme is a fucking threat to my brother and their crew," I say. "Effie, we need you to create a diversion, something that will draw your brother and the some of the Vipers away from the compound."

"Oh, I don't know. What if he finds out what I did?"

"Please. We need this to give us a chance to get in there to get her out. Do it for Esme. She doesn't deserve this."

"Okay. I'll do it. Just let me know when."

We discuss a few more delicate details of how it will all go down and who will be where, and when. Effie is on edge as her face pales with some of what we have planned, and she has every right to be. But for her and Esme to get out of this safely, she needs to let us do this my way.

Nyla is all geared up in black clothing and a beanie; someone has been watching too much TV.

"Where do you think you're going, Firecracker? Nyla, there is no way you're tagging along." He puts his finger over her lips to keep her silent. "It's way too dangerous, and we have no idea what's in store for us, so stay here and wait. She'll need you more when we get her back here."

She isn't buying it, but she agrees with Ash, and we sit down and start planning exactly how to execute this with what we know from Effie.

# Chapter Eighteen

My whole body feels ruined. I can't move from the floor, and they took away the chair I had. I want out of here so badly, but my body is giving up. The beatings Declan keeps giving me are so severe that I'd be better off dead. It's not just his fists anymore. He has metal things on his hands when he attacks me, and it's brutal. I'm black on my ribs and legs, and one eye feels more swollen than before. I wonder if I'll ever be able to see out of it again.

I hear thumping footsteps heading toward the room, and I try to cower in a corner, but I can't bend because the pain won't allow me to. I groan because it hurts so badly and then the door swings open. I breathe a sigh of relief when I see who stands before me. It's Effie.

"Jesus Christ, Esme. What the hell have they done to you?"

I splutter my words out as best I can, but I'm fading fast. I just want to close my eyes.

"Esme, stay with me, please. You need to stay strong, okay? You have to because Reid will kill me if you don't."

"Reid?"

She reaches for my hand and looks me in the eye. "Smiler is coming for you."

Tears fall from my eyes because I know he is fighting for me and he always will, no matter the cost. Effie hands me a tissue and begins telling me her story and how Reid fits into all this.

"So, you were the girl who was attacked ten years ago at the underground?"

"Yes. That was me."

"Oh my God, Effie. I had no idea. So, Leo Jenkins, he's your brother? The cop?"

"Again, yes, and he's also the Vipers' founder. He brought Declan into the fold with a purpose of getting to Reid for revenge in my honor."

"Okay, so I'm piecing it together slowly, but I don't get how I fit into the equation."

"You were never supposed to be part of the plan, Esme."

I try to sit up, but it hurts too much.

"Esme, are you all right? Let me help you."

I try with her help to sit up, but the pain is really unbearable. It's crushing into my tummy so badly, so I lay back down on the concrete floor.

"You're shivering. Here, have my hoodie."

Just as Effie puts the hoodie over my head, the door wallops into the wall again and the hoodie is pulled from me. Leo towers over us.

"Effie, leave now."

"No."

"Get out now, sis."

"Leo, I said no. God damnit, for once you're going to listen to me. I want to hear what you have to say to her."

"All right, have it your way."

Effie has some balls about her when it comes to her brother. He looks at me and smiles and then sits on the floor in front of me.

"Sweet, sweet Esme."

"Why am I here, Leo?"

He gets right in my face and his look is one of anger, but there is something else there, and my guess is pain. The pain he feels for his sister and what she went through, and that he couldn't protect her from.

"You are here because of your boyfriend and the consequences his actions caused. Because of him and Jack, my sister was attacked."

"How is that their fault? Did they tell the guy to assault her?"

I think I've pissed him off as he grabs my chin and squeezes a little.

"Let me get one thing straight. They will always be responsible. She followed Jack to the underground because she wanted to know what he was up to. He and that piece of shit Reid will always be responsible for what happened to my sister, and the life that was taken away from her. I presume he told you how Jack took his own life out of guilt?" He then makes a noise like on a game show when you get an answer wrong. "I paid Jack a little visit after I found out the truth, and the sight I found him in was depressing to say the least, so convincing others that he took his own life was easy."

"I knew you had something to do with his death. Why? Why would you do that? How could you? It wasn't his fault!" Effie says.

"It *was* his fault, and will always be his fault. Them doing illegal shit led to your attack, whether they meant it or not."

"Oh, and you're the epitome of illegal shit, aren't you?"

"Effie, everything I've ever done was to protect you and because I love you."

She stands before him and asks him to get up. Just as he does, she rears back her arm and lands him with a thump right across his nose. Blood sprays everywhere.

"I loved him, you bastard! You had no right."

"What the fuck, Effie?"

"He was everything to me and you took that away."

"No, he took it away when he didn't protect you, and consequences were to be had. Now it's time for Reid's comeuppance."

"Hey." I draw their attention back to me. "You still haven't told me where I fit into all of this."

"Easy, princess. I'm getting to that part."

"Don't ever call me that."

"I'll call you what I please. He has no say here."

I feel sick when he calls me that. It was something special shared between Reid and me, and coming from this sick bastard changes how I feel about it.

"You see, I met Declan when I was a prison officer, and it was a bonus when I found out the connection. I always planned on getting justice, and it was like a plan fell into my lap."

"So, Declan was also a pawn in your game? Does he know?"

"Oh, he was never a pawn. He was always in on whatever I planned for his brother."

I try to sit up, but the pain is excruciating, so I slump back to my side on the floor.

"You see, Declan has sibling issues too, except his run deep. He—

"—he killed our parents."

And there he is, the second part of this sick duo, Declan Taylor.

"Declan, you have to know that was an accident," I say,

"Accident? A fucking accident? I wasn't supposed to be in that car, but Reid, as usual, fucked off and never came home, so they were taking me to a sitter's house. Bet he left that snippet out."

I get why Declan's annoyed with Reid, but he can't hold him responsible for their deaths. He was eight years old and Reid was young too. He didn't know that was going to happen.

"And me? I guess *I'm* a pawn in the game. Another way to get to your brother and for you, Leo, to get at who you think is responsible for Effie's attack. Well, isn't this just dandy, boys."

"I'd curb the smart remarks, Esme, unless you wish to meet your fate earlier than I'd planned."

Poor Effie is huddled in a corner just staring at her brother like she no longer knows or recognizes him, and I feel for her. She's been through hell these past few years, and now to be stuck amongst Declan and the rest of the Vipers isn't a way of life.

"You are the best-added part in all this, sweetness. Using you as bait to get him here is better than we could've dreamed. It was like God was on our side, for a change."

"My family… why?"

"Wrong fucking timing. That's all. No biggie."

"No biggie? They were my family, you piece of shit."

My head wants to beat the ever loving shit out of him, but my body can't move. I feel myself slipping slowly and I don't know how long I can keep my eyes open.

"Maybe if you hadn't hidden, you'd be with them right now. So quit fucking whining, bitch."

I feel myself drifting now, and I can't hold on any longer. I really tried to stay awake, but the beatings were too much, and the lack of food and water, too.

"He's coming for me."

"We know. Effie made sure of that."

# Chapter Nineteen

## REID

Ash and I are near the Viper's compound, waiting on Effie's signal before we can make our way in and find my girl. We see a few leave, but it's not enough for us to gain entry successfully. I see two flashes of light from across the other side of the compound. It's our guys' sign, and I know our backs are covered for when we enter. If I've learned anything about my brother and the Vipers over these past few years, it's never to trust even those you once loved, and that includes Effie. I have no doubt they know we will be coming, so I've set my own plan in motion.

"Brother, I have your back whatever happens in there, okay?"

"Ash, always."

"Do you trust this Effie chick?"

"Honestly, I don't know. I want to, but she's been tied up with them for too long and then there's the loyalty to her brother too."

"Her brother doesn't know loyalty. It's time to show him what messing with a real family is all about."

Ash is right. I've babysat Declan for too long. Cleaning up after him when he's caused mayhem and bailing him out when he's gotten into trouble. Not anymore. He's responsible for his own actions and they start with Esme and her family. One thing I'm sure of is, at the end of all this, I will have lost him for good.

There's a lot of noise and the gates open to the compound. Jenkins and Declan leave, followed by a few of the Vipers. It's time for us to take action. I send a quick flash of light back across and they make their move just before the gate closes. I see Linc slip inside and we wait. It seems like forever, but only five minutes pass and the gates slightly re-open and we all move in. There are about ten of us, all guys from the underground, and I bark orders of where to go and the rendezvous point and then scatter about.

"Linc, you're with us. Just keep your mouth shut and do as I ask. Think you can do that?"

"Fuck you, Taylor. I take orders from no one. I'm doing this as a favor for Bruce, so don't get too cocky."

"Listen to me, you piece of shit, you will do as I tell you if you want to get out of here in one piece and not in a casket, you understand?"

"Easy, boys. Play nice. Let's go find Esme and get the hell out of here."

Ash is right. I need to find my princess fast. I have a gut feeling something is seriously wrong.

This compound is huge and derelict. Most rooms are pretty much empty, but you can tell that some are used as what can only be described as torture chambers. There are splatters of blood on the walls and floors and chains attached to the floor. Some rooms hold cages. What the fuck are they in to? I dread to think.

We hear a commotion down a hallway and see some of our guys dragging a couple of Vipers into a room. Linc decides he wants in on the action, but I grab him around the neck and he starts scrabbling as he can't breathe. I whisper in his ear.

"Last warning, Linc. Stay with us and don't fuck it up."

I release him, and he turns on me and takes a swing, but I'm too quick for him and he hits the wall.

"What the fuck, man! I broke my knuckle."

"Deal with it."

I push him forward when I notice a door that looks like the others, and there is light streaming underneath it. I signal to Ash and Linc to keep their eyes and ears alert. The others are nowhere to be seen, and there are no Vipers around, so all's good right now. In fact, it's too good.

We stand on either side of the door and there is nothing, not a sound. But then I hear a whimper. It's faint, but I heard it, and I know it's Esme. I look to Ash and Linc and they both nod. We count down from three, but I can't wait, and I storm through the door only to be met by an entourage.

"Welcome, big brother. Glad you could finally join us. Oh, and your guests, of course."

The door slams shut behind us and there are two Vipers now blocking it. In front of me stand Declan and Leo, and my girl is slumped on the floor with Effie holding her.

The sight of her has my rage boiling. She is black and blue and pretty much naked. I also notice blood on the floor around her. I move toward her, only to be met with the barrel of a gun, so I back off.

"Why? This is between us, so why involve her?" Pure silence. "Answer me!"

"You're right, Taylor. You are the main reason she's here, and because of you, she won't be leaving alive."

"If you think I'm letting that happen, then you really are stupid."

Jenkins doesn't hesitate in bending down and grabbing hold of Esme's hair then yanking her head up to show me her face. She's barely conscious. Her face is black, and that eye is really bad, but I catch a whimper, and it breaks me.

"Smiler," she whispers.

"Take a good hard look, Taylor, because I want you to remember this face when you fall asleep at night. I want this sight to haunt you day and night, knowing there was nothing you could do to stop it."

"What the fuck? Man, you are crazy. What happened to your sister was fucked up, but it wasn't on me or Jack. Let her go. You have what you want… me."

"Not that easy, brother. You've got to pay for your bad ways."

"What the hell does that even mean, Declan?"

"You know what it means."

He really does hate me over our parents' deaths. The

accident was not my fault. "Explain why, little brother, you seem to hold the cards here… along with him."

"You really are dumb. Must be all the punches to your head that's fucked you up, but you never were the clever one, were you, Reid?"

"Damn you, Dec! Spit it out." My anger's peaking, but I can't lose my shit just yet.

"The accident will always be your fault. Our parents dying, your fault. Me losing my shit, your fault. See a pattern that's formed? You were supposed to be at home that night. Instead, you chose partying over me." I try to speak, but he halts me. "You don't get to talk. They were taking me to a sitter's house just so they could have a night together, but we never arrived there."

The guilt from that night starts to seep into my body. He's right. I did choose to go partying and drinking that night, and I feel sick with the realization that I could have prevented all this.

"I became your responsibility and you didn't try hard enough. You allowed me to go to juvie."

"Jesus Christ, Declan. What was I meant to do, lock you away? No matter what I did, you fucked up. You need to own your shit, man. I'm not being held responsible for that."

"Yeah, well, I do blame you. I lost everything that day. I had no one left because of you. So, when I met Jenkins in prison and we made the connection about you, everything else slipped right into place. We had the same goals; to take you down and make you suffer like we did. And I have to say, we're doing pretty good so far."

There's no way this is going to go their way. I now know my brother's drive for all of this, and we know Leo's motivation.

"And Esme and her family. Where do they fit into all this?"

"Well you see, that was purely a coincidence and part of the initiation, but meeting my brother's woman just spiraled things, and she had to be hushed. I mean, we can't have her talking, so she needs silencing. And what better way than to be fucked quiet."

I surge forward before they realize what's coming. I knock Declan to the ground, but he's been working out and knows how to fight back. Fists are flying and Jenkins is shouting at us.

"Get the fuck up now, both of you." He fires his gun and silence falls over us all.

I grab hold of Declan, pulling him up off the floor, but he knocks me away.

"Get the fuck off me! This is far from over, brother."

"This is how it's happening. My boys will be back any second and they'll be taking Esme. This will be the last time you see her," Jenkins says.

Hell, no. This isn't happening. I promised Nyla I would bring her back and I promised Esme I would always protect her. It's time. Making my hand signal for Ash and Linc, movement happens. Declan realizes, but it's too late. Effie runs from behind Jenkins towards me and I manage to grab her hand and pull her behind me.

"Effie!" He has a pained look on his face.

He loves Effie more than anything, and she will be our

bargaining chip in all this, only she won't be staying, either. She told me what she's endured being part of the Vipers, and that she tried telling her brother about all the abuse, but it was like he chose not to accept it.

"You want her back, Jenkins, then you give me Esme. That's the deal, and then we all get to leave."

"You really think you hold all the cards now, Taylor?"

"Actually, I'd say I do. What do you reckon, Ash?"

"Definitely, brother."

Declan laughs sarcastically.

"You laugh, Declan, but he's more of a brother. I know what you tried to do to Esme, you sick fuck." More demented laughter pours from his tainted mouth. "What is wrong with you? I tried, but you can't help someone who's mentally unstable."

"You never tried, not really, and if you'd have come back to her apartment that day, you'd have seen just how much your girl would have enjoyed fucking a real man."

Ash has already moved next to me so I can't attack the bastard. He is pushing every button inside of me and the rage is becoming uncontrollable.

"She was wet for me, and I hadn't even touched her then. But the other day, that pussy was tight as fuck."

"You're a dead man, Declan." I charge forward, only to be yanked back by both Linc and Ash.

"Reid, man, remember why we're here."

I look around to see Effie scared to death. I also forget her attacker from ten years ago is now in this room. She knew he was coming, and when I told her why, she agreed, reluctantly. He, too, is going to pay for what he did. It doesn't change that she's staring at him like she's seen a ghost and he has no idea who she is, or the trauma he caused.

I then look across to my girl, and she's breathing, but not moving. I need to get her out of here fast.

"This is the deal. You want your sister back, I get to leave with Esme. It's that, or I will hand her back to the guy who caused all this in the first place."

Effie looks up at me with tears in her eyes. She's shaking now. I know saying it is a bastard move, but she agreed it was needed in order for Jenkins to believe what we're doing.

"You fucking knew who did this to her and never came forward?"

"No, I didn't know straight away, and I had no proof, just word of mouth. But I know it to be true, trust me."

"Trust you. Are you fucking with me? Look what you've put her through and you're asking for trust? Tell me who it is…"

"Give me Esme and I will gladly tell you his name."

Jenkins looks at Declan and they talk in hushed voices. They're planning something, but I'm ahead, I have to be.

"Be warned, Taylor, we aren't finished by any means, and you can be assured that I will be coming for you again."

I make my way towards my princess and remove my top to cover her as much as possible. I gently pick her up. She makes some sort of wheezing sound and I realize she desperately needs a hospital. I pass her to Ash.

"Get her out of here now, and brother, you know what to do, right?"

"I'll make sure she's okay, and yeah." Effie follows

Ash, but not before Jenkins bellows at her and raises his gun… and that's when I raise mine too. Now we're evenly matched.

"Where the hell are you going, Effie?"

"I'm leaving. Please don't stop me. I love you and hate you all at once, but I can't do this anymore. What happened to me has destroyed you and us. I can't carry on like this anymore."

"I did everything for you, Effie. You are my little sister."

"No, Leo. Making me stay in this dirty place with these fucked up guys and him." She points to Declan, "It was torture, and nothing about it was you looking out for me."

"Why?"

"Why? You want a detailed description of how they dragged me into rooms, held me against my will, and took every ounce of my soul that was left? You can work out the rest, Leo. But him…" Her eyes are trained on Declan now. "He was the worst of them all."

Dread hits my stomach, thinking about what he did to her just to get his kicks, especially seeing the damage he caused to my girl.

"I have to get away from all of this and from you. I need to find myself again and I can't do that around you, Leo. It's not just me I have to think of anymore."

"What does that mean?"

She looks at all of us and then back at Declan and then down at her stomach.

"I'm pregnant."

Shit, this really has fucked things up. Declan's obviously the father, going on her deathly look at him just now and what she said, but Leo is seething and turns the gun at Declan's head.

"Ash, get the girls out of here now! Go!" I tell him.

Linc goes to help him, but I grab him and pull him back to my side.

"You're staying."

"What the fuck, Taylor?"

Jenkins still has his gun aimed at Declan's head and he's spewing words at him with pure hatred. It's obvious Declan was just a pawn in his plan to get to me, but right now, I don't care. I want to get to Esme and take care of her the way I promised.

"Who's the big lump, Taylor?" And here is where I play my ace card.

"Now, this is how it's going to happen. I'm leaving and Declan is coming with me."

"Like hell I am," Declan says. "Time for happy families is well and truly gone, big brother."

"See, Declan, that's where you're wrong. Your family is waiting for you back at the prison. Get used to it, because you're going to spend a very long time there."

"You can't prove anything. Jenkins wiped my record clean of everything related to that bitch. Sorry to burst your bubble."

I start laughing, which makes him more aggravated. I walk towards him with Linc right at my side. He is uneasy and glances back toward the door.

"Move back, Taylor!" Jenkins screams at me.

But I want to end this all now.

My gun is still pointed in the direction of them both,

while still have my grip on Linc so he can't bolt.

Jenkins starts swinging his gun between us. I take this opportunity to remove the listening device the police gave me to help take all of them down. Declan decides to make a run for the door, but it's slammed shut and there stands my real brother, Ash.

"Going somewhere?" says Ash, as Declan runs into his fist and hits the floor.

Jenkins looks defeated. He knows he's not getting out of this in one piece.

"You and your brother will pay for what you've done to my sister," Jenkins sneers.

"You only have yourself to blame for what that piece of shit called my brother has done to her. You brought him into her life knowing how fucked up he was, so that's on you."

"A deal's a deal. Who raped my sister ten years ago at the underground, Taylor?"

"Oh, yeah. I forgot to introduce you. Linc, meet Leo. Leo, meet your sister's attacker."

"What the fuck are you talking about, Taylor? I never raped anyone."

"That's where you're wrong, Linc. You should be more careful when showing the evidence. You never know who's watching."

"It wasn't me, I swear."

Linc was stupid enough to show some idiots who get off on shit like that. He had a video and I happened to see it.

"Give me his phone NOW! You get down on your knees!" Leo roars at Linc. As Jenkins has the gun, I don't hesitate. "You mother fucker piece of shit! This is my goddamn sister you were raping." He smacks Linc clean across the face over and over. That's when we leave. As we shut the door, we hear the sound of two gunshots as the police storm the building.

# Chapter Twenty

## REID

Handing my brother over to Officer Evans was probably one of the hardest things I've ever had to do, but it was nothing compared to what he and Jenkins put Esme through. She was taken to New York-Presbyterian Brooklyn Methodist Hospital, and Ash called Nyla to meet her there, as we were being held for questioning. I needed to get to her fast and these idiots were pissing me off. I involved them for crying out loud, and I did what they asked and wore the listening device, which gave them the evidence they needed to put Declan away for a very long time. He's going down for three counts of murder, the attempted murder of Esme too, and now her assault.

"You have what you need from me, so I'm leaving.

Anything else, you can contact me at the hospital."

I start walking away when Officer Evans calls my name.

"Mr. Taylor, you don't get to say when it's time to walk, I do. That being said, you've cooperated fully. There is just one discrepancy with your turn of events and what we found in the room after you left."

"Really? And what's that, Officer?"

"Your comms went dead before any gunshots were heard. Why was that? And why did we find Lincoln Fletcher and Officer Jenkins both dead from the same gun bullets?" She eyes me suspiciously, but before I can answer, she does it for me. "I believe there was a struggle and your comms fell out during it, in which Officer Jenkins took it upon himself to destroy it so as he couldn't be implicated. Am I right so far?"

"I believe that is right, Officer." Who am I to argue? I just want to get out of here.

"Am I right in also believing that Lincoln Fletcher is the man who raped Officer Jenkins' sister, Effie Jenkins, ten years ago and he became aware of this when they met in that room tonight?"

I look toward Ash then at Officer Evans and nod. But I get the impression that Evans knows exactly what went down tonight and is on our side.

"Yes, that's correct, but we were forced at gunpoint to exit the room, leaving only the two of them in there, so we can't say exactly what went down in there after we left."

"Hmm, I see. Okay, well, you can be on your way for now, Mr. Taylor. I'll be in touch should there be anything else. Same goes for you, Mr. Adams."

I'm pretty sure we're far from out of the woods, but as I turn back to look in the officer's direction, she is still watching us walk away with a smile on her face.

I breathe a sigh of relief knowing that finally there is an end to all this. Actually, the end is not over yet. My girl is fighting for her life, according to Nyla and the text that just came through.

We speed through the city, not giving a shit for lights at all. Esme would kick my ass if she knew, and she'd have every right, too. I was careless, but I'm not thinking straight. She's my life. Every last second of it belongs to her.

We race inside to the emergency department and find Nyla pacing the floor with Jase. She sees us as soon as we enter, and she races toward us and straight into Ash's arms.

"They said she has some internal bleeding, and that was the last we heard before she crashed on the trolley as they were bringing her in."

Jase starts sobbing. I go looking for someone who can give me some answers. No one will tell me anything, so I sit and wait with the others for what seems like hours. Finally, after about two hours, a doctor appears, and we all go into a smaller room.

"Hi, I'm Doctor Felix. I take it you are all Miss Lewis's family?"

"Yes, we are," I reply impatiently.

"Okay, the surgery went well considering how much blood she lost, and that was due to a number of issues she presented with when she arrived here. The main being the internal bleeding caused by the beatings she received. We have managed to stop the bleeding, but she needs full bed rest in order to heal fully. But with the help of her loved ones and counseling, I'm sure she will recover fully."

"Can I see her now?"

"Of course. Follow me."

We follow him up to the next floor where the wards are and it's far quieter.

"Here is her room, but only two in the room at any one time, okay?"

Nyla and I enter. The lights are dimmed low and the curtain is pulled around her bed slightly. We draw it back and the sight we see is a shock and brings tears to my eyes. Nyla squeezes my shoulder and we take a seat on either side of her bed. She must sense we're there because she tries to open her eyes, but one is swollen so badly it's almost closed.

"Hey, princess."

She grabs my hand and tries to pull me toward her. I lean over her and she whispers, "I'm so sorry. I tried to stop him; I really did."

My thoughts immediately go to rape again and I need to listen to her and not get ahead of myself like last time, so I keep listening.

"Hey, listen to me, no matter what, we will get through it, I promise."

Her sobs come hard and fast and it kills me seeing her like this. Stuff the hospital rules. I gently slide her across the bed just enough for me to be able to lie next to her and hold her.

"Princess, I've got you, always. Now just sleep, please."

I look at Nyla and she nods and gets up and kisses Esme on the head.

"Hey, Es. I'll be back later. I love you." She hugs me, and now it's just me and my woman.

I lie there as she slowly drifts off in my arms, and I think about everything that happened tonight and how close I was to losing to her. Effie lost her brother and is pregnant with my brother's child. Declan's in custody and won't see the light of day for a very long time. I need to focus now on Esme and her recovery, and give her the life she deserves. I also need to let Effie know I am behind her whatever she chooses to do regarding the baby. What a fucking mess this has all been, and for what?

Just as I think Esme is fast asleep, she opens her eye and whispers the words we haven't uttered to each other yet.

"I love you, Reid." A tear rolls down her cheek.

I wipe it away with my thumb and then kiss her slowly and gently. She starts moaning, and I know this wrong, but I can't help myself around her. I stare into her blue eyes and I'm done for. The feelings inside me are so strong I can't deny them anymore. Tears fill my eyes, and it's because of the woman in my arms. The realization of how close I came to losing her, not once, but twice, has finally broken me.

"Princess, you are my future, my everything, and I love you so much it hurts."

We lie there next to each other until we both fall asleep.

Esme is given the all-clear to leave the hospital after four days. She is nervous about leaving, but we are all there, including Ash and Nyla.

"You want to walk or be carried out? The choice is yours. Your wish will be my command."

She lets out a little giggle and it's the first smile I've seen in weeks. She needs to have more of those moments, but all in good time.

"I'll walk, if that's okay with you."

And there she is, my determined girl. She holds out her hands, imploring us all to take them, and what comes next swells my heart more than anyone ever could.

"Together we are strong and fierce, because we are family."

And that's exactly what we are, family. It may have only been a month since she and Nyla breezed into our lives and caused a whirlwind of chaos, but I wouldn't change a thing. This is us, our family.

# Epilogue

## ESME

***Four Months Later***

It's been a tough few months. The nightmares continue, but Reid's been amazing, giving me the space I need to deal with everything. I've not been back to my apartment yet; it's too hard. All I see is Declan's face and the damage he could have brought to us both. There would've been no coming back from that. He could have ruined everything between Reid and me, but we are stronger than ever right now, regardless of what he did. The dates he promised me have happened at least every other day so far. Some may only be a walk in the park, but him making good on his promise means more than anything.

Declan got life in prison and won't see the light of day,

along with the other guy who was there on the night my family were murdered. It should make me happy that my family finally has some justice, but I don't know if it ever will. Maybe as time goes on, it will ease.

Reid still trains for the underground, but has yet to return. Something is holding him back, and I can't figure out what that is. In the meantime, he is thriving at the gym, and his business is flourishing. He and Ash decided to go into a partnership and take the gym to the next level.

Nyla is glowing lately, and that's because of Ash. No matter how many times she tries to convince herself that it's just casual with him, I can see she's smitten with him. I just hope he doesn't break her heart, or he'll have me to answer to.

I believe it was fate that brought Reid and I together in a twisted way that no one could comprehend. He's a cocky caveman who doesn't take no for an answer, and boy, is he overprotective. But behind all that is a fragile soul of a gentleman, who loves like no other and will fight for those he calls family, no matter the cost or the consequences. Reid Taylor is all mine. My smiler and my caveman, and damn anyone who tries to get in between us. This is our time, and it's a new beginning for each and every one of us.

# Epilogue

## REID

***Four Months Later***

My princess is healing. She is the bravest, strongest, and most determined woman I know. Sometimes I have to thump myself and ask what I did to deserve her. I've nearly lost her twice now, and I'll be damned if that's going to happen again. My brother did his best to ruin what we had, but in fact he's made us stronger than ever.

Effie is grieving for her brother, which is to be expected. He was all she had left, no matter what he did to me, he loved her, and everything he did was out of revenge. She has decided to keep the baby and Esme and I are standing by her one hundred percent. She's moved into Esme's apartment, which is hard, but she, Jase, Nyla, and Ash are renovating it. Maybe one day Esme will be able step back in there, when it's all done.

Ash has bought into the gym. We are now equal partners, and I couldn't be happier. We have big plans for the future, something I never thought I'd have a few years back, so making this work means a lot to us both. I'm training for the underground again, but I'm unsure if, or when I'll go back, even though my princess wants to see me back in the ring, something is holding me back.

When I first met Esme, I thought she was a naïve young woman who'd been sheltered by her parents. But one taste, and I was done for, there was no going back. I wanted more, I needed more, and I got more. She's my woman, and I love her. She's my everything, my future, and my family, which is why it's time for new beginnings, starting with a proposal.

The End

# Acknowledgements

In August 2016, my head was spinning with a story that was itching to be written. So, I decided to take the chance and give it a go, and here it finally is.

Rob, my darling hubby, throughout all of this you have constantly pushed me and have been my biggest fan. The late nights and never-ending hours I've spent writing and editing, and not once have you moaned at me. Even when things went wrong, you were the one who calmed me down and said, "Take a step back and all will be okay, I promise." And boy, were you right. I just hope you're ready to do this all over again. I love you more than you know.

Megan and Phillipa, you pair have been a pain in my ass sometimes, but when I have needed you both for advice, you have always given it to me. Just like your dad, you have supported me all the way and never once doubted me. Thank you girls. Momma loves you xx

Gemma Weir, lady it doesn't matter what time of day or night it is, you have pretty much always answered me and my tirade of messages. You've made me laugh when times have been stressful and helped shape my book in ways, I didn't know it needed. For this, I am truly grateful.

Rebecca Prescott, you, my beautiful friend, have been amazing with your feedback and words of wisdom. You really have no idea how much confidence you instilled in me after our facetime. I will never forget that call, and I hope there are many more of those to come.

A special thanks to all my beta readers, Chanah, Laura, Samantha, Bri, and Janice. Ladies, thank you for reading my debut book and for being totally honest with your feedback. Your honesty, suggestions, and advice has enabled my book to be its best.

And finally, Nikki Groom and Karen Sanders: both of you ladies have worked your magic not only on this book, but also on myself. I have learnt so much this past eight months, and neither of you will ever know how grateful I am that you helped make my dream of publishing a book come true.

# About Tracey

Tracey Jukes is from Wolverhampton in the UK. She's a wife, Mum of two and Nanna to Tiggy (4) and Tilly (nearly 2). Her much loved family is a little crazy, but then she would argue that she is also. She loves to blast out loud music in the car and has a fetish for designer handbags. She loves to read—especially books that involve a hot, protective alpha, and believes she will always be a reader foremost, however her dream of writing a book is now becoming a reality. She primarily writes romance with a twist and her debut adult novel, Twisted Fate, starts the beginning of her writing journey.

facebook.com/TraceyJukesAuthor
amazon.co.uk/Tracey-Jukes/e/B08HCQJP18
instagram.com/traceyjukes_author/

TRACEY Sukes
WRITING ROMANCE WITH A TWIST

Cat Weatherill is a performance storyteller, appearing internationally at literature and storytelling festivals, in theatres and in schools. She loves to travel the world, having adventures and making stories from them. She is also a best-selling author, with books translated into twelve languages.

**www.catweatherillauthor.com**

Other books by Cat Weatherill

**Barkbelly**
**Snowbone**
**Wild Magic**

Published in 2018 by Tansy Books

ISBN 978-1-912009-10-7



Designed by Matthew Lloyd

Cat Weatherill

# Famous Me

To Phoebe
Best Wishes!
Cat Weatherill

# Chapter 1

Have you ever wanted to be famous?

I was famous last year, for a short time. I can hardly believe it myself now, but it really did happen. I was in all the newspapers. I appeared on breakfast tv. I was crushed half to death in a supermarket because so many people wanted to touch me.

So why was I famous? I wish I could say it was my amazing talent (haha!) but it wasn't. It was simply because I was different, suddenly. But it wasn't just me. It happened to twenty four of us, all girls at St Mary's High School. It started in November and was over by Christmas.

Looking back now, I can see the funny side, and I know the experience changed my life for the better. But we still don't know how it happened. I guess we never will.

We know *why* it happened, though. That's easy! It began with a conversation we had in the school cafeteria, soon after half term...

We were new to St Mary's then. We'd started back in September and were still getting to know each other, making friends and sniffing out enemies. I had come up from Green Lane Primary School with Keeley Sheringham. Keeley was everything I wanted to be – tall, smart, funny and very, very pretty, with long dark hair and cat-green eyes. We'd been best friends forever. But now we were getting friendly with a girl called Carrie Ann Marsh. She had hair the colour of biscuits and giggled a lot. St Mary's was her first school. Can you believe that? Twelve years old and never been to school before. Her mum and dad had taught her at home.

Anyway, like I said, it started with a conversation...

We're sitting in the cafeteria, having lunch – me, Keeley and Carrie Ann - when Mr Derren the drama teacher comes in. He's the hairiest teacher I've ever seen. A shock of black hair on his head, uncontrollable eyebrows and a moustache like a floor brush. He even has hairs peeping out over the top of his tee shirt. He's like a werewolf.

He's carrying a poster and a jar of drawing pins. From the look on his face, he's about to do something important. He strides over to the notice board, pins up the poster, steps back and checks it's straight, then strides away again.

Keeley speeds over to it, reads the poster and comes skidding back because she slips on a patch of potato.

'It's all the things that are happening this term,' she says, throwing herself back down on the bench.

'Like what?' mumbles Carrie Ann through a mouthful of veggie sausage roll.

Keeley picks up her shoe. It is thick with mashed potato. 'Oh...yuck.'

'Like what?' asks Carrie Ann again.

Keeley slips her shoe back on. 'All kinds of things,' she says. 'A family bingo night. A Book Week. Poppy Day. And for Christmas, there's a big school play – *The Baby in the Stable*.'

I nearly choke on my poppadum. 'A nativity? Brilliant!'

This is the best news I've heard since I came to St Mary's. I want to be an actress when I grow up. A really famous one. And I know this is just a school play, but it's still a chance to be on stage with everyone clapping me. Everyone starts somewhere.

'I want to be a Wise Man,' says Keeley. 'I'll have a long robe - midnight blue - with a gold turban and my best slippers. You know the ones my dad brought back from Egypt?'

We nod. She has brought them into school twice already.

'I want to be Joseph,' I say.

'I'd like to be a shepherd,' says Carrie Ann.

'Dream on, little ladies,' says Jack Lewis. He is sitting at the next table with his best mate, Matthew Sharp. They both start grinning.

Keeley glares at them, even though they're two years older than us. 'Do you mind?' she says. 'This is a private conversation.'

'Oooh!' says Jack. 'Excuse my elephant ears.' He winks at Matthew and carries on eating.

'I could be the innkeeper,' I say, trying to get back to what we were discussing.

'No,' scoffs Keeley. 'That's a rubbish costume. It has to be a Wise Man.'

'Forget it,' says Jack Lewis.

'Are you listening *again?*' snaps Keeley. She's a tiger when she wants to be. 'It's none of your business. Anyway, what do you mean – forget it?'

Jack wipes his mouth on his sleeve. 'Wise men, shepherds, Joseph – you won't get any of those parts.'

'How do you know? Are you the one who casts the play?'

'No. That's Mr Derren. I say it because you're girls, and girls don't get those parts. Not in this school. They go to boys.'

*'No!'*

'Yeah! Derren is in charge and he doesn't like girls playing boys.'

We can't believe what we are hearing. If this is true, it's terrible news.

'Matt,' says Jack. 'Tell them. They won't believe me.'

Matthew Sharp is The Best Looking Boy in the School. Everyone says so. He has lovely hair. The kind you want to fiddle with. And he's what my mum would call a *dark horse*. He's laid-back and mysterious and never says more than he needs to. When he does speak, it's always in a quiet voice so you have to lean closer and really listen to him. Which is clever when you think about it. When I want people to listen to me, I always speak louder but it never works, especially when everyone's talking at once.

Matthew nods. 'Jack's right. Girls will get Mary or the angels. Nothing else.'

'Can't they be narrators?' asks Carrie Ann.

'Yeah, but who wants to be that?' Matthew throws her a dazzling smile. Carrie Ann turns princess pink.

'Look,' says Jack, 'this is our third year here and we've only seen one girl get a male part.'

Matthew smiles. 'Frankie Day. I'd forgotten her.'

'You see!' cries Keeley. She thumps the table so hard, the plates jump. 'It *can* happen!'

Jack shakes his head. 'Frankie was special. She was in Year 10 when we started and we thought she *was* a boy. D'ya remember, Matt?'

Matthew nods. 'She was awesome. She could trump louder than Billy Evans. And she had a quad bike.'

'It was *Joseph and the Amazing Technicolour Dreamcoat* that year,' says Jack, 'and Frankie wanted to be Joseph. Derren wasn't keen but he couldn't say no, because Frankie really did look like a boy. She wanted the part so bad, she shaved all her hair off before the auditions.'

*'NO!'* We stare at each other in horror. Carrie Ann is holding on to her plaits. I'm protecting my ponytail. It has taken three years to get it this long. I can't cut it off for a part in a school play. No way!

'There has to be something we can do,' says Keeley, turning her back on the boys. 'When a cat wants the cream she will always find a ladder.'

'There ain't a ladder long enough,' says Jack. 'Not for this cream. Sorry, kittens.' He stands up, stretches and runs his fingers through his spiky hair. 'You finished, Matt?'

They leave the table without clearing their plates. Mrs Starling, one of the dinner ladies, comes over. She's planning to tell them off, but Matthew smiles at her so it never happens. She wags a finger at them like they're naughty five year olds and takes the plates herself.

Keeley's tiger eyes flash dangerously. 'I *will* have a part in that play,' she snarls, 'and not some sissy angel. A proper meaty role, with lines and everything. I don't care what it takes.'

Carrie Ann frowns. 'You'd cut your hair off?'

'I'd grow a *beard* if I had to.'

I stare at her open-mouthed. I can't believe she would do that. And then I hear myself saying: 'Yeah. So would I.' Because in that moment, I know that I want this more than Keeley does. I want a part so badly, it hurts. There's no way – *no way* - I'm going to stand by while Keeley steals the show.

'Really?' Keeley tilts her head like an owl. She doesn't believe me.

'Absolutely.'

Now Carrie Ann is nodding and smiling. 'I like the idea,' she says. 'A beard is very manly. Very mature.'

'Time to go,' I sigh and, with a clattering of plates and a banging of trays, we finish lunch and think no more about it.

# Chapter 2

Next morning. 7.15 am.

I'm lying in bed, cosy-warm. The curtains are drawn. I can hear Mum downstairs in the kitchen, singing along to the radio. She's called me once already, but I know I have another five minutes before she calls again. So I stretch, rub my eyes, casually stroke my face – and feel something. A dry roughness, right along my jaw line. And when I feel really carefully, I can make out dozens of tiny little bumps. Measles! It has to be. That covers you in spots. My cousin Alice had it once and her face was so red and bumpy, she looked like a pan of spaghetti Bolognese. And now I'm in a real panic, because my fingers are finding so many lumps, I know I'm going to look even worse than she did.

So I'm lying in the dark with my heart thumping, and I want to look but I don't want to see. I clamber out of bed but don't open the curtains. I just run straight into the bathroom, lock the door and stand there, not daring to turn around. I'm going to be so ugly, there's a real risk the mirror will shatter and Mum's only had it two weeks.

'Emily!' Mum's voice shoots up the stairs like a rocket. 'Are you up yet?'

I don't have a voice to answer her. My mouth is dry as the bottom of a budgie cage. But I must say something. I don't want her coming to find me.

I unlock the door, open it a tiny bit and somehow manage a croaky: 'Yes. Down soon.'

Then I lock myself back in and take a deep breath. You can't stand here all day, I tell myself. You'll have to look eventually.

So I turn round, take a few steps forward, raise my eyes and look in the mirror.

*Oh!* It's not measles. There's no redness. No spots. My hair's a scraggy mess. My nose is too small. My eyes are too pale to be beautiful. But these are things I see every day. There's nothing new – except the bumps. They *are* there. I haven't imagined them. They just look smaller than they feel, if you know what I mean. In fact, I have to peer in the mirror to see them at all. But they are there. Dozens and dozens of tiny little lumps, mostly along my jaw line, though there are a few under my nose too. Are they a rash? I'm not sure. I decide to ask Mum.

Mum is banging around the kitchen, trying to do an impossible number of things before heading off to work.

'Do they itch?' she says, barely giving my chin a glance.

'No.'

'Then it's probably something you've eaten,' she

says. 'Too much sugar or something. I wouldn't worry about it. I don't think your head's going to drop off.'

But she's wrong, because my head *does* drop off, there and then. It rolls across the kitchen floor, picking up all kinds of rubbish on the way. Fluff, dust, cornflakes, fingernail trimmings... Does this floor never get cleaned? Then *doomp.* It smacks into the fridge and shudders to a stop. *Ow.* I'm going to have a lump the size of a creme egg. I lie there blinking, trying to blow a stray Rice Krispie off my nose.

Okay, I made that up. My head doesn't drop off. But would it matter if it did? Mum would just add 'Sweep up Lumpy Head' to her list of Things To Do. And for the first time today, I wish my dad was here. Because:

1. He'd have a good look and
2. He'd kiss it better even though I'm too old for that kind of thing now and
3. He wouldn't think I was making a fuss over nothing and
4. He wouldn't care if he was late for work.

But he's not here and I can't bring him back, so I just get off to school, like Mum wants.

~

As soon as I get there, I notice Keeley's face. It's pink along the jaw line, like she's been rubbing it.

'It's my own fault,' she says when I mention it. 'I tried some of my mum's new face cream last night. I don't know why. It's meant for old people. But it was such a cutesy little pot, I wanted to have a go. Then this morning, I woke up and my skin was all bumpy? I tried rubbing it with the flannel but that made it worse.'

I'm about to show her my chin, but she doesn't stop talking. 'Listen! I've just come from the library, and I've arranged a meeting there this lunchtime for any girl who wants a part in the play. It's at 12.30, so we'll have to be first in the lunch queue.'

I don't know what to say. She's taken me completely by surprise. A meeting? I wasn't expecting that. I thought we'd just go along to the auditions and hope for the best. But maybe Keeley's right. Maybe it will take more than hope to win over Mr Derren.

And now I'm kicking myself because I didn't think of it first. Keeley always beats me to things like this. She's so quick, so clever. She roars through life like a Formula One car while I trail behind her like exhaust smoke. Organising this meeting is a perfect example. I'm the one who wants to be an actress. This play is far more important to me than it is to her. Yet she's the one who's been doing something about it. I've just been picking spots in a mirror.

Then Carrie Ann arrives, and Keeley tells her about the meeting too.

'Cool!' says Carrie Ann. 'A protest meeting!'

I can't speak for *another* reason now. I'm looking at Carrie Ann and all I can see is her chin. It's pinker than the rest of her face. And when she turns sideways, the light catches it – and there are lumps. Dozens of them, just like mine. What's going on?

'Miss Bailey is well behind it,' says Keeley. 'I've never seen her so excited. She says we'll be like Suffragettes, fighting for the cause!' She punches her fist in the air and Carrie Ann copies her.

'You can be Mrs Pankhurst,' says Carrie Ann. 'I'll carry a banner.'

'We can chain ourselves to the fence outside the school,' says Keeley.

'Then chain ourselves to the police when they come to take us away!' adds Carrie Ann and they both start giggling.

'But we won't throw ourselves in front of any racehorses,' says Keeley, suddenly serious.

Carrie Ann's eyes widen in horror and she shakes her head. 'No. *No.*'

They stand there in silence, just looking at each other, then they collapse into giggles again. I have no idea what they are talking about. Racehorses, super jets... It's a complete mystery.

'We need to start spreading the word,' says Keeley

urgently. She looks at her watch. 'Five minutes to the bell. Let's get going.'

Carrie Ann nods and, with that, they both disappear, one going one way, one going the other and I'm left standing there like a lemon, not having a clue what's going on. There's only one thing I'm sure of. I *must* be in the library at 12.30!

# Chapter 3

Let me grab a moment to tell you more about myself. My real name is Emily Travis, but since I came to St Mary's, I've been asking everyone to call me Emmy. And now most people do, except some of the teachers and Mum when she's telling me off. I changed it because half the girls in the world seem to be called Emily. It was bad enough at my old school, but here it's ridiculous. If you stand in the cafeteria at lunchtime and shout 'EMILY!' thirty heads will turn around. I'm not kidding. There are almost as many Chloës and Rebeccas. Why weren't our parents more imaginative? Why didn't they choose something different? But then, there's a girl in Year 8 called Daffodil and a boy in Year 11 called Thunder, so maybe parents can't be trusted with names.

I am 1.3 metres tall, with pale blue eyes and mousey brown hair. I wish it was thick and glossy like Keeley's, but it's not. Some days it's so scraggy, it hangs down around my face like rats' tails. I will dye it one day, when I'm a movie star.

Being a movie star isn't a dream. I know it will happen. I can feel it, deep down inside. Keeley sometimes says she wants to be one too, but I can't see that happening, even if she is much prettier than I am. Keeley will run her own business, like her mum and dad, and be very rich. But a famous movie star? No.

I like singing and dancing as well as acting. Keeley and I go to classes every Saturday morning where we do all three. A bell rings at the end of each hour and everyone swaps rooms. On Sunday mornings I used to do horse riding. I really loved it. But Dad used to drive me there and Mum's too tired to do it now. She works hard all week, so Sunday is the only time she can have a lie-in.

I don't have any brothers or sisters. There's just me and Mum. Dad was killed in a road accident. That was three years ago, so I was only eight at the time, but I remember how terrible it was. Mum cried for weeks and kept saying *'I told him about that bike'* over and over again. Dad loved his motorbike. I used to sit in the garage with him while he polished it and told me stories about where he'd been.

Mum said the motorbike was dangerous and he should get rid of it because of me. I didn't understand that, then. The bike made him happy so I wanted him to have it. But I understand now. If it was still in the garage, I'd take a hammer and smash it into a thousand pieces. But the bike went a long time ago, what was left of it.

This is getting a bit sad and angry. Sorry. I didn't mean it to. I really want to keep things light and fluffy, like an omelette. And anyway, I should be telling you about Keeley's meeting. That's what you want to know, isn't it?

# Chapter 4

It's 12.25 and Keeley is hurrying me along the corridor to the meeting. Ooh! I had eggs for lunch and they scramble in my stomach as she urges me on.

'We've told all the girls in Year 7,' she tells me for the fiftieth time. 'Some of them have older sisters, so they will know too. The response we had was great, so I'm expecting it be really busy and – *oh!*'

We've reached the library but there's hardly anyone here. There's Carrie Ann, of course, with Shannon Jenkins and Lily Chung from our class. The Khan twins from Year 9, Anuja and Shailja. Caitlin Morrow from Year 8. And that's it. Keeley's face drops like a flipped pancake.

'Where is everyone?'

'Don't panic, Keeley. They'll be here soon.'

That's Miss Bailey, the school librarian. She's a smiley woman with a mass of red hair and a love of whacky jewellery. Today she's wearing a necklace made of liquorice allsorts. Not real ones - they're made of plastic or something - but they're exactly the same size and colour as real ones.

'I thought the place would be full,' murmurs Keeley. 'This is important.'

'Have faith,' says Miss Bailey. 'It isn't half-past

yet.'

Miss Bailey has re-arranged the library specially. There is a table at the far end with two chairs behind it and six rows of chairs in front. Keeley sighs and takes one of the two chairs. I'm about to claim the other when I see Carrie Ann's bag is on it already.

What's that doing there? Keeley is *my* best friend, isn't she? When did Carrie Ann take my place?

I don't say anything. I just take one of the seats on the front row. But I am hurt. I'm a bit worried too. I've been in St Mary's half a term now, and I'm getting to know things. But it's a big place, with loads of people, and I need Keeley. She's tougher than me and a whole lot smarter. I feel safer when she's around.

But now Carrie Ann's bag is on the chair beside her, and I'm over here, and Keeley doesn't seem bothered. Do you see why I'm worried? I feel like a baby bird that's fallen from its nest. I'm a fluffed-up ball of feathers, suddenly alone in a big, cold world.

~

Miss Bailey is right. The library door starts swinging like a donkey's tail. More and more girls are arriving. They are mostly from our year but there are some older ones too. Carrie Ann is sitting next to Keeley now. They're talking rapidly to each other but their voices are too quiet for me to hear. They look important, like newsreaders on tv. Miss Bailey brings Keeley a glass of water and taps her watch. It's enormous – a bright pink flower on a green strap. Keeley nods and rises to her feet.

'Thank you all for coming,' she says. 'I don't want to talk for long. We only have fifteen minutes and I'm sure you all know what this is about. Injustice! Inequality! Gender discrimination!'

BANG! A light bulb explodes in my head. Of course! Why didn't I think of it before? Keeley didn't come up with the idea of a protest meeting - her *mum* did. Keeley's mum is a lawyer. She's an expert in something called 'Women's Rights.'

But really, it doesn't matter who came up with the idea. It's Keeley who's making the speech and she's off to a flying start. Carrie Ann is clapping and soon everyone else is too. I start to feel a bit envious. I wish it was me up there. In my head, I could do it. I'm witty and clever. But in my heart, I know I couldn't. Not like Keeley. Not without a script.

Keeley waits till the clapping has stopped before she carries on. 'It's not fair,' she says. 'Why should girls miss out on the best parts in a play simply because they are girls? Why are we denied even the *chance* to audition for the best roles? Remember, sisters, we are talking about *acting* here. It's not real life. An actor pretends to be someone else. Someone older, younger, meaner, funnier – anything is possible. A girl *can* be a boy on stage. If she has acting talent, the audience will believe in her. We all know this is true.

But Mr Derren will not give us the chance to show it is true. He will not even consider girls for boys' parts.'

Shannon Jenkins puts her hand up. 'Do we know this for sure?'

A look of alarm flashes across Keeley's face. No! She doesn't know this for sure! She only knows what Jack Lewis told us, and he could have been lying. Winding us up like alarm clocks, waiting for us to ring and make fools of ourselves. It was a trap and we've walked right into it.

'Yes, we do know for sure,' says Miss Bailey. 'I spoke to Mr Derren an hour ago. He told me that he will not cast girls in the leading male roles. That means there are two speaking parts for girls and thirteen for boys.'

A gasp goes up around the room. It's worse than we imagined.

'I wish things were different,' continues Keeley. 'I wish Mr Derren would respect the rights of the girls in this school. I wish he would acknowledge our dreams and desires. But sometimes wishing isn't enough. Sometimes action is needed. Mrs Pankhurst knew that – and the women who marched beside her, carrying the Suffragette banners. Now, I'm not suggesting we do protest marches. I don't think we should attack Mr Derren with words and slogans. Behaviour like that could work against us. We do not want to be branded 'silly girls' - noisy, troublesome, irritating. *No one* would want to work with us then! No. I propose a quiet programme of protest.'

'Like what?'

That's Shannon Jenkins again, at the back of the room. She's really mouthy when she gets fired up.

'Excuse me?'

'What kind of action is *quiet?* Writing letters?' Shannon's top lip curls. 'I don't wanna do that. We need to fight properly. Make our views known.'

'I *will* make our views known,' Keeley fires back, but she's looking a bit flustered.

'How?'

*'How?'* Keeley pauses a fraction too long.

'You don't know!'

That's it. Suddenly the room is in uproar, with everyone talking at once. Shannon is shaking her head dismissively. Someone makes a joke I don't hear and a whole group starts laughing.

Keeley shouts over the top of them, really loud. 'I admit it! I don't have a plan! But that will come in time. I only found out yesterday. *Yesterday!* So give me a break, Shannon, yeah?'

Shannon nods and things quieten down.

'I will fight this thing,' says Keeley firmly. 'My

way – your way – whatever. I tell you now: I will defy Mr Derren. I will audition for a boy's part and I will get one. I will do whatever it takes. I will even grow a beard if necessary!

Another gasp goes up. My hand flies to my lumpy chin. She said that yesterday, and I said I'd grow one too. So did Carrie Ann. No. It can't be. Can it?

Keeley's really storming now. 'Are you with me? Will you grow a beard and show your support?'

I look at the faces around me. Eyes are shining, cheeks are glowing, mouths are grinning. The whole room is tingling with excitement. This is wild! It's mad and girly and impossible and we're all loving it. Yes – even me. Keeley has won me over too. I'm still upset because she seems to be dumping me for Carrie Ann, but at this moment, I can forgive her even that. I so want to be in this gang.

Keeley wants a reply and won't let any of us go until she gets one. 'WILL YOU GROW A BEARD AND SHOW YOUR SUPPORT?'

'YES!!' We scream so loud, the roof rattles.

Keeley's smile is bright enough to light up a street. 'We shall be the *Hairy Marys.* We shall fight for the right to audition for the best parts, then we will audition – and BEAT THE BOYS!'

# Chapter 5

'Emily! Are you still in bed?'

It's the next morning and yes, I am still in bed. I'm so tired, I feel like a lorry has run over me and flattened me into the mattress. I'm squished like a hedgehog. It's my own fault. I stayed up late watching a movie and now I'm paying for it.

I push back the duvet, drag myself out of bed, and fumble for my dressing gown in the dark. One of the sleeves is inside out. I stand there battling with it, like a man fighting an octopus. I step into my slippers. I've got them on the wrong feet but I don't care. I grunt and shuffle to the door. Across the landing, into the bathroom, switch on the light, head for the toilet and – *AAAARGH!*

I have a beard. A big, hairy beard. Not a few lumps and bumps like yesterday. This is a man-size beard, brown and bristly. Fat whiskers have grown overnight, in the dark while no one was watching. They've pushed through the skin of my chin. Now they are covering half my face, lying there, curling like caterpillars.

*What on earth am I going to do?* I can't go to school like this. I'll frighten children in the street. Bring traffic crashing to a standstill. Terrify the

Lollipop Lady on the zebra crossing. She'll scream so loud, her false teeth will fall out and run down the pavement, biting people's ankles.

Suddenly the phone rings. Mum answers it and shouts up the stairs: 'It's for you. It's Keeley.'

I'm not going downstairs looking like this! I go onto the landing, stand well back from the stairs and desperately try to sound calm. 'Tell her I'll see her at school.'

It goes quiet for a moment.

'She says she really needs to speak to you. She sounds a bit weird, Em.'

Does she? I start to smile. I can't help it. She's grown a beard too, I know she has. Good! I hope she is upset. Really upset. Because I am, and it's all her fault. She was the one who started it, back in the cafeteria with her big mouth. Look where it's got us now.

'I can't talk, Mum. Not now. I'll see her later.'

It goes quiet again. I know that will be the end of it. Mum won't listen to any more pleading from Keeley. Not at this time of the morning.

I go back into the bathroom and stare at the beard. There are so many hairs. Hundreds of them, thousands of them, packed tight together like a football crowd. My hand comes up, wanting to feel them, but I stop it mid-air. I don't want to touch. I don't want to know the beard is real. At the moment I'm clinging to the hope it's just a bad dream.

But it's not, is it? That's why Keeley was ringing.

I touch my face. The hairs aren't bristly. They're surprisingly soft. They move beneath my fingers and actually feel quite nice. If they were on a cat, I'd happily stroke them for hours. They're warm and comforting, like a baby blanket. I imagine they'll keep out the cold on a day like this.

No! Stop it! Stop it now! I can't start thinking like this! It's a *beard*. I can't pet it like a puppy. I have to get rid of it. Now.

'Emily? Are you still in the bathroom?'

My heart skips a beat. Does Mum need to use the toilet? I can't have her coming up. Not until I've got rid of my whiskers.

I return to the landing and call down: 'Nearly done.'

Nearly done? I haven't even started. I open the bathroom cabinet and begin searching through the bottles. There must be something here, in amongst the potion, pills, indigestion remedies and cough mixture that is months beyond its use-by date. And suddenly I wish my dad was still here, because he'd have a razor and shaving foam and – *tweezers!* I've got tweezers!

I pounce on them like a kitten on a feather. Hold them triumphantly in my hand. But then it all goes horribly wrong. Maybe I'm in too much of a rush. Maybe my hand is shaking. Whatever. I don't know. What I do know is this: I drop them into the toilet. They fall in slow-motion down into the bowl and land with a small splash in the water. I can't believe it. I stand there, staring into the toilet. I'm going to have to fish them out. But with what?

The toilet brush! I drop to my knees and reach behind the toilet. *Where is it? WHERE IS IT?* We used to have one, I know we did.

Oh... I'll have to use my hand.

I roll up the sleeve of my dressing gown and try to tell myself it could be worse. And that's true. It could be worse. Okay, I have a beard the size of Scotland and I'm about to shove my hand down a toilet, but at least the water isn't yellow, if you know what I mean, and I'm sure you do.

I fish out the tweezers, wash them under the hot tap, dry them off and stand in front of the mirror. I seize hold of the first hair and pull. *OWWWW!* Dear heaven, it hurts! I pull out a second. *OWWWW!* Does it hurt this much women when pluck their eyebrows? No, it can't. No one would ever do it. *OWWW!*

I pluck away for five minutes. The pain is appalling, my eyes are blurry with tears, and the patch of skin I've cleared is no bigger than a postage stamp.

Finally I come to my senses and stop.

*How was that ever going to work?* I ask the shaggy monster in the mirror. *You crazy girl. You need a razor.*

*'EMILY!'*

Mum is starting to get snappy now. She'll come storming up if I don't do something, and I can't bear the thought of her seeing me. And do you know why? Because I feel ashamed. I don't know why. I've done nothing wrong. But I know that under this beard, my cheeks are pink with shame and embarrassment. I can't have her seeing me like this. I just can't. I'll have to lie.

I flush the toilet.

'I'm all right,' I shout. 'My tummy's a bit funny, but I'm okay. I'm getting dressed now.'

Five more minutes. That's all I've got then she'll be up here.

I scan the bathroom, desperately looking for a razor. Mum *must* have one. Her legs are smooth, she must use something. But what? I can't see anything. And suddenly I realize, I have no idea what my mum gets up to in here. She could give herself a tattoo and I wouldn't know.

Anyway, there's no razor. But there is a flat thing for doing your feet. It's like a big nail file. It rubs away the hard skin on your heels. Would it rub off hairs?

I rub it furiously against my face. Is it working? I don't think so. I try again, harder now. My skin's going red and starting to hurt but still it's not working. And now my eyes are filling with tears. I can feel a great big sob, rising in my chest. I start rubbing again, on the other side of my face but I can't see any more. The tears are running down my cheeks, soaking this awful, awful beard. It won't come off. *It won't come off.* I need a razor and there isn't one, because my dad isn't here. He'd know what to do. I don't. I just feel dirty and ashamed and my face is sore.

And then, through my tears, I see a movement in the mirror.

'Emily?'

I turn around. My mum sees my face, stumbles backwards and grabs hold of the door for support.

'*What the -* ' she breathes. Then her hand covers her mouth and she says no more, just stands there, staring.

And that's when I know this is really, really bad.

# Chapter 6

'What's going on?' says Mum.

'I've grown a beard,' I say, like she can't see it. Then my face crumples like a tissue and I hang my head and cry. And Mum takes me into her arms, and holds me and hugs me and says: 'It's all right, Em, it's all right.' And I think perhaps it *will* be all right, because I'm not on my own now. She will be able to fix this.

'Come on,' says Mum. 'Let's go downstairs. Have a hot drink.' She takes the file from my hand. 'Leave this now.'

She puts her arm around my shoulders as we go downstairs to the kitchen. I sit at the table while she hands me a tissue, flicks the kettle to 'on' and reaches for the phone.

I start to panic. She's phoning for an ambulance! The whole *world* will see me like this. And Mum must see the fright on my face, because she raises a hand as if to say *it's okay* and then I hear: 'Beth? Hi, it's Karen. I won't be in today. Em's not well.'

I can breathe again. She's not leaving me. I'm going to be okay. Fresh tears fill my eyes.

'Hey – come on,' says Mum, putting the phone down. 'You didn't think I'd leave you, did you?'

I say nothing.

Mum looks at me, wide-eyed. She shakes her head. 'No... *No.* Why would you ever think that?' She comes behind me and wraps her arms around my shoulders. 'I'm not going anywhere. I'm here for you. I'm *always* here for you, Em. You know that - don't you?

I nod. I feel her sigh, right into my ear.

'Hot chocolate?' she whispers.

I nod again.

'One hot chocolate coming up. And while I'm making it, you can tell me what this is all about, yeah?'

So I tell her what I know. Mum listens carefully.

'I don't know what to make of it,' she says at last. 'I think you're right about Keeley. I think she *has* made it happen – though I have no idea how.'

'Do you think she's grown a beard too?'

'Yes, I do. She was a bit strange on the phone earlier.'

If I'm honest, I don't care how Keeley is. I have my own problem, right under my nose. 'Can you get rid of mine?'

Mum thinks for a second. 'I don't have a razor,' she says. 'But I have wax. Come on!' She runs up the stairs. I follow, wondering what she means by 'wax.' Candles are made of wax, and there are candles in the bathroom, but I don't see how they could work.

As it turns out, the wax she means is in strips. And they aren't in the bathroom. We go into her bedroom. She opens a drawer, pulls out a box and takes one strip out. It looks like an enormous sticking plaster. It's made of two pieces of very thin stuff with bright green wax sandwiched in between.

'Sit on the bed,' she says.

She warms the strip between her hands, then separates it into two sticky pieces. Next she places one of the pieces against my beard, wax side down, smoothes it carefully and *RRRRIPS* it off, really fast.

OWWW! I feel like half my face has been torn off but Mum is giggling. 'Sorry,' she says. 'It hurts, I know, but look!' She shows me the back of the wax strip and it's covered in hairs. 'This is better than shaving,' she explains. 'When you shave, the hairs are just cut off at skin level, but when you wax, they are completely pulled out, root and all.'

'Does that mean they will never grow back?'

'I don't know. When I wax my legs, the hairs grow back after a while. But this beard will be different.'

'Will it?'

She smiles. 'Let's hope so, eh?'

Five minutes later and the job is done. It's an incredibly painful process. You would think that after the shock of the first strip, the pain wouldn't be so bad for the next? But that's not true, because your skin starts to get pinker and sorer. Mum has to use ten strips and every one stings like a bad-tempered bee, but I am so, so happy to have smooth skin again. And once the beard has gone, I realise I'm starving hungry.

Mum makes porridge, then I have a long soak in a bubbly bath. When I come down again, Mum has changed out of her smart work clothes into jeans and a jumper. I like her much better like this.

'Let's watch a movie,' she says.

'Now?'

'Yes!' she says. 'Right now! You choose the movie, and I'll make the popcorn.'

I pick a DVD, draw the curtains and switch off the lights, and we snuggle down on the sofa together. Time goes by. Two blissful hours of cuddles and laughter. And then, all too soon, it's over.

Mum eases herself away from me, stands up and stretches. 'Ooh!' she says. 'I'm hungry! There's chicken in the fridge. I'll make some sandwiches.'

She crosses the room, opens the curtains and lets in the sunshine. Then she turns and freezes, staring at me.

I don't need to ask her what's wrong. I can feel it.

The beard has grown back.

# Chapter 7

I sit there like a statue, my hands cradling my face, my eyes staring into a horrifying future. I will never, ever be rid of the beard. It's growing on me like mould on cheese. Soon it will creep down my neck and onto my chest. I'll look like a chimpanzee with trainers on.

Mum is beside me, saying 'It's all right, Em, it's all right,' over and over again. But I can hear the fear in her voice. And then she says 'I wish your father was here,' and something snaps inside her and she starts to cry. Big, gulping sobs – she makes no attempt to stop them. I look at her, blank-eyed. She's rocking backwards and forwards. Tears are streaming down her face. She wipes them away with her hands, smearing her make up. She doesn't care anymore. Her husband is dead and her daughter is a freak. I'd cry too if I were her.

I don't try to comfort her. I can't. I'm numb with shock. I rise to my feet like a zombie, spilling the last of the popcorn. I trample it into the carpet as I leave the room. Up the stairs, into my bedroom. Then I close the door behind me, lie face down on the bed and wish I had never been born.

And I must fall asleep, because suddenly I wake up. The phone is ringing downstairs. It stops. I hear footsteps on the stairs and Mum is tapping on my door.

'It's Keeley,' she says.

'I don't want to talk to her. I don't want to talk to anyone. Ever again.'

'I think you should, Em. She knows what you're going through. Perhaps she can help.'

I don't reply, but I am considering this.

'I'll leave the phone outside the door.'

Mum walks away. I wait for a moment then open the door and pick up the phone.

'Em? Are you there?'

Keeley's voice is loud, over-excited.

'Yes.'

'Where've you been all day? Why didn't you come into school?'

The breath jumps from my body. *Doesn't she know?* I thought she had a beard too. Am I the only one? No. *No*. My legs go weak.

'Was it because of the beard?' Keeley asks. 'You do *have* a beard, don't you?'

I admit nothing. There's a squeal of laughter down the phone.

'Oh Em, you are a softie! Promise me you'll come in tomorrow, yeah? You have to be there. You have to see.'

'See what?'

'I'm not telling! You have to be there. See you then. Bye!'

And with that, she's gone. I stand there, holding the silent phone like it's a magic wand. Oh, I wish it was! I'd wave it and this would all go away. But Keeley has made me curious. What does she want me to see? And why did she sound so happy? Why isn't she sobbing into her pillow and cursing her stupid mouth? I don't know – and there's only one way to find out.

Beard or no beard, I'll have to go to school tomorrow.

# Chapter 8

I saw an old movie on tv once. It was called *The Invisible Man,* and it was about a scientist who did an experiment. But it went wrong, and he ended up completely invisible. Anyway, in the film, the actor wore a big scarf wrapped around his face and a hat and dark glasses, so no one would notice that he didn't have a head. Well, not one you could see.

I remember all this the next morning when I'm standing by the hall mirror, wrapping an enormous scarf round and round and round my face. Because the beard is still there. It hasn't grown any longer, and it hasn't spread any further – and I am *so* thankful for that – but I still look like something from the Stone Age.

By the time I'm finished, I can't see anything of my face except my eyes. But I don't look too weird because it's bitterly cold today, and everyone is muffled up with hats and scarves. But what will I do when I get to school? Oh... I don't know!

Mum gives me some lunch money. 'Will you be okay?' she says, pulling my scarf up even higher. 'You have my number. Call me if you need me. I'm in the office all day.'

I nod again. I have to. I can't speak through the scarf, even if I want to. I open the door, look both ways then venture out. I hurry along the road with my head down. I reckon if I can't see people, they can't see me. It's dangerous, though. I nearly get run down at the end of the road because I don't see a mail van coming. There's a terrible squeal of brakes and a skidding sound.

'Oy!' says the postman, leaning out of his van window.

'Be more careful, will you? You nearly gave me a heart attack then.'

I can believe that. He's as white as a candle and his hands are shaking.

'Sorry.'

He nods and drives away and I walk on through the smell of burning rubber.

As school gets closer, my steps become slower. I don't want to go. *I don't want to go.* But I have no choice. There are people coming from every direction. I'm swept up by the crowd outside the school, carried through the gates and up the drive.

Mr Derren is on duty outside the main doors. He stands there, muffled in a duffle coat, his hair rammed under a Manchester United bobble hat. His breath steams white in the November cold, and his dark eyes glower above. I put my head down and hurry past, praying my scarf doesn't slip.

Once I'm through the main doors, I wonder where to go. The library suddenly seems the safest place. I scuttle off down the corridor. But I'm only halfway there when I see the worst person possible coming towards me: Robbie Flynn.

There are several bullies in school, girls as well as boys, but Robbie Flynn is easily the most feared. It's hard to say what's nastier, his fists or his mouth. Most bullies don't say much, but Robbie Flynn does. He's short and wiry, so he can't rely on brute strength. But his tongue cuts like a laser, and it's fired by a vicious imagination.

As he comes closer, I say the same words, over and over again in my head: *don't see me, don't see me, don't see me, don't see me.*

It works. I don't know how; I'm just so glad it does. He sidles on by without even a sideways glance. I'm nothing. I'm just one more person wrapped up against the cold.

I take a deep breath… and almost forget to let it out again. Because coming towards me now are the Khan twins – and they both have beards. Smooth, black beards, shiny as satin. And yes, people are looking at them, but no one is saying anything bad. How could they? The twins look *magnificent* and they know it. They are gliding down the corridor like swans on a moonlit lake. They are proud, polished, perfect. Suddenly I feel like a tramp, my scraggy beard hidden by a smelly scarf.

As the twins pass by, their beautiful eyes don't see me either. Why should they? They're Year 9s. Then someone *grabs* me from behind and I nearly wet myself - but it's Carrie Ann. And she has a beard! A gorgeous curly beard, brown as fudge.

'Are you a spy?' she giggles. I shake my head. 'Then why are you in disguise? Take this off!' She tugs at my scarf and it starts to unravel – just like me. I don't want to face the world without it. Not yet. I grab her hand and protest through the layers of wool.

'Okay!' she says. 'Don't panic! I'll leave it alone. But there's nothing to be ashamed of, you know. You're a member of a *very* exclusive club.' She links my arm again, leads me to the library and opens the door with a flourish. 'Look!'

I go in - and find a jumble of bearded faces. Black, brown, golden... Some beards are straight. Some are curly. Some are tight to the face. Some are bushy. But there's one thing they all have in common. Above every one there is a pair of bright, dancing eyes.

'Emmy!'

I recognise Miss Bailey's voice, so I turn and – *jumping Julie!* She has an enormous red beard! It looks like she's eating a fox and hasn't finished the tail.

'We were so worried about you yesterday,' she says. 'Is everything all right at home?' I nod dumbly. Has the world gone mad? No one seems to think there is anything unusual about the situation. Yet here we are, a gang of girls, looking like we've stepped out of *Aladdin*. I haven't seen so many beards since my mum took me to a folk festival.

I grab Carrie Ann, hustle her into a corner and pull down my scarf. 'How is this possible?' I hiss, pointing at my whiskers. 'Girls with beards?'

'Well, it was Keeley, wasn't it?' she replies. 'You remember, at the meeting, we all said we'd grow a beard.'

'Yes, of course I remember *that*,' I say, rolling my eyes, 'but that only explains *why* – not how. How have we grown beards overnight?'

'I don't know,' says Carrie Ann. 'I haven't thought about it yet. I've been too excited. The boys are *so* jealous! You should have seen their faces yesterday morning. Their eyes were popping out of their heads like mushrooms.'

She giggles. I give up on her and ask Miss Bailey instead.

'How is it possible?' she repeats. 'I honestly don't know, Emmy. Does it matter? The simple fact is, we have them - and they are wonderfully symbolic. They show the world we are committed to the fight. We're hairy and proud of it!' She punches her fist in the air. 'We know *why* we've grown the beards, Em. That's enough for me. *How* really isn't important.'

Well, maybe it isn't important to her, but it is to me. And I'm just about to say so, when the library door crashes open and a bearded Keeley stands there, panting like a dog in July.

'You'll never believe what's happened,' she cries. 'The press have arrived!'

# Chapter 9

It's true. The press *have* arrived. And I'm not talking about the local newspaper. It's the national press! There are two reporters – one from *The Sun*, one from *The Times* - and a photographer.

Keeley whips a brush out of her bag and starts to groom her beard. 'They're going to want photos, aren't they?' she says. 'Oh – hello Em! I thought you were the Invisible Man for a moment.'

I'm standing there fuming. I'm not angry with Keeley – I'm angry at myself. Why didn't I bring a brush? What kind of movie star will I make? An actress is supposed to look glamorous all the time, even if she's just popping to the supermarket for a tin of dog food. There might be photographers waiting around the corner. She has to look good. The public demand it. Yet here I am, looking as wild as a holly hedge.

'This is brilliant!' says Carrie Ann. 'Mr Derren won't be able to stop us now.'

Miss Bailey shakes her head. 'I'm not so sure. I don't want to spoil the party, girls, but I can't see Mrs Burton allowing interviews and photos. Not without your parents' permission.'

'Mine will give permission,' says Keeley. But Miss Bailey still isn't convinced.

'School politics,' she says. 'Very tricky – especially these days.'

We all nod, but we don't understand what she means. We don't really care. We just want to see our pictures in the papers. Even me! Just think – five minutes ago, I was horrified at the thought of anyone seeing my face. Now I want the whole world to see me: Emmy Travis, Hairy Mary and Movie Star of the Future.

Suddenly the bell rings.

'Time for classes,' says Miss Bailey. She starts to herd us towards the door. We protest but she won't listen. 'Go on! This will take ages to sort, believe me.'

She's right. Lunchtime comes and still we haven't heard anything. I go to the school office and say I've lost my purse. I haven't, of course. I just want an excuse to stand outside Mrs Burton's office, which is next door. I might hear or see something.

Mrs Burton is the Head of St Mary's. She's tall, with silver hair, grey suits and scarily thin legs. Sometimes she stands motionless, just watching, like a great, long heron. Being outside her office without good reason is risky, and suddenly I wonder why I'm doing this.

My plan doesn't work anyway. I don't hear anything. Then, through the window, I see one of the reporters, talking into his phone. But by the time I reach him, the conversation has ended, so I have nothing to tell Keeley and Carrie Ann.

I head back to the library. But as I turn the corner of the corridor, I bump straight into Mr Derren.

'Aha!' he cries. 'One of the troublemakers.'

I open my mouth but nothing comes out. I can't think. He's standing too close. He's blocking my brain waves.

'You can't win, you know,' he says. I look at his chin. It's easier than looking into his eyes and I'm interested in chins now. He is *so* hairy. I can see he's shaved this morning, but already the bristles are growing back. There are tiny pin pricks of black all over his chin, under his nose, down onto his neck. Freaky. I wouldn't want to meet him in a graveyard with a full moon rising, that's for sure.

'It's my show,' he growls. 'I say who gets what. And I'm telling you now – the male parts *will* go to boys. I don't care who comes to this school. The press, the television... The Prime Minister can come, it'll make no difference. I won't be bullied.'

He walks away, and now I am thinking just one thing: *did he say TELEVISION?!*

## Chapter 10

It's nearly midnight. The night is clear and still. Bitterly cold. My hand almost freezes to the latch as I open the gate and enter the graveyard.

I walk down a tunnel of yew trees, my feet crunching the gravel path. Ahead looms the church, with a full moon hanging above it.

I turn left, onto the path that leads behind the church. My feet know where to go. They have been here countless times.

The grave I seek used to be the last in the row, but now there are others. Six more mounds, lying side by side like dominoes. Time moves on, even in this sleeping place.

I reach the grave. Read the inscription though I know it by heart.

*Benjamin William Travis*
*Loving husband of Karen.*
*Beloved father of Emily.*
*Taken too soon from this world*

I hear the church clock, preparing to strike the hour. A barn owl leaves the tower and flies to a quieter perch. It passes overhead, white as winter.

The bell begins. A slow measuring of time. I turn

and walk back towards the church. As the final ring fades into the night, I reach the main path and turn for the gate. Then I freeze. Look. Listen.

I can't be sure – it could just be a trick of the moon on the trees – but I swear there's something there. I saw it. Just for a moment. It was so swift, it could have been anything. But whatever it was, it's still there. In the shadows. Watching. Waiting.

My heart starts to pump faster, forcing the oxygen round my body, feeding my muscles, readying me to run. My brain is whirring like the clock in the tower, finding other paths, other gates, other options. *There's a gate in the hedge on the North side of the church. It leads to a path through the woods.*

I start walking – slowly, backwards. If something starts following, I want to see it.

*I do see it.* There's a movement at the far end of the tunnel, a shifting of shadows, and onto the path steps a werewolf. It has the shape of a man but the bulk of a beast. A squat body, bowed legs and a great shaggy head that hangs forward, eyes burning red as car lights.

It starts to run.

I turn and flee. My feet are pounding, my arms are pumping, my head is thrown back with the force of running. My heart is going to explode in my chest. I have no time to breathe. I think only of the gate, the gate, the gate.

I'm nearly there. I can see it, reach it, almost

touch it when the werewolf slams into me from behind and knocks the breath clean out of my body. I fall to the ground with such force, my mouth bites into the earth. I taste mud and blood and cold, cold fear. I spin over onto my back, legs kicking, trying to find some footing. The werewolf looms over me, snarling and shifting, pinning me to the ground with its devil eyes.

The burning red transforms into the terrible dark eyes of Mr Derren.

'You won't win,' he snarls. 'You won't win.'

Then the eyes turn grey. Graveyard grey. And the werewolf turns to stone, just like the angels on the tomb beside me. I start to feel incredibly sleepy. My own eyes close, and don't open again till morning. And when they do, I'm warm in bed, the smell of bacon is drifting up from the kitchen and I am the only hairy thing in the room.

# Chapter 11

Mrs Burton has said yes! The newspaper reporters can speak to the Hairy Marys and take photos! But they must also talk to Mr Derren, if he will talk to them. She wants their reports to be fair and balanced. *Pah!* Who cares about that? We're going to be in the papers!

Mrs Burton won't let the reporters disrupt our lessons, so she tells them to meet us in the library at lunchtime. They are already there when we arrive. Miss Bailey is having her photo taken.

'Ah, the girls!'

This comes from a glamorous woman in a tight black dress and very high heels. She looks like she should be interviewing celebrities on a red carpet, not hairy girls in a backstreet school. She smiles, and her red lips sweep back to reveal movie star teeth.

'I'm Jennifer,' she says.

'And I'm Bill.' This comes from a man sitting at one the library tables. He's in a creased suit and has teeth like a donkey.

'We're not from the same paper,' says Jennifer quietly, and we nod. But we don't care! These aren't the local guys who cover jumble sales and charity fetes and little kids dressing up for Hallowe'en. No, these are both from national newspapers, and that's all that matters! And suddenly the door opens and a *third* crew arrives, a man and a woman.

'Sorry,' says the woman. She has a nose redder than Rudolph the reindeer, and her coat is so enormously padded, it looks like it's eating her. 'Jam on the motorway held us up.'

I picture an overturned lorry and a vast, sticky sea of strawberry jam gluing down the cars. I think Carrie Ann does too, because she starts grinning.

Bill beckons to her. 'Can I talk to you, sweetheart? Over here.'

Carrie Ann frowns but goes anyway.

Jam Woman, still in a fluster, turns to Caitlin Morrow, who has just arrived. 'Hiya! Are you happy to talk? Thanks.' They move to where the second photographer is setting up.

Miss Red Carpet smiles at me. 'Can we have a little chat?'

You bet we can! I grin so hard, it hurts. She sits me down and starts asking all kinds of questions. My name, my age, why did I grow the beard, how long did it take, what are my feelings about the school play... It's brilliant. Suddenly I feel like I'm the most important person in the world. This woman has come all the way from London and now she's listening to *me*. She wants to hear *my* opinions!

I glance at Keeley and instantly feel sorry for her.

She's biting her lip and looking so lost. It's not fair she's been overlooked. Not when she was the one who got the Hairy Marys started. Without her, we wouldn't be here now.

Then her whole face brightens. The first photographer has called her over. Suddenly her face is golden and her eyes are shining.

After Keeley it's my turn to be photographed. By the time we leave the library with Carrie Ann, we feel like we're walking on air. Oh, I want more of this!

We head for the drinks machine. Giving interviews is thirsty work! And as we stand there with our cans, through the window we notice a group of boys gathering by C block. Jack Lewis is there, Matthew Sharp and at least twenty more.

'What's that all about?' wonders Carrie Ann.

'We can soon find out,' says Keeley. 'Come on!'

'No!' I pull her back. 'It's boys only. You could be in big trouble if you wade in there.'

'But I really want to know what they're *saying*,' she moans. 'I bet they're talking about us.'

'We'll soon know if they are,' says Carrie Ann. 'Follow me!'

She runs out through the doors, across the walkway and into C block, with me and Keeley sprinting behind her. We race up the stairs, along the corridor and into a classroom which should be directly above the boys' heads. We creep towards the window, craning our necks to see.

'They're there,' says Keeley, stepping back. 'Right under us.' We drop down and Keeley opens the window very slowly. Just a crack but it's enough. We have no trouble hearing. The boys' voices are loud, fast, angry.

'What do they think they're playing at?' says one. His voice is snarly, like a dog's. 'Growing beards is men's business.'

'Yeah!' cries another. 'S'not right. S'not fair.'

'You don't even want a part in the play,' sneers a third.

'That's not the point,' says Snarly Dog. 'They shouldn't be doing it, play or no play.'

'I want a part in the play,' says a new voice. It's so high and squeaky, we start to giggle. 'A proper speaking part.'

'I don't think so,' whispers Keeley. 'Not unless there's a rat in the stable with something to say.' We stifle our giggles. The boys mustn't hear us.

'You won't get one,' says Snarly Dog. 'Not if these flamin' girls have their way.'

The lads grunt loudly in agreement.

'I've been thinking,' says a deeper voice. It has to be Ajay Rampal. 'They have grown beards. Is that *all* they have grown?'

The lads roar with laughter. We can imagine their

gestures.

'It wouldn't surprise me,' says Snarly Dog. 'They seem determined to be blokes.'

Carrie Ann gasps. '*They think we want to be like them?*'

Keeley rolls her eyes.

'Growing a beard makes you more of a man,' says Ajay, and half a dozen 'yeahs' drift up.

'Does it though? I wonder.'

That's a new voice, but an unmistakable one. Soft, calm… It has to be Dominic Fellows.

'I have no intention of having a beard,' Dominic goes on, 'even when I am old enough to grow one. I do not believe that will make me less of a man. What is a man anyway?'

The lads fall silent. This has thrown them. They haven't come to talk about deep stuff.

'S'not important - is it?' Snot sounds hopelessly confused. I'm not surprised. I couldn't answer that 'man' question either, if I'm being honest.

'We're going off-road here,' says Jack Lewis. We'd know his voice anywhere. 'What matters is this: the media are getting behind them. Newspapers today – it'll be tv tomorrow. Derren will come under so much pressure, he'll have to give in.'

'There must be something we can do,' says Squeaker. 'Can't we grow beards too?'

'I've got a moustache,' S'not says proudly.

'So has Anuja Khan,' says Matthew Sharp.

'Yeah, but I had mine first. And I bet it's softer than hers.'

'I wouldn't know,' replies Matthew. 'I haven't kissed yours.'

*Aaah!* We turn to each other, wide-eyed. The boys have erupted below. All kinds of comments float up – most of them rude.

'How do you do it?' It's Squeaker again, sounding desperate now. 'How do you grow a beard?'

'Try kissing one of the Scary Marys,' says Gruff. 'Their beards may be catching.'

'If they are, Matt is gonna be *covered* in hair by Christmas,' says Jack Lewis. A howl of laughter comes from the boys and we don't stick around to hear any more. We want to be far away from C block when the meeting breaks up. Whoever that Squeaker is, we don't want his slobbery lips dribbling all over our beards!

# Chapter 12

Jack Lewis was right about one thing – the television companies *do* want to meet us. We are invited to go on morning tv! They want three Hairy Marys, so Mrs Burton picks me, Keeley and Lily Chung. We travel down to London by train with Miss Bailey, and as soon as we get to the station, people are pointing at us and nudging each other. Everyone seems to be smiling and waving. By the time we reach London, we're starting to feel like stars. And when we find there's a long black car waiting to take us to the tv studios - well, that does it! Especially when the driver holds the door open for us. Now we feel like real, solid gold celebrities.

Once we reach the studios, things get even more amazing. A woman called Milly meets us and gives us special security passes to wear. Then she leads us along corridors and through doors, up staircases and round corners, and wherever we go, there are busy, busy people. Then we see someone famous! None of us can remember his name, but he's an actor. He plays a detective in something. And he's so tall and so cool... He sweeps down the corridor towards us with his overcoat flapping dramatically behind him. He doesn't look at us. Not even the tiniest sideways glance. But as he strides by, we all feel tingly. He's a star and he knows it, and what we feel is his confidence, I suppose. It absolutely washes over us. We're like seagulls, bobbing on the waves when a boat has gone by. As for Miss Bailey... She's looks like she's seen an angel. She just stands there, looking really soppy. When we call her, she gives a big sigh and won't move until we take her by the elbow and lead her on.

Milly takes us to a special room – the Green Room, it's called – where we have to wait until we go on set. There's a table full of orange juice and fizzy water and tea and coffee – even a bottle of champagne, if anyone wants that for breakfast! And there's an enormous silver tray heaped with doughnuts and Danish pastries. My mouth goes dribbly, just looking at them.

Milly tells us to help ourselves to whatever we want. But as soon as I sink my teeth into an apple Danish, another woman comes in and asks us to go to Make Up. *Wow!* Keeley and I are vibrating with excitement. We follow her into a room full of mirrors and lights and chairs that go up and down. The make up ladies put little plastic capes around our shoulders and we think we're going to have full make-overs: hair, make up, nails, the lot. But we don't. The make up ladies just tidy our beards, powder our faces and that's it. I am *so* disappointed, because I'm not super-pretty but they can do amazing things with make up, can't they? I guess with our beards covering half our faces, they don't have much to play with. And they want us to look like schoolgirls, not supermodels.

Once we're tidied up, we are taken to a dressing room to change into our school uniforms – we travelled down in jeans and jumpers because it was so cold. Then we return to the Green Room and I look at my watch. 10.05! Back at St Mary's, they won't have had morning break yet, and we've done so much.

Then things start to get really exciting, because we meet the presenters, Adam and Alice. They chat for a while and go through some of the questions they're planning to ask. It's just to help us relax. Then they wish us good luck and off they go, into the studio because the show is starting *right now!*

# Chapter 13

The next hour whizzes by in a dazzling blur of colour and smiles and bright, bright lights. Afterwards, I can't remember what I was asked or what I said. But I do remember how I felt, sitting there in front of the cameras with my tiny microphone clipped to my cardigan. *Happy*. Amazingly, wildly, hug yourself happy. And I remember looking at Adam and Alice and thinking *you are so lucky. You do this every day and get paid pots of money for doing it.*

When the show is over, Milly takes us up onto the roof of the building. There's a balcony you can stand on and look out over the whole of London. It's fabulous: a fast, busy, wonderful city, spread out before me like a map. I can see the Houses of Parliament and St Paul's Cathedral and the River Thames, glittering like a necklace. I know that down there, on the street, it's dirty and smelly and noisy and full of people pushing into you. But up here, it's quiet and perfect. Truly magical. And I start thinking that my heart is going to burst soon. There's no more room for all the emotion I'm feeling today.

After the tv show's done, I am expecting to grab some lunch, do something touristy and then catch the train home. But Miss Bailey suddenly pulls out her phone, checks her texts and makes an announcement.

'Sorry girls, we have another interview to do. They've just confirmed. It's very last minute, I know, but it's for one of the Sunday papers. You know the glossy magazines they do? One of those.'

We are all happy to do it, so we clamber into a taxi and head into the West End. The meeting is in a place called Soho. We press our noses to the windows as we arrive. It's a crazy-busy area. We love it.

We arrive at a plain-looking door. Miss Bailey presses a buzzer and we are let in. We climb a flight of stairs and come out in a gorgeous place, with enormous sofas, paintings on the wall, huge pot plants and a studio all set up for photos.

'Welcome!' says a voice. 'I'm Cassandra.'

She is tall and thin, dressed completely in black, with tiny silver glasses perched on the end of her nose. She isn't old, but her hair is pure silver, and pulled back into a single plait that reaches down to her waist.

'I am doing the photos,' she says. 'Jon will be doing the interview - when he's finished making the coffee! And this is Shreya. She is styling the shoot.'

I have no idea what that means, but guess we'll soon find out.

Shreya is tiny and very beautiful, with huge dark eyes and the longest eyelashes I have ever seen. They flutter like butterflies. She is dressed in black too, with silver rings on every finger and pointy boots like a pixie might wear.

'We only need one of you for the shoot,' says Cassandra, and she starts looking at each of us in turn. *Really* looking, studying every centimetre of our faces. It's a bit squirmy, to be honest. She looks at me for *ages*.

'What's your name?'

'Emmy Travis.'

'Well, Emmy Travis,' she says, 'I think you are perfect for this. Shreya?'

Shreya nods. 'She even has pierced ears.'

'It's a sign!' laughs Cassandra. 'So, Shreya will fix you up, Emmy, then we can begin.'

A man walks in with a tray full of coffees.

'My tribe!' he exclaims when he sees us. His beard is bigger than ours. This is Jon.

I don't get to talk to Jon. Keeley and Lily do the interview without me. Shreya takes me to a side room and begins dressing me up. First she brushes my hair and ties it in a high ponytail. Next she asks me to put on a heavy robe with a cream collar. Then she takes a long length of silky cloth, in the most gorgeous shade of blue, and wraps it around my head like a turban. She ties it so it hangs down over one shoulder.

Then she opens a little box and brings out a pearl earring. She fixes it into one ear, takes a step back and smiles. 'You're ready.'

She leads me back into the studio.

'Oh *Emmy!'* cries Miss Bailey when she sees me. 'Wonderful. Just wonderful.'

Cassandra is thrilled too. She sits me down in front of a black velvet curtain. I don't think I have ever seen anything so black. It is amazing. Like a piece of night.

'Just look at me,' says Cassandra, as her camera clicks and whirrs. 'Don't smile. And now you're pouting! Stop it, modern girl!'

Five minutes later, Cassandra has finished. Before I leave the chair, Miss Bailey steps forward with her phone. 'One for us,' she says.

Later on the train, when Keeley and Lily are dozing, Miss Bailey pulls out her phone and looks at the photo.

'They were right. You were the perfect choice,' she says.

I don't know what she means *again*. Honestly, I'm not stupid. I do know things. But these days, there's so much I'm not getting.

'What was all that about?' I ask her. 'Why did they dress me up like that?'

Miss Bailey's eyes widen. 'Don't you know? Oh Em - why didn't you say?'

'I didn't know I was missing something, until

now,' I admit.

'They were recreating a painting. One of the most famous paintings in the world, *Girl with a Pearl Earring*. It's very old. Seventeenth century. And it's very beautiful. Wait - I'll find an image of it.'

She taps into her phone. Waits a moment then shows me the screen.

It's a picture of a girl. It's stunning. Take-your-breath-away beautiful.

'And here's you.' She brings up the photo of me again.

'Oh wow! They got it so close!' It's all there - the deep black background, the blue wrap, the pearl earring...

'And next Sunday, your face will be on tens of thousands of breakfast tables. The photo is going on the front cover of the magazine. They told me while you were with Shreya. Can you imagine that?'

No, I can't. Could you?

~

Later that night, back home, I'm lying in bed, not wanting to go to sleep. I want this day to go on for ever. It has been the best day of my life, no doubt about it. When I grow up and become a movie star, I will have days like this all the time. Some will be even better. But I'll always remember this day, because it's been so special. This will be a perfect memory.

And with that thought, I turn out the bedside light, snuggle down in bed and sleep like a puppy dog. No worries. No strange dreams.

No idea of the terrifying events the next day has in store for me.

# Chapter 14

It's Saturday. Mum drives me to my StarzOnStage classes then picks me up again at 1 o'clock.

'Do you want to come to the supermarket, Em?' she asks. 'I haven't been yet. Or I can take you home, it's up to you.'

I think for a moment. I haven't been to the supermarket since I've had the beard. I don't mind going to school, though I still wear my scarf on the way there. Yesterday was fun on the train. And I am a bit of a celebrity now, so no one will think I'm weird. Will they?

Mum senses my uncertainty. 'Honestly, Em, I can take you home. It's no bother.'

'No,' I say. 'I'd like to come. I want to look at Christmas cards.'

So we drive into the supermarket car park and wait for *ages* because half the people in England seem to be doing their Christmas shopping, even though it's still November. Then I wrap my scarf around my face and we go in.

The store is huge, with a moving walkway that takes you up to a second floor. That's where the clothes are.

'I'll go up there,' I say, pointing vaguely in that direction. 'I'll look at the cards later.'

'Are you sure?' asks Mum. She's picked a wobbly trolley. I can see she's deciding whether to swap it.

I nod. 'I'll be fine. I have my mobile on. You can call me!'

'That's not as mad as it sounds,' says Mum. 'Where have all these people come from? I've never seen it so busy.' She turns the trolley round and heads for the exit. I step onto the walkway. As it takes me up, I see Mum kick the trolley, then she abandons it completely and storms outside for another.

I carefully step off the walkway and head for the socks. They are nice in here and very cheap, so Mum doesn't mind if I slip a pair in with the shopping.

They have new ones for Christmas. So many designs! Snowmen and Santas, robins and Christmas trees... I'm so busy choosing, I don't notice the little boy staring at me. Then I hear his voice. 'Why is she wearing that scarf?'

'I don't know.' There's a woman at the end of the sock display, looking embarrassed. 'Come away, Harry.'

But Harry won't be moved. He comes closer. 'Why you wearing that scarf?' he asks, pointing a sticky finger in my direction. 'I don't have a coat.'

I know what he means. It is warm in here, and my scarf is thick and woolly. I turn away, but he starts tugging at my jacket. 'Why?'

'Harry! Come here! Leave the girl alone.'

The woman is sounding flustered but she makes no move to grab the little pest. In fact, she moves further away.

'What's wrong with your face?'

I feel my cheeks burning. I look around to see if there's anyone who could help, but I'm on my own.

'Nothing!' I hiss. It comes out muffled but he gets the idea.

He stares at me. 'Then... why you wearing the scarf?' He starts to tug at it really hard.

That's it. I've had enough. I bend down so my face is really close to his, pull down the scarf and bark: *'Go away!'*

*'YAAAAAAAAA!'* His scream is so loud, they must hear it in the car park. But he doesn't run away. Oh no. He just stands there, staring at me. Then his face wrinkles like a raisin, his eyes close and the wailing begins. Soon his whole body is racked with sobs and he's shaking like a rattle.

'What did you do to him?' cries his mother. She's storming towards me like a crazy elephant. *'What did you do?'*

I shake my head helplessly.

Harry stops crying, takes a great gulping breath, points at me and declares: 'SHE HAS A BEARD!'

'What?' says his mother.

'A beard! A big brown beard! On her face! I saw it! She showed me!'

Now his mother is staring at me. 'Is this true?' she asks, like it's any of her business.

'We'll soon find out,' cries a voice. And suddenly, someone grabs my scarf and whips it off. I'm spun around by the force – and there's a big lad standing behind me holding my scarf. He must be Harry's brother. They have the same red hair and freckles.

'Whoa! Look at that!'

'What?'

Like a fool, I turn round at the sound of the mother's voice. She sees the beard and screams with the same terrifying lung power as Harry. And suddenly there are people running over from every direction. They think someone's been murdered and want to see the blood. Within seconds there's a crowd around me, shouting and pointing. I can't get away – all my exits are blocked. Then the voices begin, firing at me from every side, so fast, I can't see who's speaking.

'I know her! She was on the telly yesterday morning!'

'She's from St Mary's, isn't she? Wants to be in the play.'

'Good on ya, girl! You show them boys!'

'On telly? Really?'

'Yeah. With Adam and Alice.'

'Is she famous, Dad?'

'How's it going, love? Got a part yet?'

'Dad – is she famous?'

I think I'm going to faint. I can't breathe. I'm trying to, but my breath is so fast, so shallow, and it's too hot in here. I have to get out.

'Excuse me,' I say. 'I have to go.' I try to push through the crowd.

'Could I have a picture with you?' It's a girl, older than me. She puts her arm around my shoulders, holds up a phone and takes a photo. And suddenly everyone wants a photo. There are phones everywhere. Some are flashing. I can't see where I'm going.

'Can you sign this?' There's a man, waving a scrap of paper under my nose.

'Why?'

'You could be *really* famous one day. It'll be worth something.'

'No. *No.*' I try to push past him. But there are more pieces of paper now. Shopping lists, magazines, bus tickets, all being waved in front of me. The crowd has a hundred heads but only one brain. Someone thinks of something and all the others follow, like a big Mexican wave.

*OWW!* I feel a terrible pain on the left side of my face. I turn, and there's a woman holding a clump of hair. My hair. From my beard.

Now there are hands grabbing my beard, my hair, my clothes. This is crazy. I'm nothing, I'm no one. I was looking at socks, for goodness' sake. Now they're tearing me to bits.

'EMILY!'

Mum?

*'EMILYYYY!'*

*Mum!* Tears spring to my eyes. I fight on, harder now, not caring if I hit people, stand on toes, knock down toddlers. I just want to get out.

'Em!' Mum grabs hold and wraps her arms around me. I bury my head inside her open coat. 'Back off!' she roars. 'Back off! She's just a kid, for God's sake.'

Then I hear loud voices. Men. Security guards. They push the crowd back and bundle us over to the lifts. The doors close behind us and there's silence.

'We'll take you to the staffroom,' says one of the guards. 'Get you a cup of tea.'

'No,' says Mum. 'No. We just want to get out of here. Are you okay, Em?' She holds my face in her hands and studies it, her eyes dark with concern. I nod.

'You can't go through the store,' says the second guard. 'They'll 'ave you again. We'll take you to the loading bay.' He presses a button and the lift starts to descend. 'Did you come by car?'

'Yes.'

'If you give me your keys, I'll bring it round for you. Can you remember where you were parked?'

'Aisle C. By a trolley bay. It's a blue Toyota. Needs a good clean.'

The man nods and leaves us as soon as the lift opens. We wait by the loading bay doors. Men come in and out, pushing huge cages full of toothpaste and tinned peaches. Down here, the world seems very grey and ordinary. And there's nothing wrong with that.

Is this what fame is like? Hiding in basements because it's not safe to be seen in the store? I've never been so terrified in my life.

If this is fame, you can keep it.

# Chapter 15

4. 25 am. Almost Sunday morning. It's so quiet, I could be the only person left in the world. Right now, that wouldn't be a bad thing. At least no one would be around to see this hideous beard.

I can't sleep. I've been going over things in my head. The same thoughts, chasing each other round and round like rabbits. I don't understand how something can be a dream one day and a nightmare the next. It's like a fairy tale. You know those ones where someone is given a key and they start exploring a castle? I'm walking along a corridor with loads of doors on every side. Open one door and I'm in heaven. Open another and I'm in hell. The problem is, you don't know what you're going to find until you open the door, and by then it's too late.

There's one thing I *do* know. I've had enough. I don't care about the play any more. I just want my face back. I don't want to look in the mirror and see a troll. I want to see Little Emmy Travis from Green Street. Not perfect, but okay. Keeley will be furious. She'll say I'm letting the Hairy Marys down, but I don't care. I have to do what's best for me.

I tiptoe to the bathroom, quietly close the door and turn on the light. The waxing strips are still on the window ledge, where Mum left them. I take a clean flannel from the airing cupboard, fold it and put it in my mouth. I take a waxing strip out of the packet, warm it in my hands, press it against my beard and pull.

*RRRRRRRR!* I'm so glad I have the flannel to bite on. I don't want Mum to hear me. I use another strip and another. By the time I've finished, I'm as pink as a prawn, but I am so, so happy with the blotchy face I see in the mirror.

I cross my fingers and close my eyes. 'Please don't grow back,' I whisper. 'Please, please, please don't.'

I tiptoe back to bed, clamber in and soon I'm fast asleep. Life is good again.

But next morning.... well, you can guess the rest, can't you?

# Chapter 16

'You don't have to go, Em. Not today. I can ring the school. Tell them you're sick.'

Monday morning. I'm sitting at the breakfast table, stabbing my boiled egg with half-burnt soldiers. 'I want to,' I mumble. 'I need to talk to someone.'

Mum sighs. 'Well... I'm going to take you in the car. And I'll pick you up again, okay? No walking. Are you listening?' I nod. 'And if there's any trouble, you give me a ring.' I nod again.

~

I find Miss Bailey in the library, as usual. She's putting plastic covers onto new books.

'Hello Emmy,' she says. 'What brings you in here?' Then she smiles, and it's so warm and reassuring, I feel the tears brimming in my eyes. And before I know it, she has her arm around me and I'm telling her everything. The supermarket, the waxing – everything.

Miss Bailey finds me a tissue. 'I'm so sorry,' she says. 'Emmy, I had no idea you were suffering like this. The other girls are proud of their beards. I know I am. I don't think anyone has tried to get rid of one. Our beards are symbols of our commitment to the cause. A badge of courage, if you like! If we ever have any doubts, or the going gets tough, we look at our beards and remember what we're fighting for. They are a source of comfort, not despair.'

'You weren't in the supermarket,' I say.

'Actually I was. Not on Saturday - on Sunday. And yes, people were pointing and gathering around me. So I asked to see the manager, and she very kindly gave me a microphone and a box to stand on, and I made a speech. Right there, by the frozen chickens! I told people why I had the beard, what it meant, what I was fighting for. And when I finished, there was a great big cheer from the crowd and everyone wanted to shake my hand. It was a wonderful moment. Mrs Pankhurst would have been proud of me.'

There it was again – that name. 'Who *is* Mrs Pankhurst?'

'She was the leader of the Suffragettes, Emmy. Have you never heard of them?'

'Keeley mentioned them once.'

'Oh, Keeley knows all about the Suffragettes! Her mother's written a book about them.'

'Really?'

'Yes. It's a fine book. Very well researched.'

'So who were they?'

'They were a group of well-educated ladies who

wanted women to have the right to vote. *Votes for Women* - that was their big slogan. VOTES FOR WOMEN! They had it painted on all their banners. Women weren't able to vote in the past, you see. It was strictly men only. Mrs Pankhurst disagreed and founded the Suffragettes in 1903.'

'Did they chain themselves to fences?'

'Yes, they did. Did Keeley tell you that? They chained themselves to the gates of Buckingham Palace. They smashed windows, burned buildings, shouted at political meetings, threw stones, went on hunger strike... It was shocking behaviour for the time. *Very* unladylike!'

'Keeley said something about a horse?'

'Oh, that was a terrible incident.' Miss Bailey shakes her head and sighs. 'Do you know what the Derby is? It's a famous horse race. Very posh. All the top people in society go, including the Royal Family. Well, in 1913 the King was there because he had a horse in the race. The Suffragettes were there too, and during the race, one of them threw herself in front of the King's horse.'

'No!'

'Yes! Can you imagine that? It wasn't an accident. Someone said she shouted 'Votes for Women' before she did it.'

'Did she die?'

'Yes, she did. Not right away. Four days later. The horse was running at full speed... Bang, straight into her. She had dreadful injuries.'

'What about the horse? And the jockey?'

'The jockey did what they always do. He fell off, but rolled up into a ball and stayed there till everyone else had gone by. He had only cuts and bruises. The horse was fine too. It fell, but it got back up again and finished the race without the jockey! There should be a book in the social history section. Come on, we'll find it.'

I follow Miss Bailey across the library. 'Why does Carrie Ann know about the Suffragettes?' I ask. Which really means *why does she know when I don't?*

'Carrie Ann knows because she has been taught at home by her parents and they have done a wonderful job. In school, teachers have to teach certain things by law. But Carrie Ann has been taught so much more. She has extraordinary knowledge and great understanding of so many things. She's a delight to be with.'

Really? I had no idea. This must be why Keeley is spending more and more time with her instead of me. I'm boring compared to Carrie Ann.

I suddenly imagine Carrie Ann is here, being delightful. Miss Bailey is telling her something and Carrie Ann's head starts to swell. There's no more room in her brain. It's chock-a-block full of facts and figures. Her head grows bigger and bigger. It's the size of a football... a beach ball... a pumpkin. The world's biggest pumpkin! And still it gets bigger and bigger and bigger and BANG! Her head explodes. The whole room is spattered with pumpkin – globs of orange dropping from the shelves, the ceiling, the lights. I try walking, but bits of Carrie Ann squelch under my feet. I'm treading her into the carpet. Then I see something lying by the main desk. It's brown and furry, like a squashed rat. I pick it up. It's Carrie Ann's beard, wet with pumpkin juice.

'Here it is. *The Suffragette Movement*. Would you like to borrow it, Emmy?'

I nod and we head back to the main desk. 'I hope it inspires you,' says Miss Bailey. 'You know, it's a strange thing... Mrs Pankhurst's first name was Emmeline and the poor woman who threw herself in front of the horse was Emily Wilding Davison. So you're following in a proud tradition of protesting Emilys!'

'Not anymore. I've changed my mind. I won't be auditioning for the play.'

Miss Bailey stops so fast, I pile into the back of her. *'What?'*

'I don't want a part in the play. I don't want to be an actress anymore.'

'Because of what happened yesterday?'

'Yeah. If that's fame, I don't want it.'

Miss Bailey shakes her head. 'Well, if you give up so easily, you didn't want it in the first place.'

'I did want it! I've wanted to be an actress for years and years. It wasn't a dream or a game. I really wanted it. Friday at the studios was brilliant. The best day of my life. But yesterday was scary. Really scary. I don't want people mobbing me when I'm shopping. I don't want photographers following me down the street.'

Miss Bailey frowns. 'Hang on, Emmy,' she says. 'I think you're getting confused here. You're talking about acting and fame as if they're the same thing. They're not. There are thousands of actors who aren't famous. They're working people, doing a job they love, making a living. They probably won't be rich, but that's not important to them. They love performing. Travelling. Meeting other people. My cousin's an actor. He does theatre and radio. He's really good, but you wouldn't know him if he came in here now. So what did you want to be, Emmy? An actress – or just someone famous?'

I can't answer her. She sighs.

'You need to think carefully about this. If you don't know what you want in life, you will never, ever get it. And if you decide it's the *acting* that is important, not the fame and glamour, then you should audition for the play. Because once you're up there, on that stage, you will remember why you wanted it in the first place. And you will know whether you made the right decision.'

## Chapter 17

All morning, I try to find time to think about what Miss Bailey has said. Keeley loses patience with me at breaktime. She's trying to tell me something but I'm just not listening. So she gets all huffy and makes a point of eating with Carrie Ann at lunchtime. Just Carrie Ann.

I don't care. I buy a sandwich and take it to the corridor by the Drama Studio. It's always warm there. On my own at last, I can think about things.

I try to remember when I first wanted to act... It was two years ago. I was at my old school, there was another Christmas play – *Helen and the Helpful Reindeer* – and I was Helen. I had loads of lines and I was only nine. But I remembered them all and sang a song on my own. At the end of the show, when it was my turn to take a bow, the audience clapped and cheered like they'd never stop. Looking back now, I think they were just being kind, because Dad hadn't been gone long and Mum was sitting there on her own. It was our first Christmas without him. And I remember Mum crying afterwards and saying, 'Your dad would have been so proud of you, Em.'

That was when I decided I wanted to act. Half because it made me feel good and half because it seemed to make other people happy. It had nothing to do with fame or glamour or wanting to be a celebrity. I didn't even know what those things were back then.

So I decide: I *will* audition for the play. I *do* want a part. I want Mr Derren to see how good I am. He can give me any role and I will win over the audience.

As for the beard, I still don't like it but I will try to see it as a positive thing. A beard is a manly accessory – so I *should* have a man's part. Mr Derren can't argue with that. Without the beard, let's face it, I don't stand a chance. And it's strange how I can't get rid of it. It's almost like there's someone watching over me, wanting me to succeed. And look where I'm sitting now! Outside the Drama Studio – the exact place where the auditions will take place! That has to be a sign.

All this thinking makes me feel hungry again. I decide to go back to the dinner hall to buy a yoghurt or something. But as I get up off the floor, I don't look where I'm going and *DOOF!* I bang straight into Jack Lewis. His bag flies from his shoulder, falls to the ground and everything spills out.

'Oh, I'm sorry!' I say. 'Here, I'll help.'

'No!' says Jack, and he pushes me out of the way to get at his things. 'I'll do it.'

He scrabbles on the floor, shoving books, pens, money, all kinds of things back into his bag. But I can see a plastic bottle that's rolled away under a low table. I pull it out.

'*His-n-Hair?* What's this?'

'Give it here!' Jack leaps to his feet and lunges at me, but I turn my back and read the bottle. 'Is this to make your hair grow?'

Jack snatches it from me and throws it into his bag.

I don't understand for a moment. Jack has thick blond hair. Then I get it. 'You're trying to grow a *beard!*'

'No,' he says, but his eyes tell another story.

'You are!'

'I'm NOT!' He storms off down the corridor.

Would you believe it? Jack Lewis is jealous of the Hairy Marys! Jack Lewis is jealous of *me!* He wants a beard! He is spending his pocket money on silly potions in the wild hope he will grow one. Hah! I can grow a beard in two hours. Maybe I should tell him *that!*

~

My chance comes during afternoon break, the next day. I'm on my own, walking past the hall when I see Jack coming towards me. But he's not alone. Matthew Sharp is with him. I won't embarrass him in front of his best mate. That's mean.

Jack's eyes narrow as he nears me. He doesn't say anything and neither do I. We pass, and I can almost hear his sigh of relief as he walks on by. That makes me smile. But not for long. Because now Robbie Flynn is coming towards me, and you don't want *him* to think you're laughing at him. So I kill my smile, and that makes *him* smile – a real bully-boy smirk. And as he passes me, he goes: '*Brrrrrrrrrrrrrrrrrrrrrr.*'

It sounds *exactly* like my Dad's old motorbike. I stop dead. I can't breathe. What did he mean by that? *What did he mean by that? Ohh...!* He's heard. Someone's told him about my dad, dying on a bike. He knows. And now – *ohh!*

I don't know how I get to the next class. Don't know how I get to the end of the day. Is it the beard? Is that why he's noticed me, out of *all* the new Year 7s? Or would it have happened anyway?

Probably. It's the kind of story people repeat. It was never going to stay secret. There are too many here from my old school who knew me when it happened. And here's me, wanting to be special in a school full of Emilys. *Which Emily do you mean?* they'll say. *Oh – Clever Emily? Tall Emily? Emily with the Long Hair?* No. *Emily Whose Dad Died in a Motorbike Crash. Oh... that Emily.*

Do you sometimes wish you could turn back time? I'd go back to when Dad was still alive, then I'd smash up that flamin' motorbike before he got on it.

I don't think I'll ever stop wishing that.

# Chapter 18

Another day, another lesson. Science with Miss Carter.

Miss Carter looks like a model. She has gorgeous long blonde hair that tumbles over her shoulders and swings from side to side when she walks. It's like watching a shampoo commercial. She always wears lovely clothes and fabulous shoes. Today her shoes are grey suede with spiky heels. I can't wait till I can wear high heels. Mum won't let me wear them because she says I'm still growing. But I don't think I am. I'm second to shortest in the class. *That's* why I want heels.

Miss Carter starts talking about homework. 'Read pages nine to thirteen,' she says, 'then answer the questions on – *oh!*' She frowns and looks at the empty folder she's holding. 'I didn't do the photocopies at lunchtime.'

'Too busy flirting with Mr Jacobs,' whispers Keeley into my ear.

Miss Carter has really slipped up. She knows it, *we* know it, but maybe she can get away with it? She smiles at us and bites her lip like a little girl. Ooh, that's clever! We soften like ice cream on a warm afternoon.

'I'm sorry,' she says. 'I forgot. Emmy - could you

run to the Print Room for me?' She hands me a piece of paper. 'Thirty copies, please. Thanks.'

I walk slowly to the Print Room, glad to be out of class, trying to make the job last as long as possible. I lift the top of the photocopier, put the paper face down, key in '30' and press the big green button. The machine whirrs and the copies start shooting out. But then it stops. There's a flashing light and a message: *Insert paper into Tray 2.* It's showing a diagram of the machine too, with a big flashing arrow to show me exactly where Tray 2 is. I'm sure I can sort this out, if I can find more paper. *Where is it?* There's nothing by the machine except an empty box. I'll have to ask Mrs Dunn, the school administrator.

I go to her office. The door is open but she isn't there. I decide to wait. So I sit down on the sofa in the corridor, and then I hear voices. Loud voices, coming from Mrs Burton's room. The door isn't shut properly. I can easily hear them.

'Please, John, calm down,' says Mrs Burton, sounding flustered. 'I'm just asking you to think about it.'

'I *have* thought about it!' says the other voice. Mr Derren! 'Over and over again. And I don't see why this year should be any different. I'm in charge. It's up to me who gets what. I've done the Christmas play for six years, Judith. *Six years.* They've all been brilliant – everyone has said so – and do you know why? It's because I've kept it real. Boys in the male parts, girls in the female. What's wrong with that?'

'Nothing,' says Mrs Burton, 'but you have to agree, John, the best parts this year are all for boys.'

'Of course they are! It's the Christmas story, for heaven's sake.' I hear the scrape of a chair. I picture him on his feet now, pacing up and down like a gorilla in a cage. 'I'm only doing what's there in the Bible. Shepherds, Wise Men, innkeeper, Joseph, Herod – they're all male. Strictly speaking, the angels should be male too, but I'm letting a couple of girls have a go.'

'That's very generous of you,' says Mrs Burton evenly.

Mr Derren isn't listening. 'There's Mary and the innkeeper's wife. She's not in the Bible - I've added her specially. So there are parts for girls. Not as many as they would like, perhaps, but they *are* there.'

Mrs Burton gives a big sigh. 'I know they are. Don't get me wrong, John, I'm not criticising you. Every year you do a wonderful job. The Christmas play has become a highlight of the school calendar, for the children, parents, teachers, everyone. But this year it *is* different, whether you like it or not. First the newspapers, now the tv. The eyes of the world are watching us, John. Waiting to see what will happen.'

I hear heels tip-tapping down the corridor. Oh,

please don't let it be Mrs Dunn! I want to hear this out! Ah... it's Miss Harvey. She goes into a classroom. I listen again, but it's harder now. Mr Derren has calmed down and stopped shouting.

'Are you saying that I should give the lead parts to girls just to please the media?'

Mrs Burton doesn't reply.

'What is fair about that?' he exclaims. 'We should be true to ourselves, to the play, to the story. We shouldn't be making decisions just to look good on the evening news.'

'We don't want to look *bad* on the evening news,' says Mrs Burton. I can hear the worry in her voice. 'Please John, you must think of the school.'

'I *am* thinking of the school. And more importantly, I'm thinking of the boys. Do you know why I chose to do *The Baby in the Stable?* It's because we have so many good lads in school at the moment. There are a dozen *really* good actors, most of them in the top classes, and I wanted to give them a chance to shine. As many as I could, before they leave us.

'The girls don't need this opportunity, Judith. Not really. Girls shine all the time. Half of them do classes out of school - dancing, singing. They have their moments. But boys – no. It's only here, in school, in the Christmas play, that they'll suddenly feel confident enough to stand up in front of everyone and have a go. For some of those lads, it will be the only time they do it. *Ever*. For others – and I'm thinking of Joshua Maruru now – it could change their lives. Make them see that they could *be* something in this world, if only they used their talents.

'*That* is why I chose a play with plenty of good male roles - to give those boys a chance. And that, to me, is something far more important than keeping the newspapers and tv happy.'

Everything goes quiet. I keep quiet too, but it's a real struggle. What a speech from Mr Derren! I've never heard him talk like that. It was brilliant, like something in a movie. My heart is filling my chest. I feel like leaping to my feet and clapping. He's changed me. With just a few words, he's turned everything on its head and made me see things completely differently. I hadn't thought about the boys – not like that. Pinching the best parts from under their noses, yes. We've laughed about that: me, Keeley, Carrie Ann, all the Hairy Marys. We've always said it will be a triumph. We'll be WINNERS and we'll dance around the room. Now I'm not sure how I'll feel.

I think Mr Derren's words have touched Mrs Burton too. She doesn't say anything for ages. I hear more footsteps on the corridor. This time it really is Mrs Dunn. I cross my fingers, close my eyes and make a wish. *Let me hear Mrs Burton's reply*. I desperately want to hear it. Suddenly it seems the most important thing in the world.

When it finally comes, it's a question. 'Why didn't you say this to the press?' she says quietly. 'It would have made all the difference in the world.'

'Why should I?' Mr Derren replies. 'Why should I explain myself to people who don't even know me?'

Mrs Burton goes quiet again. 'I'm glad we've had this talk, John,' she says at last. 'You've given me a great deal to think about. But these girls with their beards...As Head of this school, I must *insist* you consider them for male parts. '

Now it's Mr Derren's turn to stay silent.

'John?'

'The best parts will go to the best people,' says Mr Derren finally. Then he sweeps out of the office, and he's so caught up in the emotion of it all, his dark eyes don't even see me – little Emmy Travis, hiding behind my beard.

# Chapter 19

That night, after tea, I don't watch much tv. Instead, I go to my room to think about things. I sit in my favourite place, on the window ledge, and gaze at the world outside. It may sound like an uncomfortable place to sit but it's not. The window ledge is low and very wide, so I can get both feet up. I put a pillow under my bottom and a blanket around my shoulders, make sure all the lights are switched off, and then I can watch all the comings and goings in the street below.

It's dark outside. The street lights are on, splashing golden pools of light onto the pavement. It's cold out there. Mr Nelson, our next door neighbour, comes by with his dog, Gracie. Mr Nelson has a woolly hat pulled down hard over his ears and his breath is hanging in front of him like a ghost. Gracie doesn't mind the cold. She's a golden retriever and has the softest, silkiest fur. I wish I could get my beard as smooth as her coat! Gracie's eyes are beautiful too. Warm and kind. Brown as buttons.

I'd love a dog like Gracie. Sometimes, on a Sunday, we have roast chicken for lunch. Mum always offers me the wish bone. We wrap our little fingers around it, close our eyes, make secret wishes and pull. I always wish for a dog like Gracie. It hasn't happened yet. I don't think it ever will, not until I'm grown up. Mum says we can't have a dog. They need walking, and who will do that, with me at school and her at work all day?

I want to think about what Mr Derren said. He's really unsettled me. I can't stop thinking about the boys now. Mr Derren was right, they don't shine very much. Matthew Sharp does. He can't help it, not with his face and that hair. And Jack Lewis does, because he works hard at it. But the rest of them just merge into one big blob of Boy.

They're like brown birds.

Last year, Mum and I went to Devon on our holidays. We stayed in a caravan, and every day we walked down a lane to the beach. There were hedges on either side and they were full of birds. One day, we sat on a bench halfway down and started to count all the different ones we could see. Some were easy: blackbirds and blue tits and robins. But the rest of them were just little brown birds. We could see they were a bit different to each other. Some were speckled. Some were plain. Some were shy and flicked their tails a lot. Some were bold and sang beautifully. But what I'm saying is this: we really had to sit and look carefully to see those things. If you gave a casual glance, all you would see is brown birds. The boys in school are like that.

All Mr Derren wants to do is to give them the chance to be robins or blackbirds, even if it's just for three nights. That's a lovely thing.

I remember what Jack Lewis said the other day: Mr Derren could get into real trouble over this whole affair. Maybe even lose his job. Would he let it go that far? I don't know. He's making a stand too, isn't he? He's standing up for what he believes is right, just like the Hairy Marys. Just like the Suffragettes. Maybe he would think losing his job was worth it, if it made people listen. Emily Wilding Davidson thought losing her *life* was worth it, to make people listen. *Oh…!* These people are so much braver than I will ever be.

A car pulls up at the house opposite. It's the Lenskas. Mr Lenska gets out first, opens the passenger door and helps Mrs Lenska out. She's having a baby soon and her belly is *enormous*. Perhaps she'll have it on Christmas Day? That would be so sweet. If it was a girl, they could call her Holly. Or Angel. Or Snow. Don't know what they'd call a boy. Joseph? No. *Star!* That would be a brilliant name.

Mr Lenska holds his wife's hand while she walks to the front door. It must be getting icy out there. When I was little, Dad used to sit here with me. I'd sit in his lap and he'd wrap the blanket around both of us. We'd look out at the street and he would make up funny stories about the people who walked by. And when it was cold, like tonight, he'd say: 'Look Em, the frost fairies are out.' Then he'd describe what they were doing. They'd be peeping in at windows, tip toeing across the roof tops, sliding down car bonnets, chasing each other up and down the street like squirrels. Wherever their feet touched the ground, they left a silver sprinkling of frost. They would dance in the glow of the street lamps, but they didn't cast shadows, they were so light. And no one could see them but us. Me and him, sitting cosy on the window ledge.

And I really *could* see them. They were bright and shining and real, because he made them real. And now I look into the street and so want to see them, but I can't. They've gone. Perhaps I'm too old now. Perhaps I wouldn't be able to see them even if Dad was still here. But he could *always* see them, so age must have nothing to do with it.

I wish I could still see them. I wish they were playing the street now, silver as starlight.

I wish you were here, Dad. It's cold on this window ledge without you.

## Chapter 20

Days go by. There's no more excitement for the Hairy Marys. No interviews or tv. We're just waiting for the auditions. The boys haven't managed to grow beards, despite their potions and prayers. Ours are getting longer by the day, but they're boring now. Mine gets itchy sometimes. I don't like that. And I don't like it when bits of dinner get stuck to it. Soup is the worst. No matter how careful I am, there are always drips clinging to my whiskers when I'm finished.

*Whiskers.* What a strange word to use. Cats have whiskers. There must be a better word for the hairs that are sprouting from my chin. *Bristles?* No, that makes me sound like a paintbrush. *Stubble?* No. Stubble is short and my beard is long now – 12cm from chin to tip. And stubble sounds hard. My hairs are quite soft. A bit wiry, perhaps, but definitely not hard and scratchy.

Keeley has a beautiful beard. It's conker brown and softer than a Persian cat. She says she brushes it a hundred times before she goes to bed every night and uses loads of hair conditioner when she washes it.

The Khan twins use almond oil on their beards. Miss Bailey told me. Their beards are The Best.

They are long and shiny and perfectly straight, like horses' manes, and such a deep midnight black, they look almost purple.

Carrie Ann's beard was very tight and curly when it first started growing. Now it's longer, it hangs in shiny brown ringlets. It's very pretty. And one Monday morning, she surprises us all by coming to school with bright coloured braids in it.

'I went to a festival over the weekend,' she says. 'I was going to have some braids put in my hair and then I thought *no* – I'll have them in my beard!'

I am so jealous. They look lovely. There's a pink, a red, a green and a blue. And I look at her and think *You didn't really need them. Your beard was pretty to begin with. But mine .... well...* Oh, this has got me thinking! Keeley is excited too, I can tell. She fingers Carrie Ann's braids, saying nothing, but I know she's plotting something.

And sure enough, when Keeley comes to school the next day, she has threaded beads onto the tips of her beard. Shiny red beads, like holly berries. She is massively proud of them. But she can't outdo me, because I have plaited ribbons into mine. Pink and blue ribbons, finishing in a row of tiny bows at the bottom. I look like a shire horse.

Caitlin Morrow must have been inspired by Carrie Ann too, because she turns up with her beard woven into twenty tiny plaits with sequins glued on.

But this is nothing compared to Lily Chung. She has the longest beard. It isn't very thick, and it only sprouts from her chin, not along the jaw line like the rest of us. But today, she has parted it into two plaits, and the plaits are pinned up on top of her head with diamond hairgrips! She looks amazing.

When Miss Bailey sees our creative efforts, her eyes nearly fall out of her head. Miss Bailey, you may remember, loves all kinds of accessories and has a huge red beard, as thick as a holly hedge.

'Why on earth didn't I think of doing something?' she cries. 'All this time gone by... I could have been having such fun.' Her eyes start flicking like a fruit machine as ideas zing round inside her head. We can't wait to see what she looks like tomorrow.

She doesn't disappoint us. When we next see her, she has six stuffed birds tucked away in her beard. They have real feathers and little glass eyes.

'I was inspired by the limerick by Edward Lear,' she tells us. 'I'm sure you know it:

*There was an old man with a beard*
*Who said: 'It is just as I feared*
*Two owls and a hen,*
*Four larks and a wren*
*Have all built their nests in my beard.'*

This is just the beginning for Miss Bailey. As

the days go by, her creativity blossoms bigtime. Ribbons, bows, shells, sequins, lace, buttons, jewels, silk flowers – they all get woven in or stuck on. Some days she dusts her beard with glitter. Some days she sprays it with temporary hair colour – red, green, blue or fluorescent pink. One day she keeps the natural foxy red colour but adds black and a touch of white so she looks like a Bengal tiger – it's absolutely brilliant!

But my favourite moment comes one day when she's looking quite ordinary. She has a simple green ribbon tying the tips together, so the rest of the beard is billowing above it. I'm making some notes but my pen runs out. I ask if I can borrow one, and she reaches *inside her beard* and pulls one out.

I can't believe what I've just seen. 'Have you got anything else in there?' I ask.

Miss Bailey nods and pulls out a pencil, a plastic ruler, scissors, two toffees and a pair of reading glasses. And all the while, she's acting like it's the most natural thing in the world.

All the Hairy Marys love Miss Bailey to bits. She's so warm and funny and kind, and very entertaining. She gives us something to look forward to every day. She always makes us smile. And the days keep slipping by, almost without us noticing, until one day we realise something.

The auditions are tomorrow.

# Chapter 21

Where is Keeley? I stare at her empty seat as Mr Morris, our class teacher, takes the morning register. She can't be sick today. She can't! Not *today.*

I put my hand up when Mr Morris has finished.

'Yes, Emmy?'

'Please, Mr Morris, do you know where Keeley is?'

Mr Morris frowns, though it's hard to tell. He's really old. His face has more lines than a road map. He thinks I'm being nosy. Keeley's location is really none of my business. Then his face softens and he smiles.

'Ah, it's a big day for the Hairy Marys, is it not? I understand your concern now.' He reaches inside the register and pulls out a sheet of paper. 'There is a note here. Keeley's mother rang this morning. Keeley is unwell today.'

Unwell? How unwell? I glance across at Carrie Ann and know she's thinking the same thing. Keeley would drag herself out of a hospital bed to be at the auditions. There must be something really, really wrong.

We don't get a chance to talk until morning break. As soon as the bell goes, we hurry outside.

'Did you speak to her last night?'

Carrie Ann shakes her head. 'No. I called her mobile but it was taking messages. I left one, but she didn't call back.'

'Do you have your phone with you? Yes! Let's go.'

I don't need to say anything more. She knows where we're going. We're not supposed to use our phones in school, but everyone does, and the best place to do it is behind the recycling shed.

Carrie Ann dials, listens and pulls a face. 'Answer phone.' She leaves a message, asking Keeley to text her.

'Was that her home? Try her mobile.'

Carrie Ann dials again. 'Oh, this is taking messages too! Where on earth can she be?'

'She might be at home but in bed,' I say. 'If she really is sick, she will be resting, so she can come in tonight for the auditions.'

Carrie Ann isn't convinced. 'Why would the answer phone be on? Why isn't her mum answering? *She's* not sick. She phoned the school this morning.'

That's true. I have no idea what's going on. I can only hope Keeley makes contact soon. But she doesn't. Lunchtime comes, afternoon break, and there are no messages on Carrie Ann's phone. It's a complete mystery.

We check one last time after school. Nothing.

'I really think there's been an accident,' I say, not

for the first time. 'What other explanation is there?'

'I don't know,' says Carrie Ann. 'Whatever it is, it's just the *worst* luck in the world. She's waited for weeks and wants it so bad. To be sick on the day it really matters... How rotten is that?'

'What time is your audition?'

'4.00. I must be one of the first.'

I nod. 'Mine's not till 6.30. Do you mind if I go home?'

Carrie Ann grins. 'Of course not! I don't expect you to hang around and hold my hand!'

'Okay. You don't need to do it for me, either. I'll just see you tomorrow, yeah?'

'Yeah.' She gives me a double thumbs-up. 'Good luck.'

'You too.'

I think we're both going to need it.

## Chapter 22

Well, this is it. I'm standing outside the Drama Studio with six other people. I've learned my speech and combed my beard. There's nothing more I can do.

The studio door opens. Miss James comes out. 'Mark Hughes?'

A tall boy with sticky-out ears stands up and goes with her. I look at the list on the wall for the twentieth time. He was two places ahead of me. One more then it's my turn.

I feel my throat going dry and start fishing in my bag for a cough sweet. I'm so busy looking, I don't see Keeley arrive. But suddenly she says my name, I turn – and my jaw drops.

*'Where's your beard?!'*

Her chin is as smooth as a baby's bo-bo.

Keeley grins and grabs me by the hands. 'I so wanted to tell you,' she says, 'but I couldn't. Not till it was over.'

'Till *what* was over? Where have you been? We've been calling you, over and over.'

'I've been in London,' she says. 'I've had an audition!' She pulls me down onto a seat. 'Last night, I got home from school and Mum was *really* excited. There'd been a phone call from London

– from a top movie agent! She'd seen me on the *Adam and Alice Show* and – '

'That was ages ago.'

'I know! But she'd remembered me all that time. Anyway, she was looking for a girl to play the lead in a movie and thought I would be perfect. Would I like to audition? Oh, now let me think... Would I? YEAH! There was just one problem. The beard.'

'David Turner?'

David follows Miss James into the Drama Studio. I'm next.

'I didn't want to lose it,' Keeley goes on. 'I'd given it so much time and effort, and it was just starting to look right. But it had to go. So I shaved it off last night and went for the audition this morning.'

'Was it scary?'

'Oh yes. A lot scarier than this.' She waves her hand dismissively and I can't help feeling annoyed. Okay, this isn't exactly Hollywood but it still means something to me. 'We went to London last night. Mum and Dad both took time off work – how mad is that? We drove down and stayed in a gorgeous hotel. It had a swimming pool and a rooftop restaurant.'

I grab hold of her arm and shake it, wanting her to shut up about the hotel. 'What about the audition? When will you hear?'

'I have heard. They phoned half an hour ago. I didn't get the part.'

I stare at her. I don't know what to say. She seems so cheerful. I think how hard it's been to live with my beard. All the pain and trouble. If I had shaved it off then found out I'd done it for nothing, I would be a complete mess. 'How can you be so calm about it?' I say. 'Don't you care?'

'Of course I do! Especially now I'm standing here, seeing everyone going in. I'm still going to audition, though.'

'You won't be a Wise Man. Not without the beard. No way.'

Keeley smiles ruefully. 'I know. It's weird not having it, Em. I feel quite naked! But I still have my secret weapon.'

She winks but I have no idea what she means.

'My voice!' she says, laughing at my blank face. 'The voice of an angel.' She flutters her eyelashes.

'Emmy Travis?'

My hearts jumps in my chest. Suddenly I have a mouthful of feathers and can't remember a single word of my speech.

Miss James is holding the door open for me. Looking past her, I see Mr Derren sitting at a table.

'Are you all right, Emmy?' Miss James asks.

I nod and manage a smile.

Keeley takes hold of my hand and gives it a squeeze. 'Knock ,em dead, girl.'

I take a deep breath to steady my nerves. Kiss the tip of my beard for luck. Slip past Miss James into the

Drama Studio and she shuts the door behind me.

There's no turning back now.

~

That night, lying in bed, I go over and over the audition in my head. Mr Derren was a little cold but not unfriendly. He asked what part I wanted, then grunted when I said Joseph. He asked me to do the piece I had prepared. I remembered my words and delivered them as well as I could. He thanked me. Miss James said, 'Well done, Emmy,' and I started to go. But just as I reached the door, Mr Derren said something I really didn't expect to hear.

'I admire your determination, Emmy, and your courage. It can't have been easy for you at times. Whatever the outcome tomorrow, I want you to know that.'

Can you believe that? Deadly Derren being nice to me? I was well pleased!

# Chapter 23

Next morning, when I arrive at school, I see two tv news vans parked outside. The parts have been announced! The film crews are already inside, filming by the big notice board in the entrance hall. Of course, they go mad when they see me – a Hairy Mary. They start pushing people out the way, trying to get a good shot of my face as I read that all-important cast list.

I scan down the list of characters. Narrator... Angel Gabriel... Innkeeper... Innkeeper's Wife... Mary... *Joseph!* I run my finger along the line.... Carrie Ann Marsh. *Carrie Ann? Carrie Ann is Joseph?* No! It can't be. It *can't.* I stare at her name, almost forgetting to breathe. Then I start to panic. Forget Joseph - did I get any part at all?

I run my finger down the list of names. Daniel Pardoe... William Day... Desmond Nkosi... Rosie McDonald... Rachel Carver... Carrie Ann Marsh... Anuja Khan... *Emily Travis!* Thank heavens for that. Who am I? *Balthasar.* Is he one of the Three Wise Men? He is! He's one of the Three Wise Men! I've done it! I've won one of the lead male roles!

Someone squeals behind me. It's Carrie Ann. She's just seen she's Joseph.

'I can't believe it!' she cries. 'I can't believe it!' She

grabs hold of me and we squeal together. Jump up and down. Throw ourselves into one of those mad mimes footballers do when they score a goal.

'It's amazing,' I gasp. 'Just fab.'

'What about Keeley?' says Carrie Ann suddenly. 'Did she get anything?'

There's quite a crowd around the board now, but I manage to wriggle through and scan the list. 'Angel 1,' I grunt as I elbow my way back out again. 'I think she'll be pleased with that.'

'Did any more girls get boys' parts?'

'I couldn't see. We need to come back later, when everyone's gone. Then we can really study it. See who got what.'

'Good idea,' says Carrie Ann. 'Let's just celebrate now. Champagne?'

'Of course!'

'Girls! Girls!'

We can't go anywhere. Not till we've spoken to the tv people. They won't let us pass. They want to hear the story of the Hairy Marys again, right from the beginning. That takes so long, the bell rings before Carrie Ann and I can have our champagne. We have to wait till morning break.

We stand by the drinks machine with two cans of cream soda in our hands. Okay, it's not champagne, but it's sweet and fizzy, and that is good enough for us.

'To us!' says Carrie Ann. 'The best bearded ladies

ever to stand on a stage.'

'To us! A Joseph and Balthasar to remember!'

We take long swigs. Ooh, it's cold!

'It's a shame Keeley can't be here with us,' I say. 'What a day to go to the dentist.'

Carrie Ann nods. 'That girl has terrible timing.'

We start to giggle.

'I knew it would good news when I saw the cameras,' says Carrie Ann.

'Why?'

'Well, think about it. Mrs Burton wouldn't have let them in if it was bad news for us. There could have been a riot or anything.'

'We could have chained ourselves to Mr Derren in protest!'

Carrie Ann shudders. 'I don't think so, Em. You have to draw a line somewhere.'

We take another long swig of our soda and Carrie Ann burps.

'That wasn't very lady-like,' I laugh.

'Neither is this!' she replies and tugs her beard playfully. She raises her can. 'To the Hairy Marys,' she says, quietly now. 'We did it, Em.'

We grin at each other, clink our cans and drink again. And we're so hot with excitement and pride, we hear the cold soda hissing on our tongues.

~

Later on, when everyone has gone, Carrie Ann and I return to the notice board to have a good look at the cast list. Only four girls have been given important male roles. Besides Carrie Ann and me, there's Caitlin Morrow – she's won the part of Benjamin, one of the shepherds – and Anuja Khan. Like me, she is one of the Three Wise Men. My heart sinks when I see who the third is. It's Jack Lewis. I can't believe it. I'm going to have to face him at every rehearsal and share the stage with him every night.

Mr Derren has been pretty fair. If you count Mary and the innkeeper's wife, girls have six speaking roles and boys have nine. As for the angels, there are eight girls and only two boys, but that's hardly a surprise. I can't see many lads willing to wear their mum's nightie and sing 'Hallelujah.' Not with their mates grinning on the front row.

Keeley, on the other hand, will adore being an angel. She'll have a dazzling snow-white costume, her hair will be curled and dusted with silver glitter, and she'll have the best wings this side of heaven. She will! Just you wait and see.

# Chapter 24

In all the excitement of yesterday, I suddenly realise I haven't asked Keeley an incredibly important question. How did she get rid of her beard? I only remember when I see Shannon Jenkins without hers. And she's not the only one. Today, all the Hairy Marys who didn't get parts have come to school without their beards. Miss Bailey is bare-faced too. How is that possible?

'I shaved it off,' says Keeley when I ask her.

'And it didn't grow back?'

'No.' She's frowning at me like she really doesn't understand why I'm asking. 'It wasn't hard. Just a bit of shaving foam and a razor.'

I ask Chelsey Wintour and Gwen Davies, Shailja Khan and Isabel Fletcher. They all say the same.

'I don't understand,' I say at lunchtime. We're sitting in the dinner hall, just like we were when all this started. 'I tried to get rid of my beard twice but it grew back both times, and waxing is supposed to be better than shaving. I don't see what's so special about a razor.'

'It's metal,' says Carrie Ann. I wait for her to say something more but she doesn't. She just slips a spoonful of strawberry yoghurt into her mouth.

'So?'

'Metal works against magic,' she says. 'I thought everyone knew that.'

Keeley and I shake our heads. She's forgetting she has been taught differently to us.

'It's nothing secret,' says Carrie Ann. 'If you study the folklore of Britain, you'll find it mentioned all the time. It's meant to be especially good at protecting you from witches and evil spells. That's why people used to nail horseshoes onto their front doors.'

I take hold of my beard. 'Are you saying this is magic?'

'Well it's not natural, is it?'

Magic. Wow. I've often wondered how the beards came to be, but believe it or not, I've never considered magic. When the newspapers first told our story, there were endless theories, from food additives to something dodgy in the school water supply. Someone even said it was alien light beams, shooting down from the sky and zapping us in our beds. But now I start to wonder... Could it be magic? Is there a witch, somewhere in school? Someone who's been listening to our thoughts and conversations, casting spells, making magic? Who could it be?

I scan the room. Mrs Broomfield, the head of Year 8? She's old and beady-eyed. Wrinkly like she's sat too long in a bath. It could be her? No! Miss Carter! It has to be. She's a science teacher, so she's always mixing up potions.

But she's too pretty to be a witch. Unless that's another one of her spells? Maybe she's a hideous old woman at other times?

Miss Carter lives in Toll House Cottage, out on the edge of town. I've seen it. It's a lovely place, shaped like a hexagon, with roses growing round the door. But maybe that's an illusion. Maybe it's only a shell of a house, with a leaking roof and broken windows and a foul pit inside. And as soon as she gets home at night, she sheds her pretty skin – peels it off like a banana – and underneath she's wet and warty. She slithers into her pit and wallows all night long in a bath of bats' blood and farmyard muck. Then in the morning, she clambers out, dries her loathsome body with a moleskin towel, dusts herself with graveyard dirt, slips back into her skin and comes into school.

But how would she have heard our conversation? She never comes to this end of the hall. She always sits at the teachers' table, flirting with Mr Jacobs. He drives a silver sports car and has a gold filling in one of his teeth. Ha! She wouldn't be able to kiss him, would she? Gold is metal. No. It can't be her.

Oh - I know who it is! She's coming towards us right now. She's in disguise. A blue and white checked overall with thin bare legs poking out of the bottom. White socks and chunky trainers. A white cap stuck onto an explosion of grey hair. *Mrs*

*Starling.* You see? Even her name is witchy.

'Y'all right here, girls?' she says, wiping the table with a greasy cloth.

Keeley nods. 'The pizza was gorgeous today. Can you tell the cook I said so?'

'Yes, me duck,' says Mrs Starling. 'It'll make her day.' She moves on to the next table.

'Do you think it was her?' I hiss. 'Do you think she's a witch?'

Keeley hoots with laughter. 'No, you mushroom! It wasn't her. She's just a dinner lady.'

'Then who did it? Who made the beards grow?' We both turn to Carrie Ann. She's the only one who might know.

'I'm not sure,' she says. 'I've thought about it a lot. I don't think it's the work of a witch – not even a good one. Because there *are* good witches, you know. My mum knows quite a few. I thought Miss Bailey might be one for a while. But now I think it might be the work of an earth spirit. Some people say there are friendly spirits around us all the time. We can't see them, but they're busy all day long. They help vegetables to grow. Help babies to open their eyes for the first time. And they'll help us, if we want them to.'

'Are they fairies?' I ask.

'Some people might call them that. Others would call them angels.'

'I don't see why they would want to help us,'

argues Keeley. 'I mean, getting a part in a school play isn't that important, is it? It's not a matter of life and death.'

'No,' Carrie Ann agrees. 'But fairies have always been fond of making mischief.'

Keeley isn't convinced. 'I don't believe in fairies,' she says, 'but I do believe in the power of the mind. I think if you *really* want something, with all your heart and soul, you can make it come true.'

'There's a saying, isn't there?' I put in. '*Be careful what you wish for because you might just get it.*'

We fall quiet, thinking our own private thoughts.

'I don't think we'll ever know how it happened,' says Keeley eventually. 'It just did.'

'*There are more things in heaven and earth than are dreamed of in your philosophy*,' muses Carrie Ann.

We look at her, blank faced. 'It's Shakespeare,' she says. 'From *Hamlet*.'

We nod, like we knew it already. But we didn't. Oh, it must be brilliant to know as much as Carrie Ann!

# Chapter 25

Later that night, I'm sitting in my bedroom, on the window ledge. I'm thinking back over the day, and that conversation in the cafeteria when I suddenly have a shocking thought.

*I can get rid of my beard.*

I can go to the shops tomorrow, buy a razor, get rid of my beard and it won't grow back.

There will be no more tears. No more wailing into the mirror when I see myself looking like a pirate. No more attacks in supermarkets. I'll be normal again.

But I'll lose my part in the play.

You see why I'm shocked now? Rehearsals begin tomorrow. I can't believe I haven't thought of this already. So what do I do? What is more important? Being normal or being special? Being an actress or being me? Can't I be both? Not at the moment, it seems. I can have the fun of the rehearsals and the wild excitement of the shows if I am prepared to be weird and ugly offstage. Or I can be free again. Free to walk down the street without people pointing. Free to be quietly unremarkable, unnoticed by the likes of Robbie Flynn – if I am prepared to see someone else on stage in *my* role, getting the applause.

I have been so strong in all this... I know, that's sounds wrong, after all the crying fits and the moments when I've felt as lost as a baby bird. But I am still here. I have survived. I *have* been strong, even if I haven't felt it. And I have carried the dream. Held on tight to that shining image of me standing on the stage, beneath the bright lights, bursting with happiness. I won the part of Balthasar fairly. I auditioned along with everyone else. Mr Derren would *never* have given it to me just to keep Mrs Burton happy. He thought I deserved it. And he said, didn't he, at the audition, that he admired my courage and determination?

It hasn't been easy for me. I've been up and down like a rollercoaster. But tomorrow I could leave this wild ride. Shave off the beard and it will all be over.

All of it.

# Chapter 26

So it's here. Today rehearsals for *The Baby in the Stable* begin. All morning my head is spinning like a tumble dryer, but I don't tell anyone. At lunchtime, Keeley announces we're going to the shops. Huh? It's cold and snowy. But that's exactly why she wants to go. She wants a lip salve.

And so we go into the exact shop that sells razors. I'm standing next to a whole display of them while Keeley chooses between mint and strawberry. How freaky is this? I could buy a razor right now, go home, shave the beard off and still be back in time for the afternoon bell.

'Sorted!' says Keeley. She links my arm and whisks me out of the shop. I didn't even see her pay, but she's carrying a paper bag.

The afternoon passes. Carrie Ann smiles as we leave the last classroom.

'Ready?'

My silence speaks for me. Her smile fades. 'Are you okay, Em? She says. 'You've been quiet all day.'

'Just tired,' I lie.

We start walking to the Drama Studio. I'm fighting the urge to run away. I don't know what to do. If I'm going to pull out of the show, I need to tell Mr Derren right away, before he even starts the rehearsal. But he will be *so* angry. He'll make some comment about weak-hearted girls, and say he should never have trusted me with a part.

I will be letting down the Hairy Marys. I can imagine the look of disappointment on Carrie Ann's face...

And I've been looking forward to today so much. I'm proud to be in the cast. I'm going to be working with Jack Lewis and a whole load of Year 8s and 9s, and that's scary. But exciting too. I can feel my heart thumping in my chest. I don't think I have ever felt so alive.

'Come on in, girls! It's lovely to have you here.'

It's Miss James. Warm, kind Miss James, who will be helping Mr Derren.

'I'm so glad you got the parts,' she whispers. 'Well done you!' And she winks.

Carrie Ann gets hold of my sleeve and leads me like a toddler to a free seat. She's frowning, and still I don't feel I can tell her what's wrong. How bad is that? When you can't share your problems with one of your best friends?

Mr Derren strides to the front of the group and pauses. He looks at every one of us in turn. He's in no hurry. Then his face breaks into a broad, hairy smile. He opens his arms wide, takes a deep breath and begins.

'Welcome to you all,' he says. 'We've made a long and difficult journey to be here today. But that's the past. Now we need to look to the future. You're here because you're the best. That's what I believe, and I know you'll prove me right on the night.

Everyone expects great things from the Christmas play. Parents, governors, staff, students – they all sit there, waiting to be impressed. And I don't need to tell you, this year the pressure is really going to be on us.

But we can do it. There's going to be a lot of hard work ahead. Hours of rehearsals for those on stage. Hours of sewing and painting for those behind it. But there will also be laughter and excitement. New friends will be found. Memories will be made. And in the years to come, when the photographs have faded, people will still remember us and say: 'I was there, I saw the show and it was wonderful.' Because it *will* be wonderful. We shall make it so. You and me together. A team, stronger than steel.'

He pauses, and I feel like leaping to my feet and crying: 'GO ON! GO ON!' I am completely overwhelmed by his words, his energy, his passion. All my doubts have been washed away by the tsunami of his vision. And I know I'm not alone in this feeling. The air seems charged, tingling. We're hanging on his words like washing on a line. Then his eyes narrow and his voice deepens.

'But I'm warning you now. Never forget who the boss is here. And I am telling you this: any bad thoughts, any differences you have between you

- leave them outside that door. I will not tolerate them in here. If I hear *anyone* making comments about boys versus girls, I will throw you out so fast your backside won't touch the ground. And that goes for me too. I know I've said and done things in the past, but that is where they must stay now - in the past.

So, what do you say? Are you with me? Do you want to make this play the best St Mary's has ever seen?'

There's a lot of muttering and everyone is nodding, but that's not good enough for Mr Derren. He fills his lungs and bellows like a bull: 'ARE YOU WITH ME?'

'YES!'

'ARE YOU WITH ME?'

'YES!'

We shout so loud, they must hear us in the High Street. Terrified pigeons fly from the rooftops. Ice breaks on the windows. The caretaker gets such a fright, he drops a metal bucket on his foot and swears so loudly, he should get detention. It's a brilliant moment. I grab hold of Carrie Ann and squeeze her and she squeezes me back. Oh, to think I nearly pulled out of this!

# Chapter 27

Mr Derren is right. Being in the play is hard work. He calls endless rehearsals. Makes us do things over and over again. Sometimes I get so tired, I crawl into bed as soon as I get home. But it's never boring. It's thrilling, amazing, fascinating – all because of Mr Derren.

He is so good. So clever. We all think we know the story of the Nativity, but we don't. Not really. He pulls it apart. Makes us look at it from every possible angle. Suddenly, we see it through Joseph's eyes, through Mary's eyes – through *everyone's* eyes, even down to the donkey in the stable! He makes us really think about our characters. Who are we? Why are we doing these things? Why are we saying what we're saying? How do we feel about the things that are happening around us?

He makes us look at the way we're moving. He reminds Jack, Anuja and I that the Three Wise Men have been riding on camels for days on end, so they wouldn't bounce into Herod's palace like five year olds at a birthday party. They would be creaky and tired. Mary is being played by Rachel Carver, and he makes her wear a 'baby bag.' It's a cotton sack filled with three kilos of potatoes. She ties it on with ribbons and it completely changes the way she walks. It gives her a pain and, without thinking, she starts rubbing her back, trying to ease it.

'Rachel!' he cries. 'Notice what you're doing. Remember it. Use it.' And she does. Even when she stops wearing the sack, she rubs her back when she's waiting for Joseph to find them a room for the night and it looks great. So real.

Suddenly this dry old story is dazzling new. It's like Aladdin's lamp. We've polished off the dust and *abracadabra!* It's shining again and there's magic in the air. Real theatrical magic. I feel so lucky to be a part of it.

Mr Derren is right about the other things too – finding new friends and making memories. I'm not seeing much of Keeley because the angels aren't rehearsing with us. They are working with Mrs O'Neill, the music teacher. Keeley starts hanging around with Sarah Matthews, one of the other angels. One day, Caitlin tells me Sarah has supper at Keeley's most nights so they can go over the songs together. And it's strange – I don't mind. If that had happened at the start of term, I would have been deeply upset. But now, I feel nothing when Caitlin tells me. Because I have Carrie Ann. She's been at nearly all my rehearsals and we've become best friends. Simple as that.

Things are much better with Jack Lewis. He's very funny when he wants to be, which is most of the time. And I really like Anuja Khan. I used to think she was snooty. I'd see her with her twin, Shailja, and they always seemed far away, in a world of their own, like ours wasn't good enough for them. I didn't like that. But I was wrong. Anuja told me they couldn't speak English when they came to this country, and that's why they stayed together all the time. They felt safer. Now it's just a habit, and they both wish they could break it. But they're such fun when they're together. They have a wicked sense of humour.

I also know Joshua Maruru now. You remember he was the boy Mr Derren talked about when he had the argument with Mrs Burton? Josh has a bad reputation. He broke fifteen windows when he was in Year 7, set fire to the bike shed in Year 8 and deliberately caused an explosion in the Science Lab in Year 9. He's in Year 11 now and has calmed down a bit, but he's still mouthy to the teachers – except Mr Derren. Josh shows him nothing but respect. Jack and the other boys are the same. Mr Derren is firm with them. He won't stand for any talking or messing around when he's working. But he's fair, and the boys seem to like that.

Mr Derren has given Josh the role of King Herod, the hardest part. Do you know his bit of the story? The Three Wise Men are following a star, hoping to find a new king who has been born. Along the way, they stop at King Herod's palace. Herod is furious when he hears there's another king somewhere, but he doesn't show it. He asks the Wise Men to call again on their way home, to tell him exactly where this special baby can be found. Secretly he plans to have baby Jesus killed. But the Wise Men are warned by an angel not to tell him, so they travel home by another road. When Herod finds this out, he flies into a rage and orders his soldiers to kill all the newborn babies for miles around. It's horrible.

When Josh does that scene, it's terrifying. He's worked really hard with Mr Derren to show a whole range of emotions. He's not a monster. He's just a man who's out of control. It's very clever.

Josh is someone I would never, ever have known if it wasn't for the play. I'd have been too scared even to look at him, to tell you the truth. But now I'm working with him, I'm seeing a different Josh. He's actually quite shy and thoughtful. Very intelligent and hugely talented. He says he wants to go to Drama College. He's working hard to improve his reading because he'll have to read scripts out loud in front of other actors.

Blimey, I suppose I'll have to do that too, when I'm an actress. I'll have to practise!

# Chapter 28

It's the big day! The show opens tonight! I'm so excited, the morning flies by and then it's lunchtime, and I'm standing in the queue wondering what on earth I should eat. My stomach feels full of frogs. There's no room for food.

'You should have something, me duck,' says Mrs Starling. 'You'll need energy tonight. It's better you eat now than later. Give your tummy time to settle.'

She's right, I suppose. But the chips look dry and the smell of the pasta sauce is making me feel queasy.

I move along and study the puddings. The custard looks good. Hot and creamy with a thick skin on top. What is there to go with it? Rhubarb crumble. *Hmm...* I'm not sure about that. But then the boy in front of me asks for it and, when I see it in the bowl, my mind is made up. It's a lovely, warm, comforting swirl of pink and yellow.

Carrie Ann and I eat together, but we don't say much. We're saving our voices for tonight. Before we know it, lunch is over and we're back in lessons. But I still can't concentrate. And by two o'clock I have something else to worry about. I'm starting to feel sick.

First I notice the heat. I seem to have a fire inside me. I put my hands on my cheeks and feel them glowing. I take off my cardigan and open my top two shirt buttons. Look around the room. Is anyone else feeling this? No. They're all listening to Mr Scott. He's telling them about the Fire of London. How it began in a shop in Pudding Lane. Who cares? *I'm* generating more heat than Pudding Lane. You could fry pancakes on my face. Put a potato in my mouth and it would come out baked.

I look at the clock. 2.10. Break is at 2.20. If I can just hang on till then.... But I don't know if I can. My stomach is churning. I have sweat coming out on my forehead. My hands are so clammy, I can't hold my pen. I wipe them on my skirt. 2.15. Will this flippin' lesson never end? I don't care about Samuel Pepys. I don't care about the Great Plague. You want to see sickness, Mr Scott? It's over here. I may look like a girl, but I'm not. I'm a hot, bubbling volcano and I'm going to blow.

2.20. The bell rings and I'm out of the door like a greyhound, hand over my mouth. But running is making me worse. My mouth is dripping wet – I'm going to throw. Down the corridor, round the corner. GET OUT OF MY WAY! I don't say it. I can't say it. I just scream it in my head. I wave my free arm, clearing a path. Down the stairs, into the toilets, into a cubicle *HUURGH!* My whole stomach heaves. Great waves of vomit rattle into the toilet bowl. They splatter the seat, the floor, my shoes. My eyes are pouring. My nose is pouring. I have sick clinging to my beard. The smell makes me throw again. The toilet is a riot of pink and yellow. Lumpy custard. Stringy rhubarb. It looks no different to when I ate it. My stomach has done nothing to digest it. It's just been lying there, festering in the dark of my belly, waiting for this moment. This hideous, stinky, mess of a moment.

I'm swaying on my feet now. The blood has rushed to my head. I think I'm going to faint. I hold onto the toilet seat and pray I don't. The feeling passes. I become aware of voices behind me. There are people crowding round, hoping for a look. Why? Who would want to see this?

'Leave her! Go on! Leave her! There's nothing to see. She's been sick, that's all.'

Carrie Ann. She must have followed me. I have never been so happy to hear her voice. I could cry. Perhaps I am crying. My face is so wet, it's hard to tell.

'Go on – out! Now! She doesn't want to see anyone. Out!'

I hear footsteps, moving away. A door closes. Carrie Ann has made them all go away.

'Em? Are you okay?' I feel gentle hands on my shoulders. Carrie Ann helps me to my feet. 'Here. Wash your face. You'll feel better.'

She fills a basin with water. I wash my face then look in the mirror. I look terrible. Staring, bloodshot eyes, pink as the rhubarb I've left in the toilet. A wet, stinking beard.

'Use the soap,' Carrie Ann suggests. 'I'll find some towels.'

Between us, I get cleaned up. But I still feel awful. Really, really sick and weak.

'Can you walk?'

I nod. Carrie Ann links her arm through mine and we leave the toilets.

'Well, well!' says a voice, as soon as we come out. 'Look what the cat threw up!'

It's Robbie Flynn, standing there with three mates. Of all the people I could meet now... I have no fight in me. I just want to crawl under a stone and die.

'Ignore him,' whispers Carrie Ann, but that's easier said than done. Robbie moves in front of us, blocking the way. Oh, he smells. Stale sweat and cigarette breath. I feel my stomach starting to churn again.

'Ah... Little Weirdy Beardy. What you gonna do? It's your big night tonight, innit?'

'She'll be okay by then,' says Carrie Ann. She tries to get me past him but he moves to block us again.

'I don't think so,' he sneers. 'I pity the poor beggars on the front row tonight. 'Come Mary, let us go to *JeRUUUUGHsalem!'* His mates laugh but Robbie suddenly turns serious.

'This is what comes of messing up the system,

see?' he says. He grabs hold of my arm and starts to squeeze. 'Derren should have stuck to his guns. Given the parts to boys. Girls can't cut it, see? Weak stomachs. Girly nerves.'

'Leave it.'

There's a new voice behind me. I know it but I can't place it. My head is spinning.

'You what?'

'I said leave it.'

I know who it is. It's Jack Lewis. He's with Matthew Sharp. Robbie's fingers relax, just for a second. Carrie Ann somehow senses this and moves me on to safety.

'What's it to you, Lewis?'

'Everything. I'm in the play too and we need her.'

'Like hell you do. She's a jumped-up, interfering freak. Anyone could play that part.'

'Oh yeah? Like you, you mean? I don't think so. They'd smell your stink on the back row.'

That's when it all kicks off. There are no more words. Just scuffling and grunting and smacking sounds. I don't see what happens. I don't turn round. I just let Carrie Ann lead me away. And as we turn the corner, I start to pray. To God, the fairies, the earth spirits, the angels – whoever is listening. *Please, please, please...Please let me be alright for tonight.*

*And please let Jack be alright too.*

# Chapter 29

Mrs Dunn phones Mum. I sit in the office with a bucket between my knees, waiting to be picked up. Eventually Mum arrives.

'Dear Lord!' she says when she sees me. 'We're taking you to the doctor's. Now.'

'No,' I protest weakly. 'I'm all right. It's just the rhubarb. I'll get over it.'

'You look *awful*, Em. Like you've been dragged out of the canal.'

'Thanks.'

'I'm just being honest.' She stands there, looking at me, trying to decide what to do, while my head spins.

'Mum – can we just go? Please?'

She nods and helps me to my feet. I walk to the car like a toddler. I can't believe how weak I am. I have to hold onto Mum's arm. When we get home, she puts me to bed and gives me a cup of boiled water.

'It's good for your stomach,' she explains. 'It'll calm things down.' She draws the curtains and leaves me alone.

It's 3.15. I have to be back at school by 6.15. The show starts at 7.30. I set my alarm clock and close my eyes.

I must fall into a deep sleep, because suddenly I'm woken by the clock dancing a jig on the bedside table. Time to go.

I stumble to the bathroom and start brushing my teeth. *Whoa...* The room starts spinning. I have to grab hold of the wash basin. Perhaps I just got out of bed too fast? I hope so.

I manage to get dressed, then carefully go downstairs, holding onto the banister like I'm eighty or something.

'Oh, Em!' says Mum when she sees my face. 'Sweetheart! You look like a skull.' This is true. My skin is deathly pale and my eyes are lost in two dark shadows. 'You need a bit of make up. Sit down.'

Mum fetches me another cup of boiled water then starts to do my face. 'How are you feeling?'

'Not so bad,' I tell her, but it's a lie. I feel as sick as a pig. I take a deep breath and try to keep calm. There a sob somewhere in my chest. I can feel it. It's so hard, it hurts. If I don't stay calm, it will punch its way out.

I can't believe this is happening. After everything I've been through. The worrying and bullying. The mobbing in the superstore. Learning and rehearsing.

My hopes and dreams are falling apart like cheap shoes.

And now tears are filling my eyes and I can't stop

them. I hear the sob as it claws its way out. 'It's not fair,' I wail. 'It's not fair. I've worked so hard and I feel so bad.'

Mum takes my head in her hands. 'What do you want to do? Are you too bad to go?'

I don't know. I suddenly picture Robbie Flynn, pretending to puke on the front row of the audience. Can you imagine doing that? I'd never live it down. Never. I'd be *Emily Who Threw Up on Everyone* forever.

'Shall I ring them and say you're not coming?'

'No!' Now I'm seeing Mr Derren, giving his speech at the first rehearsal. *You're the best... I know you'll prove me right on the night. A team, strong as steel.*

'I have to go, Mum.'

She smiles. 'The show must go on, eh?'

I nod.

'Mr Derren will be proud of you. I know I am. And your dad would be too.' Her eyes start to fill as soon as she says this, so we both have a good sniff and fetch our coats before we start howling like babies.

Mum drives me to school. The first person I see when I reach the hall is Miss James.

'Emmy!' she cries. 'Thank God you're here. That flamin' rhubarb. We've already lost Daniel Pardoe and three angels.'

*Angels?* 'Is Keeley all right?'

'Yes, she's here. She's been looking for you.'

I wander on, heading for the PE changing rooms behind the hall. Tonight they are dressing rooms for the show. I meet Anuja Khan. She's looking gorgeous in her Melchior costume: a long velvet robe, ruby red with gold trimmings; gold slippers with toes that curl up at the end; a fabulous golden turban. And best of all, golden beads plaited into her long, super-silky beard.

'Em, you're here,' she says, in her lovely, soft voice. 'I was so worried when I heard. Are you okay?'

'Sort of.'

'Daniel Pardoe is really ill. They say he might have to go into hospital.'

*'What?'*

'Food poisoning can kill you, Em. I'm amazed you can stand up.'

*Whoa!* I knew it was bad, but I didn't think it was *that* bad.

Anuja pats my arm, wishes me luck and moves on. Next I bump into Jack Lewis. He is also looking wonderful, in a purple robe with a shiny golden crown, but my eyes are drawn to the bruise on his cheek.

'Robbie punched me,' he says. 'It wasn't too bad, though. Matt stepped in and sorted him out. And, I'm pleased to say, there's not a single mark on Matt's face. If he'd been damaged, a hundred girls would never have forgiven me!'

He leans forward and kisses me on the cheek, then strolls away. I stand there, stunned. Did that really happen or is it the fever, making me imagine things? I don't know any more.

I reach the dressing room and half-collapse onto one of the benches. Carrie Ann is already in there, dressed in her Joseph robes. She pulls something out of her bag and immediately comes over.

'I'm so glad you've made it,' she says, giving me a hug. 'You couldn't miss tonight. Are you any better?'

I shake my head miserably.

'I have something for you.' She shows me a small glass bottle. There's a dark brown liquid swirling round inside it. 'My mum made it for you. She says it will make you feel better.'

'What is it?'

'Herbs and things. You know what my mum's like.'

I take the bottle, open it and swallow a mouthful.

'Urgh! It's disgusting!'

'Sorry! She put ginseng in it to give you energy. It's not nice but it will work, I promise.'

'Do I have to drink it all?' Carrie Ann nods. I hold my nose and drink it down. *Aargh!* I can taste it even when it's gone. But it does seem to work. Five minutes later, I'm feeling well enough to change into my robes.

Miss Bailey and her team have worked incredibly

hard on the costumes. I think mine has been made out of old curtains, but you would never guess it. It's gorgeous. There's a long, velvet robe with a matching cloak, both in peacock blue. I have a plaited silver belt to tie around my waist and a silver turban with sapphire blue beads sewn on. For my feet, I have a pair of flip-flops. They're disappointing, I have to admit. They're just plain brown leather. The kind of thing you would expect a shepherd to wear, rather than a Wise Man. But they look okay, I suppose. At least they fit.

Once I'm dressed, Carrie Ann wants to sneak backstage to watch the audience coming in. I'm still feeling a bit wobbly, but I tag along and we peep through the closed curtains on the stage. So many people! The rows are filling up really fast. But there seems to be someone missing. My brain is so befuddled, it takes ages to come to me, but then I realise who's not here.

'Where are the reporters?' I whisper. 'The press and tv?'

'Banned!' replies Carrie Ann. 'They wanted to be here, but Mrs Burton said it wasn't fair, what with the sickness and it being first night. So they're coming on the last night instead.'

We return to the dressing room. Keeley's in there now and she pounces on me right away.

'I am *so* pleased to see you!' she cries. 'I couldn't believe it when I heard you were sick. I really thought you were going to miss it.'

She looks beautiful. Absolutely stunning. Her dress is very simple, just a long, white gown. But there are tiny mother-of-pearl beads sewn all over the bodice, so when she's under the stage lights, she will sparkle. Her hair is loose and curly and sprinkled with glitter. On her back are the most magnificent wings I've ever seen. They're made of feathers. Real feathers, soft as snow and twice as white. They're tied on with long white satin ribbons. Has St Mary's ever seen a lovelier angel? I don't think so.

'Look!' she says. 'I have something for you.'

She reaches for her bag and pulls out her special slippers. The ones her Dad bought in Egypt. They're blue velvet and covered in jewels.

'They're only to borrow. Sorry! I can't give them away, I love them too much. But I really want you to wear them. They're just perfect, aren't they? The right colour and everything. And so much better than those tatty old things you're wearing.'

She tugs off my plain flip-flops and slips the velvet ones on. They're a perfect fit. I feel like Cinderella before the ball.

'Thanks,' I say. 'It's really kind.' I look into her soft brown eyes and she smiles. And in that moment, we both know things will never be the same between us, ever again. We'll always be friends. But we've both moved on and found a new special friend. And that's okay. We're both very happy.

'Have a good show,' she says. Then she stands up and goes over to the other side of the dressing room, where Sarah Matthews is waiting for her.

'That was nice of her,' says Carrie Ann. 'They're gorgeous.'

I don't have time to answer because Miss James pokes her head around the door.

'First positions, girls,' she says breathlessly. 'We've got five minutes and then the curtain goes up!'

# Chapter 30

Wouldn't it be wonderful if life was just like the movies? My opening night would go like this:

1. Carrie Ann's Miracle Medicine cures me completely and I leap onto stage with the energy of a banana-fuelled baboon.
2. I give the most incredible performance in the history of the St Mary's Christmas play. People leap to their feet, shout my name and clap till their hands bleed.
3. A famous film director just happens to be in the audience. He tells me to pack my suitcase, because tomorrow I'm flying out to Hollywood to be a movie star.
4. Matthew Sharp suddenly tells me I'm the most beautiful girl in the world. He says he loves me with all his heart. But he wants me to go to America to be a star. He says he will wait here until I return, rich and famous, even if it takes ten years. He just wants me to be happy.
5. Mr Derren apologises in front of the whole school. He says he was wrong to ever doubt the acting ability of girls and I, Emmy Travis, have just proved that. Can I forgive him? 'YES,' I say, and give him a good old bear hug to show everyone I mean it.

6. The Hairy Marys stand on stage with their arms around each other, glowing like Christmas lanterns, while Mr Derren shouts: 'Three cheers for the Hairy Marys!' and everyone joins in, including Robbie Flynn.

Sadly, this isn't what happens. I'm sorry to disappoint you. I know you want the Big Happy Ending. But the truth is more like this…

Carrie Ann's strange medicine *does* work. I don't start turning cartwheels or feel I could run a marathon. It just keeps me on my feet and stops me fainting or throwing up on the front row. It untangles my brain so I can remember my lines, and it gives me the energy to say them with some feeling.

But I don't give an incredible performance. I can't. The sickness has stolen my breath. Frozen my fire. But I don't let it beat me. I stand on that stage and hold on. Fight with every fibre of my being. At the end of the show I'm still there, taking the applause with the rest of the cast. And that may not sound like much, but it is. I'm a winner.

Mr Derren knows what a struggle it's been for me. At the end, when he makes a speech, he mentions me by name. Tells the audience how hard I've fought. And he makes them applaud again, just for me, while I take a bow on my own. Just a little one. I know if I bend over too far, I might pass out, so I'm careful. But it's still a good moment.

Then it's all over. There's no film director. No Robbie Flynn. No Matthew Sharp, swearing undying love. I see him chatting up Caitlin Morrow. She tells me later he was asking about her beard. Will she shave it off after the play? Yes. Will she go on a date with him then? Yes. Does she like pizza?

I'm so tired. I need my bed. Mum takes me home and I collapse into it. The frost fairies are outside again. I can see their work shimmering on the window. The world is quiet, sparkling, sliding into sleep.

There's only time for one more thought. It's more like a wish, really.

The play has two more nights to run. *Please let me be better tomorrow.*

# Chapter 31

Yes! YES! I am better! I am so happy, I leap out of the window, slide down the drainpipe, run down the street in my jim-jams, kiss the postman, climb a lamp post and start singing 'Any Dream Will Do' with the neighbourhood cats joining in on the chorus.

Actually I don't do any of this. But I am better. That's true. Not a hundred per cent better, but I feel well enough to shower and wash my hair, get dressed and go down to breakfast. I feel very hungry but want to be careful, so I have a Baby Bear-sized bowl of porridge and nothing more. Then I go to school and find everyone is buzzing about last night's show.

'It's going to be much better tonight,' says Keeley. 'Some people were a bit nervous last night and there were a few mistakes. The cow sat down on top of the manger, did you know? It would have squashed baby Jesus if Rachel hadn't grabbed him in time!'

I laugh out loud. This is the first I've heard of it. I was so fuzzy last night. So much passed me by.

The whole school is talking about Joshua Maruru. The ones who saw the show say he was awesome. A real star. Those who have tickets for tonight and tomorrow are really excited they'll have the chance to see him. It's too late to get a ticket now. Both shows are completely sold out.

I hear good things about Carrie Ann too. People are saying she's really special, but I want to make my own mind up about that. I'm going to watch her tonight from the 'wings' - the side of the stage. I can't wait!

~

They are right. Carrie Ann *is* special. I see it tonight with my own eyes. She was good in rehearsal, but in front of an audience she's dazzling. I don't know what it is. She comes alive, somehow. I watch the scene where Mary tells Joseph she's having a baby and it isn't his. Carrie Ann – Joseph - just stands there, looking at Mary. She doesn't say anything, but the expression on her face... Wow. I have tears in my eyes by the time it's over. And I'm not the only one. I peep through a hole in the curtain and there are tissues all over the hall. Little white flags, waving in the dark.

I wanted to be Joseph, but now I can't help wondering - could I have done that? Made people cry? I don't think so. I'm good, but I'm not *that* good. I can't believe I'm saying this. Me, the one who wants to be an actress more than anything in the world. But it's true. I love being on stage. I love the tingly feeling I get in my fingers and toes when I'm waiting to go on. I love the lights and the darkness beyond them. I love the laughter and the applause. But is loving it enough? If I'm going to succeed as an actress, won't I need something more? That special 'something' that Carrie Ann has?

Tomorrow night is our final performance. Will I find it in me by then? I hope so.

# Chapter 32

They're here! The newspaper reporters and the tv people! I see the vans parked outside the school gates when I arrive for the last night of the play.

I don't know what the atmosphere is like in the hall. But I do know this: backstage the air is so thick with excitement, you could slice it like birthday cake. The cast is fizzing like a mouthful of sherbet. Everyone wants to do their very best. Not just because the cameras are here, along with the Mayor, the town council, the school governors and most of our parents. No. We want to do it because this is our last chance. We can't blow it, not tonight. Especially the Year 11s. They won't be here next year.

Mr Derren gathers us together before Curtain Up and wishes us well. The music starts. The show begins. And the next two hours are a perfect dream of colour and light, music and magic, laughter and love. Yes – love. I know it sounds soppy, but it's true. Big Love is in the building tonight. The audience is full of parents, grandparents, carers and friends, and there's so much love coming out of them, we can feel it on the stage. It washes over us in big warm waves. It's a fantastic feeling. And there's love on the stage too. We're all friends together, doing what we most want to be doing, sharing these magic moments and no one can stop us.

But it's not just about us: the cast and crew. Tonight it's about the story. The Nativity story – the story of how Jesus was born in a stable then visited by shepherds and three wise men from the East – is an old, old story. It's more than two thousand years old and it's been told a million times before. But suddenly it becomes as thrilling as a real, live dragon flying over the heads of the spellbound audience. And the raging heart of this dragon is Joshua Maruru.

He is truly awesome. He isn't playing at being Herod. He *is* Herod. In my scene with him, he sits on his throne, quizzing the Three Wise Men about the baby they are seeking. The new king that has been born. I say my lines as usual: 'When we find him, your Majesty, we shall return. You have my word on that.'

*'Do I?'* he says, and for the first time ever, he looks me straight in the eyes. His gaze is so strong, it punches through my chest and skewers me like a kebab. I can't look away. I'm trapped.

'I must find this child,' he says softly, but his eyes are darker than December. 'I too have a... *gift* for him.' I feel the hairs rising on the back of my neck. My own eyes widen in horror because I see the gift he means and it's the cold, clean blade of a killing sword. And out of the darkness behind my brain, I hear a woman's scream and the cry of a baby - then nothing. Silence. And in my ragged heart, I know I would die sooner than return to this terrible king.

By the time I reach the wings, I'm shaking. What was all that about? He's Joshua Maruru from Year 11. He's not a king. And yet....

I stand in the wings to watch Josh do his final scene, the one where he flies into a rage and orders the killing of the babies. He is absolutely terrifying. Bhasker Patel is the soldier he shouts at, and I can see him trembling. He's like a butterfly pinned to a board. There is no escape. I peep through the hole in the curtain to look at the audience and they are mesmerised. They aren't in St Mary's anymore. They've travelled back in time more than two thousand years. Now they're trapped in a palace with a mad king. There's not a sound out there. Not a cough, a rustle or a wriggle. And when the scene's over – *phew!* Everyone breathes out and smiles in relief because Josh didn't pick on them.

Soon the wings are getting so crowded, we're nearly spilling out onto the stage. There are only five minutes to go and everyone is dying to soak up the applause. Five, four, three, two, one – that's it! It's all over! There's nothing now but smiles and applause, hugs and tears, speeches and photos. I'm blinded by flashbulbs. Mrs Burton banned cameras and phones during the performance, so now there's a filming frenzy. The clapping and cheering goes on and on and on. The crowd won't let us go. We take so many bows, we're up and down like seesaws. I see Mum on the second row. She's smiling but there are tears running down her face. Is it because she's proud of me or because she's missing Dad again? A bit of both, I think.

Once I come off stage, the reporters try to mob me. But Miss Bailey puts her arms around me like a shield and says: 'Two minutes please, ladies and gents! Two minutes!' She takes me through the swing doors into the corridor behind the stage.

'That's better!' she says. 'What a wild bunch they are! They can have you in a minute. I just want a quick word first. I want to tell you how proud I am, of you and all the others. You have been wonderful. So strong and inspiring.'

I shake my head. 'I nearly pulled out. I hate this beard *so much.* When Keeley came in without hers, and I saw I could shave mine off and end it all – I nearly did. I've never told anyone that. But I came *this* close to doing it.'

I pinch my finger and thumb almost together.

'But you didn't,' says Miss Bailey. 'Don't be so hard on yourself, Em. You have been *amazing.* One day, you will look back and see that. Some girls would have refused to leave the house. You got out there and faced the world. And you took on Mr

Derren, and fought for equality and won a role in his play. That is amazing, whatever you say. And that is why *they* want to talk to you.' She points at the swing doors. 'So go!'

I hug her first. Her spiky necklace catches in my beard. It's made of metal, with sharp holly leaves and bright red berries. She giggles as she untangles me. 'Go!'

So I return to the hall, and the reporters surround me instantly. They are all desperate to interview a Hairy Mary, and there are only four of us left now: me, Carrie Ann, Anuja and Caitlin. They're especially keen to talk to me because I am the only Mary who was ill. I have to tell my story eight times, and each time it gets a bit more dramatic. By the time I've finished, it goes like this:

*I was so sick in the toilets, I fainted with my head down the bowl. I would have drowned, but Carrie Ann found me and carried me in her arms all the way to Mrs Burton's office. Mrs Burton phoned for an ambulance. It battled through a snowstorm to get here but I refused to go to hospital. No, I said. The show must go on. The ambulance crew wouldn't leave me, so they sat in the wings with a tank of oxygen. When I wasn't on stage, I lay with an oxygen mask strapped to my face, desperately trying to remain conscious. It was touch and go.*

*My temperature rose to a dangerously high level during the interval and they wanted to shave off my beard to cool me down. But again, I refused. Luckily they found an ice pack in the ambulance and saved my life with that.*

The reporters seem to believe me. They want something to grab people's attention and I'm happy to give it to them. I'm loving it so much, I can almost forget the horror of the superstore. Fame feels good again. The bright lights, the applause, the congratulations – it's brilliant.

The last reporter I speak to is Jennifer, the glamorous woman who interviewed me when this all began.

'So, Emily,' she asks, 'do you still want to be an actress when you grow up?'

I open my mouth, the breath goes in, I'm about to answer, then my gaze falls on Joshua Maruru. A woman has hold of his hand. She's shaking it really hard and her mouth is working away. I can't hear the words but I know she's telling him how wonderful he was. Mr Derren is standing behind Josh, waiting to say something. But he's not being impatient. He's smiling. He'll wait as long as it takes.

The woman leaves and Josh turns to Mr Derren. They don't say anything for a moment. They just smile at each other. Then Josh says something and I read his lips. Two words. *Thank you.*

'Emily, do you still want to be an actress?'

Mr Derren nods and playfully punches Josh on

the shoulder as if to say *Well Done*.

'Emily?'

I turn my attention back to Jennifer. 'No,' I say. I glance over at Mr Derren again. 'I don't want to be an actress. I want to be a drama teacher.'

# Chapter 33

Where did that come from? Wanting to be a drama teacher?

I'm sitting on the window ledge in my bedroom, gazing out at the snowy street, thinking back over the night I've just had. It was glorious, which makes my answer even stranger in a way. If it had been a complete disaster, if I'd forgotten my lines and fallen over my own feet on stage, you could understand my wanting a change of career. But with it all going so smoothly, and the reporters being so nice to me at the end, you'd think that would make me want to be an actress even more, wouldn't you? The Big Dream would be shining brighter than the Christmas star. But it's not.

There are two reasons, I think. The first is to do with me and the 'something.' Do you remember I talked about Carrie Ann and how she seemed to have a certain 'something' on stage that made her shine? And I was hoping I'd find it in me by Saturday night? Well, I never did find it. Don't get me wrong, I'm not saying I'm bad at acting. I gave a good performance, with lots of energy and focus. I loved being up there on stage. But there was something missing. Now matter how hard I tried, I couldn't conjure up that extra bit of magic that

Carrie Ann has.

As for Joshua Maruru, he has so much of it, he crackles like a bonfire. He doesn't have to work for it. It seems to come as naturally as breathing. I really hope he goes on to Drama College because he'll be such a star. I know he will.

The second thing is to do with Mr Derren. Would you believe it? Deadly Derren, Mr Werewolf, is my hero now! I can hardly believe it myself. But I look back at everything he's done and he's been amazing. He worked so hard to get the show right. Night after night, he stayed behind after school to rehearse with us. I bet he didn't get paid for that. And when all the newspapers were shouting at him, saying he was wrong to pick boys over girls, he stayed quiet and dignified. He knew the real reason he was doing it – to give the boys a chance to shine. And on the night, they *did* shine. He took those little brown birds and made them as proud as peacocks. Gave them memories they will keep for the rest of their lives.

I didn't see the reporters fighting to speak to Mr Derren at the end. No one wanted to hear his story or take his photo. But I don't think he'd care about that. Joshua Maruru said thank you, and I bet that meant more to him than having his picture in the paper. Tonight, Mr Derren gave Josh a future and Josh knows it. He will be grateful forever.

It must be brilliant, being Mr Derren. Having the

power to change lives for the better. To give people hope and dreams. And he spends all day doing drama. How fab is that?

So that is why I said what I did to that reporter.

I look at the sky. It's as plump as a duvet. Snow is beginning to fall. Down on the street, Mr Nelson has let Gracie outside for one last sniff-around before bedtime. It's all very peaceful.

Hold on – what's this? Mr Lenska from the house opposite is out on the pavement, without a coat, looking up and down the street. Mr Nelson is going over to see what's the matter. And now there are blue lights, bouncing off the houses. An ambulance! Mrs Lenska must be having her baby.

I run into Mum's bedroom and wake her up. She gets out of bed and we sit on her window ledge, huddled together for warmth, waiting to see what happens next. Mum even opens the window a tiny bit so we can hear voices. It feels a bit weird, watching other people like this. We wouldn't do it if someone was sick. But this feels right, somehow. It's like a fairy tale. A baby being born in the middle of the night, with the snow falling like feathers all around.

Suddenly we hear a cry. A baby's cry, cutting through the night. Mum and I gasp in delight and turn to each other, our eyes shining like little moons.

'A baby!' says Mum. 'No more than a minute old. *Oh!* It's so lovely.' She gives me a hug.

An ambulance man comes out of the house and says something to Mr Nelson. He's been waiting for news, even though it's bitterly cold. Mr Nelson nods his head and starts to grin then he crosses the street and looks right up at the window where we're sitting. He must have known we were there all the time!

'A boy!' he announces. 'Very healthy and Mum is fine too.'

We wave and thank him. He calls to Gracie and they head off down the street.

'She's a beautiful dog, isn't she?' says Mum a bit dreamily. 'I'd love one like her. What do you think, Em? Shall we get a dog like Gracie?'

I can't speak. Is this real?

'Yes,' I manage at last. 'Yes!'

Mum beams. 'Let's get one in the spring,' she says. 'When it's a bit warmer.'

I nod. It is too cold to be walking a puppy now.

'You need to get back to bed,' says Mum. 'You've had a long day.'

I don't argue. I'm super-tired. I sleep till 10 o'clock the next morning and only wake up when Mum brings me a cup of tea. She opens the curtains, turns – and starts smiling.

I peer at her, gummy-eyed. 'What's funny?'

Mum doesn't answer. She just reaches for the mirror on my dressing table and hands it to me.

I look at my face – blink hard – and look again.

My beard has gone.

# Chapter 34

It's the last day of term, lunchtime, and we're sitting in the cafeteria again. Me, Carrie Ann, Keeley – and Sarah Matthews. I don't mind her being with us. She's good fun. And she's just invited us all to a sleepover this Saturday.

Mr Derren comes into the hall. He goes to the notice board and starts unpinning the old notices for the play.

'Just think,' says Keeley. 'This is where it all began. How many weeks ago?'

'Six,' says Carrie Ann.

'Is that all?' I say. 'It feels longer. Everything was still new then. But now it feels like I've been here forever.'

'We know a lot more people,' says Keeley. 'Loads of Year 8s and 9s.'

We all nod. That would have been unthinkable before half term.

'So next year,' says Keeley, 'are we all going to audition for the play again?'

'Yes!'

'It was awesome!'

'Amazing. The best fun ever.'

'And we were famous for fifteen minutes,' says Carrie Ann.

'Longer than that!' I protest.

'No, it's a quote,' says Carrie Ann. '*In the future, everyone will be famous for fifteen minutes.* It's from Andy Warhol. The artist? From the Sixties? Did all those faces of famous people. And soup cans. He did a picture of soup cans. Doesn't anyone know who I mean?'

'NO!' We all collapse into giggles, and Sarah throws a grape at her.

'You are so ignorant,' says Carrie Ann, but she's grinning.

It goes quiet. We've all gone dreamy-eyed, thinking back to our favourite moments.

'You're stroking your beard!' squeals Keeley, suddenly digging her elbow into my ribs.

'What?'

'Just then, you were stroking your chin,' she says. 'Like this. Like you still had your beard.'

'No!' I squeal, laughing it away. But she's right. I do still stroke my beard. I've caught myself doing it a few times now. It's when I'm thinking really hard about something. My fingers stroke my invisible whiskers, teasing them into a long point, just like a wise old man.

It's a strange habit to have. Perhaps, deep down, I miss having my beard. For a while, I really was someone special. I was a Hairy Mary. I went on breakfast tv and had my picture in all the papers. I grew a beard that was 12cm long.

How many girls can say that?

Also by Cat Weatherill

**Wild Magic**

When a beautiful stranger comes to town,
Marianna follows him into a world of wild magic.
Soon she is alone and being stalked by a fearsome beast who needs someone to break a centuries-old curse.
But the price of breaking the curse is a terrible one…

**An ancient spell, a spirited heroine and a desperate villain clash in a fast-moving adventure, full of unexpected enchantment and danger.**

*Don't miss reading this book. Like the Piper's tune, it is so real you can taste it* – **GoodReads**

Also by Cat Weatherill

**Barkbelly**

Barkbelly has always been an outsider in the village,

and now a terrible accident means he

has to run away to save his life.

**From the glitter of Carmenero's Circus to the pirate ship**

**Mermaid and an island at the edge of the world,**

**Barkbelly follows his dreams.**

**But will they come true when he gets there?**

*'Glorious… A beautiful and touching story'* – The Observer

Also by Cat Weatherill

**Snowbone**

The adventure continues as Snowbone fights against the slavery of her people. An exploding volcano, a strange prophesy, man-eating plants and a hero who flies without wings - they're all here, in a second whirlwind adventure set in the world of Ashenpeakers.

*'A dazzling book, inventive in plot and rich in language'*

**- Carousel**

A Special Thank You

To Year 5 at Ettington Church of England Primary School for all their help and enthusiasm, and especially to Jove Stirling-Evans for coming up with the book title.

Also huge thanks to everyone who entered the competition to design and draw the book cover. Congratulations, Alicia Walker from Billingham, Cleveland!

Illustration by Mariya-Racquel Amato